WENDY LYNN DECKER

WHISPERS OF SEA GLASS

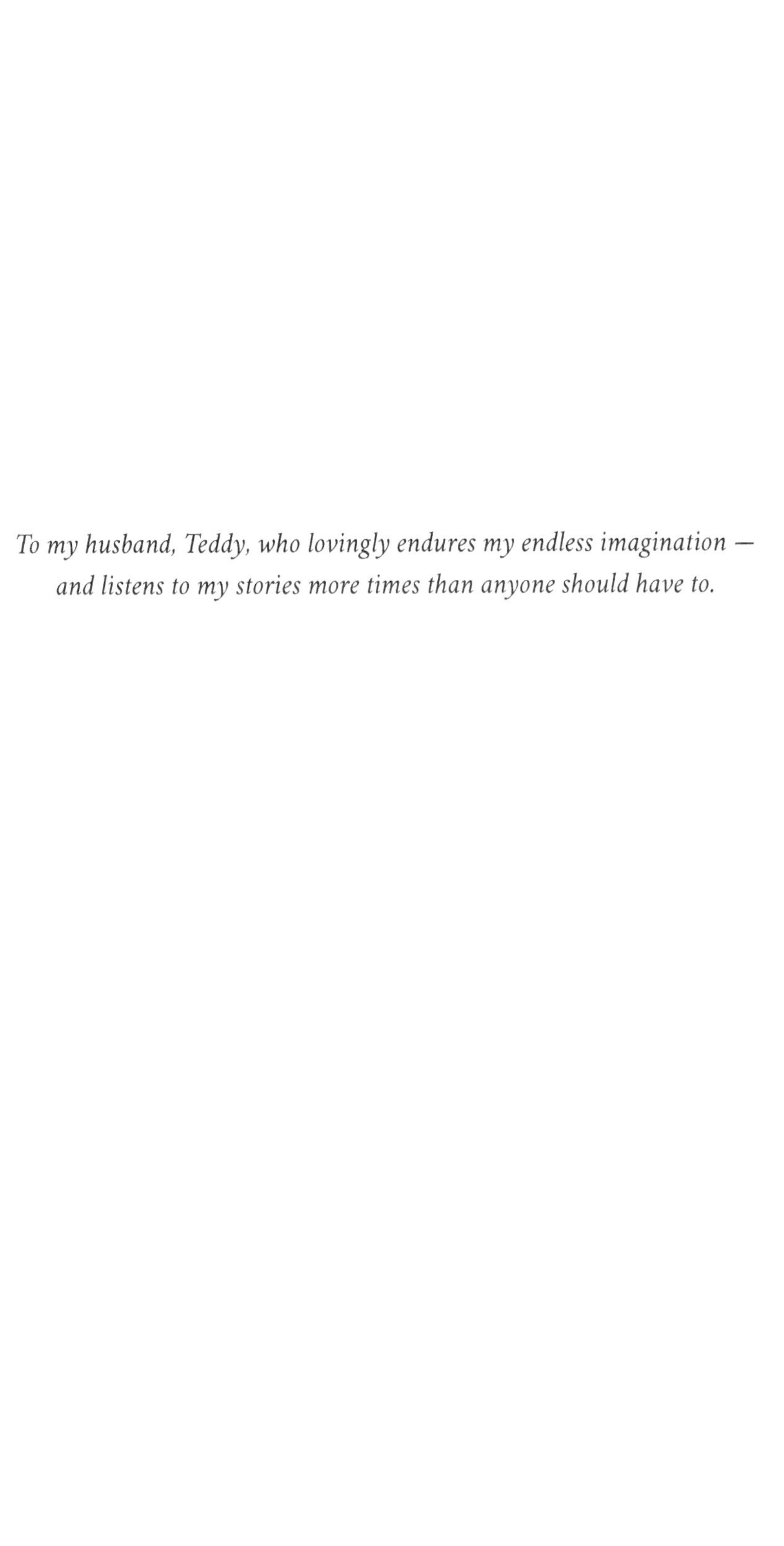

*To my husband, Teddy, who lovingly endures my endless imagination —
and listens to my stories more times than anyone should have to.*

"I've always had the feeling that nothing is impossible if one applies a certain amount of energy in the right direction. If you want to do it, you can . . ."

-NELLIE BLY

Contents

Acknowledgments

As always, it takes many eyes, ears, hands, and hearts to complete a book. Without the support of my friends and family, this story would not exist.

Thank you to **Patricia Florio**, my Catholic guide. To my daughter, **Alyjah**, my first—and many-times-over—reader. To my son, **Zane**, who answered every text at lightning speed and worked his technical magic with every back-cover revision.

Thank you to **Stephanie Mandel** for her thoughtful, in-depth notes, and to **Donna Correll, Michele Milia, Annie Alberta, and Lori Kalli** for their generous feedback and encouragement.

Susan Rosenberg, meeting you was serendipity—your meticulous proofreading is a gift I'm deeply grateful for.

Thank you to **Jolene Weiss** for sharing Andrew's story, which led this novel in unexpected directions, and to **Lenore Hart Poyer**, whose guidance from its earliest days stretched me as a writer and helped give it direction.

CHAPTER ONE

1973

We never talked about how Mo came to join our family. The scandalous rumors had long died down by the time she was old enough to attend school. Those who knew the story had been instructed by the church not to gossip, and the rest had moved away. Only one other person knew Mo before me, and she had been missing for fifteen years—until now. As hard as it would be, I had to tell Mo she existed and why we hadn't seen her since 1958.

.

1958

In my Junior year at St. Teresa's Catholic School, Mother Superior began stopping by our classroom for surprise pocketbook checks. She had done it sporadically in the past, but one day the event took a turn.

"Release and Surrender!" She shouted as her steel-blue eyes glared at us from under the severe habit headdress.

On command, each girl opened her purse and dumped the contents onto her desk. The nun strolled up and down the rows. Her enormous crucifix and rosary beads hung from her belt, clicking and clacking as she strolled by.

A ray of sunlight filtered through the large windows, raking streaks across the blackboard onto the desktops. It also illuminated the tiny patch of whiskers on the tip of the nun's chin. Suddenly, fear crept in like a slow-dripping faucet as the nun moved down the row of desks. I knew at least one girl would get caught with something the nun seemed to be expecting to find. She stopped abruptly at the side of Stella's desk, which was next to mine.

"What else is in there, Stella?" She tapped the girl's purple peacock print handbag with the ruler in her hand.

"Nothing, Mother," she said with a flat tone.

The only items that fell onto Stella's desk were a pen, a pencil, and an old, shell-shaped, floral change purse.

Not convinced by Stella's answer, the nun tucked the ruler underneath her arm and grabbed the purse by its handle, lifting it high.

"A fancy purse for school, Stella. Not at all appropriate. Where did you get it?"

"My mother's closet," she said, folding her arms with a sudden attitude.

The nun turned the handbag upside down and shook it. A tube of lipstick, a sanitary napkin, several pieces of sea glass, and an empty vodka bottle clattered onto the desk.

Mother handed Stella the empty purse after she scooped up the pint-sized bottle by its capless neck. She held it up for all to see. "What do we have here, Stella?" The nun strolled to the front of the room again and set the liquor bottle and the ruler on her desk.

"It's not mine," Stella said softly while rolling her olive-green eyes as she shoved her other belongings back inside the purse.

Gasps and snickers hissed in the classroom. The nun's sharp stare silenced the sea of girls. No way did I want to draw attention to myself because I had several of Denny Carson's cigarettes hidden in my compact.

I'd been holding them since Christmas break when Laura and I ran into him at Foley's Diner. Hot cocoa and marshmallows filled the air that day. Denny had strutted over to the table and sat down next to me as if I'd been waiting for him.

"Hey there, Ivy," he'd said with a raspy voice that reminded me of the singer Johnny Ray.

"Hi Denny," I'd responded almost as a question.

Denny and I had worked together the summer before at Mr. Fudge & Saltwater Taffy on the boardwalk, but I'd barely known him. The extent of our relationship had been grazing shoulders behind the counter and exchanging sidelong glances between customers.

That day, Denny's charm and quick wit had me beaming and laughing on a whole new level.

I remember how he licked his bottom lip between sips through his straw, his dark coffee-colored eyes locked on mine in a way I'd never experienced. Still, they often darted around the café, as if searching for someone, while his leg bounced restlessly under the table. His fingers grazed mine as he traced the condensation on his tall glass, sending a small thrill through me.

Then, a sharp rap on the window beside him broke the moment. Snow was falling hard, and I couldn't make out the face of the man signaling him. Denny looked up, and snap, the flirtation between us faded.

"Sorry, gotta split," he'd said and pinched my cheek. Then Denny rushed out, leaving a half-finished milkshake and a pack of cigarettes on the table.

I stirred my cocoa with his shake straw, staring out the window, hoping he'd come back. The school dance at St. Joe's Boys School—the school Denny attended—was coming up, and I'd been praying to see him again.

Now, I silently prayed the nun would pass me by. Sweat seeped through my blouse as her footsteps drew closer, and I clutched my purse, dreading she might ask for it next.

"To whom does it belong then, Stella?"

Stella cleared her throat. "I picked it up from the sidewalk so a little kid wouldn't trip on it."

"Why not toss it into the trash then, Stella?" Mother scratched the side of her cheek with the pale-yellow nail of her pointer finger.

Stella straightened her posture, raised her square chin, and set her pouty lips in a faint scowl at Mother Superior. If she stood, she'd be face-to-face with the tall nun. I stayed seated, my five-foot frame nearly disappearing.

"I thought I might paint it and turn it into a vase. It has a unique shape, Mother, don't you think?" Stella said.

Gasps of shock filled the classroom as anticipation of what was to come hung in the air. What the heck was Stella doing? She'd always been snarky, and because of this, she often got whacked with the ruler, but this behavior was on a new level.

"I find that hard to believe, Stella, but in any case, I can't allow your possession of something as troubling as an empty liquor bottle to go unpunished," Mother Superior said.

Stella's pretty eyes narrowed into angry slits. "Or maybe I found it on your desk, under a big, black book."

Suddenly, speculative whispers filled the classroom. For years, rumor had it that the nun kept a book, known to us as "The Book of Ill Repute," but no one knew for certain. One thing for sure: you didn't want to be in it. And no one had ever challenged Mother Superior this way before. My mouth grew dry as I continuously twisted the same strand of blonde hair around my finger while my heart pounded furiously, waiting for the nun's next move. In a flash, she turned on the stunned classroom, head whipping around quickly. I swear, if she were a cartoon character, the habit headpiece would have still faced one way, and her head the other.

"ENOUGH!" she shouted, then clasped her hands, tilted her head without changing her disdainful stare, and said, "Laura, bring me the stick."

Laura's light freckled face immediately turned pale. But she sprang from her seat, adjusted the white band that held her long, chestnut hair back, and obeyed Mother's request. Laura, Mother's pet, didn't have much popularity with the students. Always chosen to light the blessed candle. Always praised for making the sign of the cross upon hearing the sirens of an ambulance (which happened regularly as the hospital was up the road). Not to mention, the only girl who had never received an infraction for her skirt length.

Fortunately for Laura, I'd been her one constant friend since first grade. Our parents moved in the same social circles, so she came preapproved, giving me more freedom to leave the house without raising suspicion. By association, I probably dodged more than a few knuckle-thrashings because of it.

Laura returned with the ruler, holding it out on her palms like a royal scepter, her expression as solemn as Mother Superior's. I believed the head nun's fondness for her was also based on the fact that her parents tithed more money to the church than any student's family. And her mom never missed a night hosting Bingo.

The nun knocked on Stella's desk—the hollow rapping of those large knuckles, directing her to prepare for penance. Stella knew the drill; she'd been through it many times before. With a scowl on her face, she stood and thrust her left forearm forward. Mother Superior tapped Stella's right hand. Stella couldn't outsmart the nun, of course. She knew Stella was left-handed and would not be able to write neatly after a whack on her left. During the first two years of high school, the nun had attempted to break her left-handedness to no avail.

First, Mother Superior cracked the ruler against the edge of the desk. We all flinched, and then she whipped it smartly against Stella's knuckles. The snap stung my ears, but the shock of watching it break in two caused me to cringe. I knew that empty vodka bottle belonged to her mother, though I didn't understand why she would be carrying it to school.

I often saw Mrs. Lawrence stumble out of Cafferty's Bar on my way home from Laura's house. Laura lived on the other side of Deal Lake in the tiny beach village of Loch Arbor. I lived on the Asbury Park side, where vacationers appeared in droves during the summers. The locals referred to them as Bennies, short for the out-of-towners who hailed from Bayonne, Elizabeth, Newark, and New York. Dad had another name for them, which got him a slap on the wrist from Mother when he used it.

Stella blinked back tears, biting her lip, gazing toward the bright incandescent lights shining from the ceiling. Laura disliked Stella, but I could see her eyes fill at the rim of her lids. That and her shaky hand led me to believe she empathized with the poor girl. The nun handed the broken ruler to Laura. She marched to the front of the classroom and dropped it in the trash.

Did Mother Superior know or even care about the shame Stella had endured because of her sister and mother's trespasses? I wondered that day because she pulled a tube of lotion from her pocket, squeezed a bit into her palm, and began caressing Stella's flaming red knuckles. She'd never done this after whacking anyone before. Our eyes, gleaming saucers, were glued to her every move. While doing so, she spoke to the class in a quieter tone than she had been using.

"We must release the sins from our possession so we can resist temptation the next time it sneaks upon us."

The sweet floral scent, combined with the visual of the soft circular motions, confused me. Mother Superior seemed to be rubbing away the pain she had inflicted. How bizarre. The nun was behaving more erratically than usual.

That Spring, I had no clue she had more on her mind than penalizing students for their transgressions. And my self-absorbed plan interfered like the hem of a school uniform entangled in a bicycle chain.

1973

When Mo first came to us, the dynamics of our home changed in many ways. Mostly for the better. Mother removed her focus from me. I had been the hot pepper in her apple juice, the red lipstick on her white collar, and the sand in her sea scallops. Mo ate up the newfound attention like a starving puppy. The three-year-old became a beloved member of our family, and my parents formally adopted her a year later.

Throughout the years, Mother often commented, "Ivy Jean, if you had been as compliant as our sweet Mo as a child, I wouldn't have turned gray so young."

I supposed she was right, so I never argued. After all I'd put my mother through the summer before Mo arrived, it was amazing she had hair at all. Our city by the sea had begun its descent. Mother had tried her best to shield me from the so-called "riffraff" that had suddenly appeared on our side of the lake. Only, she had no idea I had already dipped my toes into the red tide.

***

I had come home for Mo's high school graduation. With plans to leave for college at the end of the summer, I knew I'd be seeing her even less moving forward. And, with the town's charm fading like an old pair of dungarees, my parents announced they were going to sell the house. This visit would likely be our last time together in Asbury Park—a fitting moment to tell Mo the rest of her story—actually, the beginning.

CHAPTER TWO

M o was searching for an outfit to wear beneath her graduation gown while I sat on the old bentwood rocker in the corner of what used to be my bedroom. One after the other, she yanked clothing from the hangers in her closet. The scent of mothballs overpowered the Aqua Manda perfume lingering in the air. Mo held each item up to her chest in front of the full-length mirror, scrunching her nose at the reflection, then tossing each into a pile on the bed.

"Nope, too dressy. Nope, too boring. Nope, too pink—I hate pink."

"Why do you even have a pink dress in your closet?" I asked curiously.

"Mother thinks redheads look appealing in pink."

"Well, you're not *really* a redhead anymore. I'd say auburn, now."

Mo shrugged, then shimmied into a navy dress and stepped into a pair of black pumps. She stood in front of the mirror, her knobby knees peeking out from beneath the hem, then immediately pulled off the dress and shoes and tossed them onto the bed. She pulled on a pair of dungarees and slipped on moccasins.

I raised an eyebrow and tilted my head. "You'll break Mom's heart if you dress like a hippie."

"She'll get over it, Ivy," she said with sass in her voice. "You broke her in good for me." A devilish grin appeared on her face.

I had moved to New York a year after Mo joined the family, and wasn't part of her daily life, but I made many weekend trips to visit over the years, as well as during holidays. We had a unique relationship considering our age difference. Now and then, I'd secretly steal her away and expose her to small rebellions my parents would frown upon, such as movies requiring adult supervision and ice cream for lunch.

On her fifteenth birthday, I bought her a pack of cigarettes, so she'd experiment in front of me with hopes she'd get it out of her system before being lured into the temptation from peer pressure. That one could have backfired for sure, but Mo did not have the same inquisitive nature as I had as a teenager. She had a plan for her future from the moment she watched her first TV episode of "The Nurses." Mother bought her Barbie Nurse for Christmas. Soon after, her toy box was filled with stethoscopes, thermometers, and bandages swiped from the medicine cabinet.

"I'm going to help doctors make patients get better," Mo proclaimed at nine years old. We did not doubt that she would.

I opened my purse and grabbed the new lipstick I had brought for her, then held it out while remaining seated in the chair. "It's called Moon drops—it's shiny."

"Thanks." She clutched it in her long fingers, then twisted the base, and brought it to her face, puckering in front of the mirror and spreading the peachy gloss onto her full lips.

Just before snapping my purse shut, I pinched the newspaper clipping hidden inside and read the headline one last time, hoping to gather the courage to share it with Mo. Secrets have a way of slipping through the cracks, and I couldn't risk Mo peeling back a layer of phony wallpaper in search of the truth—as I had, the year before my own high school graduation.

"I'm proud of you," I said.

"What for?"

"For knowing what you want in life. You've said you wanted to be a nurse since you were a little girl, and soon, that's what you'll be."

Mo grinned. "Yeah, at least I won't have to worry about what to wear every day." She glanced back at the pile of clothes on the bed. "What about you? Did you know what you wanted to be when you were my age?"

"The only thing I knew for sure was that I wanted to get out of Catholic school," I said definitively.

Mo smiled without showing her teeth and admired herself in the mirror, running her fingers through her shag-styled curls. "Aah, solidarity, dear sister," she said. "I attempted that once myself. Obviously, it didn't work out for either of us." A reflection of Mo winked at me from the mirror.

"Well, for me–it kind of did—but not the way I expected it to."

Mo squinted with intrigue. "Sounds like there's a story."

I stood up from the rocker, nervously wrapping the strap from my purse around my finger. "Would you like to hear it?"

She turned from the mirror and glared into my eyes, blue like my mother's, covered with a light layer of black mascara.

"Of course."

"Okay, then." I released the strap, and it twirled loose.

She placed her hands on her hips, standing a head taller than me as if she were the older one. "Well, spill!"

I repositioned the purse strap diagonally over my body, flipping my long, dirty blonde ponytail out of the way. "Not now, of course, it's much too long." I took a deep breath. "After the graduation party, we'll take a walk down to the beach, and I'll tell you everything."

"Everything?"

"Yup, everything."

* * *

After the graduation party, I followed Mo back to our room—her room—my room. The familiar scent of Pond's cold cream filled the air. Mo pushed her hair away from her face with a plastic headband, smoothed on a layer of cream, and removed her makeup with a tissue.

"Why are you looking at me so weird?" she asked.

I grabbed one end of the belted sash hanging from my yellow dress and wrapped it securely around my finger. "You remind me of a friend I had back in high school."

"How so?" She deep-stared at me, waiting for an answer, the same way I used to do with Gramps when he would lure me into one of his tales with a morsel of intrigue and then leave me hanging for the rest.

"One, she was stubborn, and two—messy—very messy." I pointed to the pile of clothing still on top of her bed.

"I'm not stubborn," she smiled. "Are you still friends?"

"Not anymore."

"Why not?"

"It's a long story."

"Oh yeah, by the way, don't you already owe me a story?"

"You bet. I'll meet you out front after I change."

On my way out the front door, I waved to Mom and Dad. They sat on the floral loveseat facing the TV, where Gramps's old chair used to be. "We're going for a walk on the beach."

"Be careful," Mom said. "Make sure you stay near the streetlights."

Still a worrywart, I nodded at her command and followed Mo, allowing the screen door to slam behind us.

Mo bent down, picked up two large beach pails, and handed me one.

"Maybe we can find enough sea glass to finish that Mosaic table you and Gramps abandoned."

I grinned slightly. "Yup, maybe this time, we'll find the right pieces to fill in the gaps."

It would be a long story, but it was important that I start from the beginning. After all, I did promise to tell her everything.

CHAPTER THREE

1958

The year before I started at St. Teresa's, I begged and pleaded with my mother to let me attend public high school. Whenever I brought up the topic, she proclaimed that every female in her family had graduated from Catholic school, and the tradition would carry on if she had anything to say about it.

"Catholic school will ensure you receive all the attributes to become a proper young lady," she declared. "Public school will destroy that! Your father and I have made many sacrifices for you to attend St. Teresa's. We are protecting you—not to mention, half the girls in public school end up pregnant."

"I'll be the other half," I countered.

The conversation always ended with Mother saying, "End of discussion."

As far as I was concerned, I had completed the sacraments and received the benefits from these teachings. Communion, Confirmation, and endless confessions. Hail Mary's, Our Fathers, and a mountain of Eucharists had prepared me for a righteous path. Cooped up with the same group of girls year after year, destined to become wives, seamstresses, or secretaries, bored me to tears.

I desired a future that would allow me to become something

extraordinary. The freedom to make a difference in the world—
somehow. I wasn't quite sure what that difference would be; however,
I believed public school would offer me more opportunities than
Catholic School ever could. No one I'd ever known from St. Teresa's
went to college. At least in public school, a girl had the chance to hear
about college and possibly other things that could guide her future.
Back then, though Mom and Dad paid for Catholic School, they would
never have paid for college.

Before finishing up my junior year, I had to make one last attempt
to convince them to allow me to complete my senior year in the
public school before it was too late to enroll. In my last-ditch effort, I
knew I could obtain support from my ally and confidant—my dear
old Gramps.

Gramps had moved in with our family after Gram died; I was seven.
He had always supported my desire for unorthodox pursuits. A thin,
lanky man with white hair, mustache, and a beard, he resembled an
underfed Santa.

I couldn't remember a time when he did not make room in his day
to support my curious shenanigans.

At nine, when I appeared outside Gramps's truck, dressed in a pair
of overalls and a cap (I had convinced the boy next door to lend me),
Gramps had no problem letting me tag along with him to work. Only
my father, a stern man with little room in his imagination, didn't see
my explorative nature in the same light as Gramps.

"Where do you think you're going, young lady?" Dad had asked.

"I'm going to work with Gramps," I explained, while holding a
paintbrush in one hand and a yellow beach bucket in the other.

"Little girls do not paint houses," he scoffed.

"There's no harm in letting her tag along," Gramps told him. "It's
good for her to see the work I do; she might learn something."

"Ivy, it's best you stay home and help me in the kitchen today," Delores, my always put-together-perfect-submissive mother, interjected.

I stomped my feet. "Please," I begged.

My father scowled. "You know what—let her go!" he said, swatting the air. "It'll be good for her to see what manual labor looks like. One day, when she's considering a husband, she'll be sure to avoid one who is employed as such."

"I don't want a husband; I just want to paint."

Gramps laughed and replaced the neighbor's cap on my head with a painter's hat. My mother handed me an old towel, which I put in my back pocket like Gramps, and we strode out the door.

At ten, I declared a career with the circus would be best suited for a girl like me. A girl determined to have the freedom to flip and fly through life and travel the world. Gramps generously funded gymnastic classes once a week until I broke my arm.

"How the hell are you going to do your schoolwork and help around the house?" My father screamed as he drove me home from the hospital. "I should never have agreed to those ridiculous classes. Why couldn't you have taken up sewing like your mother?"

I managed to get through the last four weeks of school that year with a cast on my arm and a C in penmanship, which I probably would have received anyway. No matter how much I loved to write, doing it neatly was a challenge. My brain moved faster than my hand ever could.

At eleven, Gramps bought me a set of Nancy Drew books and a library card. Those books changed my world. Nancy became the sister I didn't have, keeping me company through the ugly years of adolescence. Nancy filled my mind with adventures and ideas. Nancy gave me hope that a girl had choices in life.

Gramps conspired with Nancy by providing me with clues to solve the disappearance of the missing household items he had secretly hidden. The numerous books I read during those years educated me in various ways. Mostly, I learned to observe my surroundings. And that breaking rules sometimes yielded positive results.

As I grew older, I learned about war. I gained an understanding of the gift of freedom we had been given because of those who fought for it. Spending evenings, weekends, and summers lost in pages following women of espionage inspired me as well. So, I asked, "Gramps, should I join the military?"

"Unless you have a desire for tending to the wounded or taking dictation, I doubt that would satisfy your thirst for knowledge and adventure."

Not long after, I imagined working as a military infiltrator on behalf of our country to keep the commies out. The idea intrigued me. After all, I'd spent half my life living the existence of a sleuth through the glorious pages of books that offered an adventure outside of my bedroom and little beach town.

However, it occurred to me that a girl from a Catholic school in Asbury Park, New Jersey, was even less likely to obtain a career in military espionage than to become a coach for a national football team. Nevertheless, Gramps indulged me.

"Gathering information is an honorable skill if used for good and reasonable purposes." He scratched his beard. "Let me think on that one."

Gramps always had an answer for my inquisitive mind. Though when I asked him questions about his own life before he had become my grandfather, he'd turn quiet. Usually, reaching for a half-smoked cigar stub, which always seemed to be waiting for a flame in the heavy glass ashtray. He'd sit back in his chair, holding the stub between his lower lip and nicotine-stained mop of a mustache, flicking the alligator skin table lighter until it sparked to life and the red embers began to glow.

With closed eyes, he'd puff and gradually lean back into his ugly lime-colored chair. Then, he'd blow a plume of smoke into the sea air and digress by sending me to retrieve a handful of pretzel sticks or a root beer.

So, I decided it might be best to retreat from asking questions and instead ask for support with my latest quest—transferring to the public school for my senior year. He had to agree that I deserved to expand my horizons. I deserved to go to college. And the educational teachings of a nun could never make that possible.

In any event, after witnessing Stella's recent lashing, I decided it would be best to express my fear of Mother Superior to Gramps. I could tell him she'd gone off the deep end. She's out of touch, I'd say. She doesn't know what's going on in the world. She doesn't even have a college degree like the teachers in public school. Then, he would share the information with my mother, and I could use it as a catalyst for my pursuit. Although I hadn't been a recipient of the nun's wrath, lately, she'd begun staring at me with an inquisitive eye. My gut told me I should watch my step. Then again, I thought, maybe I shouldn't.

CHAPTER FOUR

other Superior often declared God had blessed her with the gift of prophecy. She told us she could foresee Satan's temptations before they confronted us. In truth, I believed she set out to hose down our fiery hormones before they got us into trouble. Whenever I thought about Denny Carson, mine reached temperatures that would make me sweat.

And it was true. Temptation lurked at every corner, threatening my good sense. The Friday night after Stella's knuckle thrashing, Laura and I went to the dance at St. Joe's Boys School. I had a good feeling Denny would be there. Now and then, I'd seen him from afar on Main Street and Cookman Avenue. Always by himself—and in a hurry—he tore about town in his rebel black leather jacket as if he were on a secret mission. Except when I caught sight of him near St. Joe's. At those times, he wore a uniform and could have resembled any other Catholic schoolboy. But the dark bundle of curls accompanied by his confident strut, which the others lacked, helped me spot him quickly.

The school dances only happened twice a year, and the anticipation was grueling, not to mention Mother Superior's list of 'dos' and 'don'ts'.

"Remember, girls, when you dance with a boy, make sure to leave enough space for the Holy Ghost. Give Him plenty of room because you'll need him to intercept your lustful desires."

* * *

When Laura and I arrived at St. Joe's School, the dancing hadn't yet begun, so I ventured off to the girls' room to check my hair in case I ran into Denny. No one knew for sure why he attended St. Joe's. Rumor had it he was a charity case, like Stella, and he lived at the boys' home on Bangs Avenue. Other than that, I didn't know much more about him than the fact that he played guitar and was too cute to ignore.

The battleship gray linoleum floors were not much different from those at St. Teresa's. However, sports team banners and photos of graduates adorned the pale green walls. And trophies for baseball and football sat on glass-encased shelves.

The alabaster hallways of St. Teresa's boasted bulletin boards with boring paper borders displaying honor rolls, club photos, and typed announcements under the large crucifix. Plus, the framed pictures of former nuns with no smiles and dull eyes. I enjoyed soaking in the different scenery of the boys' school.

On the right-hand side at the end of the first hallway, a makeshift sign hung on the bathroom door that read, 'Girls' Room.' Before I entered, I spotted Denny bent over a water fountain. Donned in a pair of tight dungarees and a black leather jacket, his dark curls were now slicked back above his ears. My footsteps must have alerted him because he turned around, his grin so wide I thought I'd pass out.

"Hey there, Ivy," he said and moved toward me with his suave demeanor. His chest protruded out several inches more than the rest of him, the way a confident or arrogant football player appears when he's greeting his opponent. Though Denny's build was too small for football, the twinkle in his eye caught mine like a wide receiver.

I batted my eyes and smiled. "Hi, Denny, I didn't think you'd show up."

"Aren't you happy to see me?" He moved closer, took my hand, and spun me around. "You sure look peachy."

I could feel my face blush. "Where's your suit jacket?" I thought it odd he wasn't wearing one and wondered how he got in without it.

"Shh." He put his finger to my lips. "That's just a technicality." He clasped my hands with his and led me toward the white cement wall in the corner, and gently pinned me against it. He wiggled his right foot in between both of mine, widening my stance, getting closer to me than ever before. His warm breath breezed into my ear as he whispered, "I've been looking for you since the minute I got here."

My heart raced, and my mouth grew dry. Denny let go of my hands, brushed the pin curls hanging from my barrette over my right shoulder, and started kissing my neck.

I stepped back. "Want a mint?" I attempted to dig inside my purse.

He grabbed my hand again and clasped it with his. I should've pushed him away with the other. That was the right thing to do. But when the tips of his fingers began roaming along my neck, shoulders, and ribs, in the dark corner of the hallway, pulling away from Denny was more difficult than disengaging from an ocean rip current.

Denny had swirled me into the quicksand of temptation. My body experienced nice little spasms in places I'd never known before. I'd never kissed a boy, and my mind was fighting to force my tongue to protest. But I had become mute—until his hands slid beneath my blouse and touched my bare skin, creeping up toward my bra. I gripped his forearm as if I were Sleeping Beauty, awoken from a trance, and pushed him off me.

"Denny, stop!"

"I'm sorry," he said and stared down at his feet.

I did an about-face and rushed inside the bathroom.

Thank God my mind had won the battle against my weak flesh. Being in that hallway at school, not shut inside a car, was my saving grace. Several girls had been discussing that scenario at the lunch table the prior week. Denny didn't have a car, family, friends, or any ambitions that I knew of. Aside from his playful smile and dreamy brown eyes, I wasn't sure why I found him so appealing. My mother would have called him a "hood." I was afraid to even imagine what Dad would have called him.

I'd hoped to run into Denny, but not so literally. Laura would be wondering what was taking me so long. Unless she finally worked up the nerve to speak to one of the more popular boys hanging around the bandstand, she'd probably come looking for me soon. I was surprised she hadn't accompanied me to the powder room as usual. Never had either of us ventured into the halls of St. Joe's alone. One of Mother Superior's 'don'ts.' Now, I knew why.

The sight of urinals in the bathroom reminded me that, despite the sign on the door reading, "Girls' Room," I was indeed in a boy's bathroom, which felt wrong. There wasn't even a mirror above the sink, which made it difficult to maneuver my hair back into place. The tortoise-shell barrette had fallen loose on my head, and strands of beige ringlets had fallen onto my forehead and cheeks. I pulled it back by memory and ran my hand across, smoothing it into place. Next, I splashed cold water on my face to cool the pink flush. Evidence of the lustful encounter with Denny.

No mirror in my compact, only Denny's cigarettes that I hadn't returned yet, and a pack of mints. I couldn't check for smudged lipstick or tell if my flushed face had melted my mascara. This would certainly earn me an infraction if one of the nuns noticed. Denny had vanished by the time I came out of the bathroom. Keeping my head low, I strolled back down the hall to Laura. The scent of popcorn filled the air, and music spilled out from the gym. My heart rate returned to normal, but my body still felt the heat of Denny.

* * *

My eyes darted down each corridor as I followed the music. Maybe Denny would jump out from one of the classroom doorways and grab my hand, spin me across the hallway in pirouettes, and into the gym where everyone would see us together. But he didn't. "Rock Around the Clock" played, and shiny-toothed grins plastered the faces of my classmates. Their ponytails danced, and skirts sashayed as they glided along the gymnasium floor.

A hollow feeling in my chest rose to my throat that I'd never experienced before—I didn't like it. Maybe Denny rushed ahead and beat me to the gym. I scanned the large room in search of his devilish grin, but he was not there. Where had he gone? Why had he gone? The "Still of the Night" began to play. Slow-dancing, high school juniors joined into couples. Their hands delicately touching one another's shoulders. The Holy Ghost properly positioned to obstruct any opportunity from engaging in an intimate embrace.

Denny was nowhere. And I had led him to believe I might have agreed to offer something more to him in a hallway corner! Not that I would have. Only slutty girls did such things. I was no slut. But the message might have begged differently, and the word 'easy' might have rung in his ear.

Mother Superior's voice trickled into my brain. Lust is for the wicked. When you feel the impulse to heed its power, pray for strength. I breathed a sigh of relief and hugged myself tight. Perhaps her prayers had interceded on my behalf after all. Because, when the time came to resist temptation, I hadn't thought to pray—I had only thought to sin. So, I closed my eyes and crossed myself, whispering in my mind another apology to God.

After a deep breath, I pasted on a 'who-cares' smile and strutted toward Laura. Within a second, she grabbed my arm and dragged me to a seat near the back of the gym, beneath the basketball hoop. Freckled and perky, her ponytail hung like pulled chocolate taffy, and her eyes were large and dark with lashes I'd die for. When she plopped down on the folding chair next to me, her poodle skirt spread out over each side, exposing her long calves and skinny ankles. Matching pink anklets sagged slightly over her saddle shoes.

"Holy mother of God, you're a mess." She pulled a tissue and a compact from her purse and handed them to me.

I licked my finger and used the saliva and tissue to fix my lipstick and blot the mascara I had feared would be beneath my eyes.

"I followed you to the bathroom a few minutes after you left. But when I turned the corner, I saw Mother Superior grab Denny by the collar and yank him toward the fire exit door," Laura said with one long breath. "That nun is much stronger than she looks!"

"Amazing. That woman can sniff out sin like a cat stalking a field mouse." I suppose Mother already knew her words had not taken root in my soul. "She would've made an excellent spy," I said morosely, twirling a piece of hair around my index finger. "Maybe she was a spy before she became a nun."

Laura snorted. "I highly doubt that. Women become nuns because they have a calling from God, or maybe their parents shipped them to a convent because they were pregnant or out of control." She grinned. "That's probably it—she was railroaded by her parents. Now, she's a crabby old woman who never got the chance to be a teenager!"

Suddenly, the hurt and anger that enveloped me only minutes before disappeared. Laura and I both chuckled at the vision of Mother Superior as a defiant teenager, smoking Lucky Strikes and swearing like a sailor. Then we sauntered to the snack table and bought a couple of sodas. We smiled at the boys who were smiling at us. And I stopped thinking about Denny—until Monday.

CHAPTER FIVE

On my way to first period, Mother Superior called me into her office. The nauseating scent of English lavender hit me hard. The fragrance seemed to emanate through the halls when a nun strolled by, but it weighed heavily in the stagnant air of the small office. I counted each step in my head from my locker to the office, which approximated twenty-five size seven shoe steps.

"Ivy." She goaded with her crooked finger. "Come in. Sit down." She pulled a tissue from a plain white box and laid it on her desk before me. "Your gum, please."

I spat out the cinnamon Dentine into the tissue and handed it to her.

"Lipstick." She handed me another tissue.

"It's Vaseline!" I sucked my lips inward to discreetly rub off as much as I could.

"I have never seen pink Vaseline—remove it."

She ripped another tissue from the box and held it out.

I was stripped of my gum, pink lip balm, and the last shred of belief that our little chat would end on a positive note. What else had she planned for me?

"Are you hard of hearing?" She cracked the wooden ruler on the edge of the desk.

I flinched. "No, Mother. I don't think so."

She placed the ruler down and folded her arms. "Tell me why you allowed that boy to grope you in the hallway at the dance Saturday night."

Of course, she was referring to Denny, and I feared the inquiry was a trick question. Had she really seen us? How could I answer? If I told the truth and said, "It felt really nice, Mother," I'd still be in trouble. If I didn't tell the truth, it would be a sin. So, I sat like a mannequin and braced myself for a whack on the knuckles.

Instead, she reached into a tote bag sitting on the side of her chair. She pulled out a magazine and slapped it onto the desk. Next, she tapped her finger on the cover photo. It was a picture of a pregnant teenager. "Do you want to end up like this?" She closed her fist and pounded the cover, then raised both hands in the air. The fire in her eyes made her seem more possessed by the devil than by God.

I shivered. "No, Mother," I said, with my head bowed.

She got up from her seat and strolled behind me. I sat stiffly. Suddenly, her hot breath rushed down my neck as she wrapped her hand around my ponytail and yanked it with such force, I thought my neck would snap. "I didn't hear you!"

"No, Mother! I do not want to end up like that." Tears welled up in my eyes, and I sniffled.

"I pray you don't." She sat back down and snapped the skewer against the desk. "Explain to me why I should not call your parents."

"It wasn't my fault, Mother. He cornered me unexpectedly."

"Well, then, why didn't you report him to me?" she probed.

Nothing else had come to mind as to how to dig myself out of the hole. Why couldn't I be quick-witted like Stella?

I counted the pencils in the jar on her desk to calm my nerves before I attempted to drum up a valid response. "I don't know, I guess I *do* like him—and sin took hold of me—it just took hold of me!" I blurted, not sure whether she'd buy it.

Mother Superior stared hard into my eyes as if she were trying to see if the Holy Ghost really did reside there and whether it would direct her decision. She inhaled for several seconds and then said, "After school, go see Father Joe for confession and receive your penance. And be certain, I will be documenting this in your permanent record. Now go to class."

I traipsed out of her office feeling sick to my stomach with an even greater disdain for Catholic school. None of this would be an issue in public school. Boys liked girls. Girls liked boys. Nuns didn't run students' personal lives.

** * **

Father Joe assigned me six *Our Fathers* and five *Hail Marys*. The following day, in health class, instead of continuing our discussion of the four food groups as we had the previous day, he spoke to us about marriage.

"Marriage is not a reform school, girls," he said. "The man you marry will be the same person after you marry him."

Stella raised her hand and asked, "Isn't that a good thing?"

Several girls in the glass giggled.

Father responded, "It is a good thing if you have a good man."

Laura raised both her hand and chin as an anxious turtle in a school of guppies would and stated, "But if he lies or cheats on you before you marry him, he's going to lie and cheat on you afterwards."

Perhaps Laura had a subscription to magazines I hadn't seen yet. Her response surprised me, and I planned to grill her on it.

Father Joe was a small man with a round face and a large head. His forehead reached far past where hair may have been once, and grayish porcupine-like stubs covered the rest. His nose, flat and wide as if the bone were missing, turned down at the tip. His ears were slightly different in size. However, his teeth were perfect, and his smile counteracted all his oddness. Father strolled over to Laura's desk and patted her head. "Yes, dear, that is the lesson about marriage. When a man shows you who he is, believe him."

* * *

By the end of the week, I was ecstatic to leave school for the weekend, and I forgot my knapsack under my desk. When I rushed back inside to get it, I noticed Mother Superior's office door slightly ajar, but she wasn't inside. A sudden rush of bravery and insanity took over my being.

I stepped into her office.

The combination of terror and curiosity blurred my ability to think rationally. Temptation ensnared me once again, and I decided to find out if the rumor of "The Book of Ill Repute" was indeed true. If so, was my name listed among the sinful? My goal—remove the pages and return the book on Monday without Mother Superior ever noticing it missing. Then, I'd make my case to my parents that the nun was crazy. They would heed my warning and let me leave the school before it was too late. Of course, they'd meet with Mother Superior, who would open the book to expose my transgressions. There would be none—only her word with no tangible proof.

* * *

I glanced to the left, then to the right, and stepped further inside. It was wrong—really, wrong, but I couldn't stop myself. Heart pounding and sweat trickling down my forehead, I scurried to her desk, opened the top drawer, and explored, glancing at the door every few seconds. Nothing. Frantically, I pulled the next drawer open and sifted through papers, pens, and rosary beads. I found a few compacts and lipsticks that the nun must have confiscated from students.

What the heck was I doing? The existence of such a book was a rumor that had been going around for years. I could be taking a considerable risk for nothing. If Mother found me, I'd be in so much trouble that there'd be no way I'd escape the ruler and who knows what else. If Mom found out, she'd *never* let me out of Catholic school. It could all backfire; yet I couldn't stop myself.

Only one more desk drawer to open. I pushed the soaking wet bangs off my face with the back of my hand and opened another drawer. Still nothing. Somewhat relieved, but at the same time dissatisfied, I had to accept that the rumors were just that. I shut the last drawer and glanced around one final time. Before I could exit, the sound of footsteps shuffled toward the room.

I had to think quickly! I'd tell Mother Superior I had stopped by to say goodbye, and I suddenly felt faint. Perhaps I'd tell her that a pack of hoodlums were taunting me from across the street. Maybe, I'd say I was afraid and ran back inside for help. Just before I practically peed my pants, the scent of ammonia preceded Mr. Jack, the school custodian. He appeared with a bucket and mop.

"Hi there, Ivy." He grinned, exposing a perfect set of Jersey corn-colored teeth. "You're here awfully late for a Friday, young lady." His right eyebrow raised. "Did you forget something?"

Mr. Jack was taller than any man I'd known. His head was akin to Frankenstein's monster, large and rectangular, though the janitor possessed zero traits of anything scary. With dusty brown hair and shiny, blue eyes that smiled all the time, he was more popular than Father Joe or any of the nuns. He'd spent many years cleaning the halls, the bathrooms, the lunchroom, and the classrooms at St. Teresa's. He knew all the girls by name and spoke to us as if we were his own.

"Oh—yes, Mr. Jack!" I swallowed a gulp of air. My mouth was as dry as summer. "I left my knapsack behind. When I saw Mother's door open, I stopped in to wish her a nice weekend, but she's not here." I shrugged.

"You girls would forget your heads if they weren't attached." He smiled. "I'm in a rush, myself, to get home; going to see my daughter's first ballet recital."

"That's nice." I shuffled toward the door, fearing he'd hear the pounding of my heart. The remorse I felt about lying to the janitor seemed to weigh more heavily on me than the sin I was about to commit.

"Oh, dang, I forgot my keys in the gym." He smacked the palm of his hand against his forehead. "I guess Fridays are forgetful for the bunch of us, looking forward to the weekend and all." He abandoned his mop and bucket and rushed out.

Seizing one last chance, I inched toward the closet where Mother Superior kept her sweater and reached up to the shelf above. The space was dim, and I had to rise onto my toes, stretching until my fingertips brushed against something smooth and cool. My thumb traced faint ridges across the cover, raised like Braille. With a quick tug, I pulled the book down. It was indeed black, made of leather. Its title, glinting faintly in the light: *Records*, was stamped in worn gold letters. Not quite as exciting as "Book of Ill Repute." I quickly shoved it inside my knapsack.

Just then, Mr. Jack reappeared. "Lucky for you, Mother Superior is still here," he said. "She's on her way back, now."

I froze for an instant. "Unfortunately, I gotta run—just realized my mother is waiting on me. Thanks." I bolted out of the office.

I was a thief in the night, stealing precious jewels. I never looked back as I dashed the four blocks home. My knapsack contained secrets I was about to unveil. The act I had just committed excited me as if I were Mata Hari or Edith Cavell. Mata Hari, the exotic, dancing spy, used her seductive abilities during World War I for the greater good. However, Mata Hari had first escaped to France from an abusive husband, not a nun. Nevertheless, she found a career. Edith Cavell, on the other hand, was a nurse and spy who treated wounded soldiers from both sides, without discriminating, during the Great War. Ironically, both were killed by a firing squad. I shivered at the thought.

The rumor of the book was true, and in my possession. Now that I had it, what would I do with it? First, I'd make sure to remove any page where my name appeared. Perhaps I'd share the other confidential pages for money? My father often spoke about the luxuries of being an entrepreneur. I chuckled at the thought. Maybe I'd keep the information to myself and smile each time I stared a page-dweller in the eyes, knowing they didn't know what I now knew.

These thoughts ran through my mind as I passed Freedman's Bakery on Main and breathed in the scent of powdered sugar and jelly doughnuts. I caught a glimpse of the crossing guard. Maybe I'd find notes on her daughter, the phony Goodie Two-Shoes.

A German shepherd leaped against the chain-link fence from behind the corner gas station. He barked at me as if he sensed what I had done. The traffic light turned green. I rushed across the street, ahead of two elderly women, toward the brick ranch house with the statue of Mary in the garden. My house.

Mary's fresh crown of rose buds and lilies was still vibrant two weeks after my mother and I crowned her. Mother would undoubtedly say it is because our home is blessed, and I'd agree. Mary undoubtedly would not be pleased with me. So, I crossed myself before I rushed inside, nearly tripping over a stack of books Mom had left for me to return to my room. Bolting up the stairs, two at a time, to my bedroom, my curiosity about to cause me to explode, I pulled the book from my knapsack. Before I opened it, I prayed, *Dearest Holy Mother, Most Holy Mary, please forgive me.*

It took me half a second to push past the guilt, and I opened the front cover and turned to page one.

CHAPTER SIX

The first name on the line read George S. in beautiful script writing—much nicer than mine could ever be. Next to the name was a room number, and beneath it was what appeared to be a description . . . or directions. It read:

No hugs.

Likes to hold hands

Must cut and butter bread and place napkin on lap when dining

Who the heck was George S.? And why did Mother Superior want to cut and butter his bread? I moved my finger to the next line, it read:

Jack H. – Room 412

 Likes hair fondled at the nape of his neck

 Martinis with three olives

 Shoulder rubs over shirt

The book made no sense. Why would a book hidden in the head nun's office of a girls' Catholic school contain this information? Not to mention, who would even be allowed to drink martinis while getting . . . a shoulder rub? The excitement for the book I'd hoped to find disappeared, and intrigue replaced it.

Confused, I read on and stopped when the content changed…

J. FINETTI – LIAR!

The other notes in the book didn't make sense to me. No doubt it was Mother Superior's handwriting, though. The pit that formed in my stomach now reached my throat, inhibiting my ability to breathe. As I read on, I realized I may have taken something very personal, more personal than the *Book of Ill Repute*—if one existed at all. This book had the possibility of so many connotations. My mind reeled. I needed to share this with someone who would be as curious as I was to dig into this book—someone who had something to gain or lose—like me.

* * *

The book encompassed twenty pages of content, written in blue ink, that triggered a circus of confusion in my mind. I read it repeatedly, each time, believing it might make sense. Was it some kind of code? Had Mother written all this nonsense and placed it in her closet, knowing a student would fall into her trap and search for it? The joke would be on them—on me? If so, the onus would fall on me.

Perhaps Mother was gathering notes for a novel about men whom she fantasized about taking her places in town where she would never be seen. Although nuns couldn't marry, I figured they must have some feelings about men. Whatever her story was becoming, I knew one thing for sure: it might just be my ticket out of Catholic school. And more than ever, I was determined to uncover who Mother Superior really was beneath that habit.

As I pondered who would be best suited to help me decipher the information in the book, it occurred to me that it should be somebody non-judgmental—someone I could trust not to share my secret. Even though Laura was my best friend, I couldn't risk telling her. Her secret-keeping skills were worse than her inability to refrain from bragging.

I'd learned that back in sixth grade, when a note landed on my desk that said, *Ivy got her period.* I immediately recognized her handwriting. The note would not have upset me so much if I hadn't been the *only* girl in class who had been blessed with what we all eventually referred to as "a visit from Aunt Flow."

I considered asking my neighbor, a girl who had always been a step ahead of me in matters of maturity. Long braids and charcoal eyes, she bore a striking resemblance to Pocahontas. On weekends, she'd release the braids, and her silky, long locks would fall down her shoulders like unraveled black licorice. There was not one inch of fat on her body. No curves either. The two of us met up now and then during the summers, despite my mother's attempts to cut our friendship off after she caught her showing me how to stuff my bra with toilet tissue.

"She's fast, that girl," Mom said. "That's because she's in public school." She spat out the "p" in public like it was a worm in her sandwich.

My relationship with her was one of convenience. When neither of our closer friends was available, we'd find each other. Though after more thought, I feared the neighbor girl might not be trustworthy. She might share the information with her public-school friends, who would most definitely not keep the secret. I also worried she might think of me as naïve or just plain stupid for not having a clue about the book's contents, despite how unusual.

Stella Lawrence came to mind. She seemed the perfect candidate. But, if I called Stella, what would I say? I couldn't imagine she'd have any more success deciphering this book than I would. But she certainly had more reasons than anyone else I knew to have a look-see.

* * *

The house stank like fish. We always ate fish on Friday because it was a sin to eat meat. Jesus sacrificed His flesh for us on Good Friday, and therefore, Catholics refrained from eating meat in His honor. My mother once told me that eating meat on the day when Christ suffered is like biting into His wounds. That visual alone almost caused me to abstain from eating meat altogether. Fish and chips were my favorite—my least favorite—linguine with clams. I strolled into the kitchen and sat down. "

"How was school today?" Mom asked.

"Fine," I answered. *I just stole a book from Mother Superior's office, and I need to figure out what it all means. I'll let you know when I do.* "What's for dinner?"

"Linguine and clams."

My appetite crumpled.

The screen door slammed. Gramps shuffled in, whistling along with Glenn Miller's big band orchestra blasting from the transistor radio inside his painter's pants pocket. The scent of turpentine followed him into the kitchen. His tanned and leathery skin, acquired from years of working outside, added a ruggedness to his slight features. Gramps moved along the kitchen floor to the music with an easy grin on his face. He resembled an eccentric *creative* painter rather than the exterior house painter he had been for most of his years.

"Hi, Gramps." I looked up for a brief second from my position at the kitchen table, then rested my chin back upon my elbows and continued staring out the window.

"A penny for your thoughts," he said as he glanced up while he scrubbed Robin's Egg Blue paint from his hands.

I sighed. Despite our close relationship, as much as I wanted to tell him what I'd done, no conversation would be had about what I'd found in the nun's office, nor how I came to find it.

He grabbed a towel from his back pocket and dried his hands. He turned off the radio and laid the towel and his keys on the kitchen counter. "Or a silver dollar for your secrets?" he said in a deep whisper, the way a character in an old film noir would. His eyes, little blue flashlights, dug into my soul as if he knew.

"Just trying to solve a small problem." I changed positions, crossing my arms around my chest, and sighed again.

"Hmmm, from your expression, I get the feeling your problem isn't as small as you say." He combed his white mustache with his right index finger and raised one bristly eyebrow.

My secret—had no price . . . at least not until I found out the meaning of the contents of the book.

"Just girl stuff," I said and left it at that. At this point, all I'd done was take something that didn't belong to me—that was bad, especially since I'd stolen it from a nun. Even worse, I had no intentions of giving it back until I knew its value. Unscrupulous! Who had I become?

CHAPTER SEVEN

After dinner, Gramps got up from his ugly green chair and began jingling his change. "I think I hear the ice cream truck." Sure enough, a second later, the Good Humor truck rang his bell. Since childhood, Gramps had repeated the ritual of jingling change in his pockets simultaneously with the truck until I'd find him in the house. When I did, he'd hold both fists stretched out and ask me to tap one. I'd always find a dime in the hand I'd chosen. Though I was too old for this tradition, I went along with it so as not to draw any more attention to my unhinged guilt and tapped his right hand.

He grinned widely, exposing his nicotine-stained teeth and a dime in his palm.

"Thanks, Gramps. You want something, too?"

"Naah. Gotta watch my waistline." He patted his belly.

I shook my head at his comment. If anything, he could have used some fat in his diet. He seemed to be getting thinner, unlike most of my friends' granddads, who looked as if they'd swallowed a small watermelon.

The truck pulled up to the corner of my house, and a group of kids from the neighborhood rushed up the street and surrounded it. Dressed in a crisp, white uniform and a black bow tie, the attendant wore a hat that resembled that of a ship's captain. He hopped out of the truck and stood in front of the icebox. I scanned the various choices on the yellow strip on the truck's side while he waited to accommodate me. No one's ever too old for ice cream, after all.

"What can I get you, young lady?"

"A coconut bar, please."

The attendant yanked the lever of the heavy door to the ice box, and cool air spewed out. He handed me the ice cream bar. In turn, I handed him the dime, and he inserted it into the silver change dispenser that hung from his belt. With a quick tear, I ripped the wrapper off. Cold smoke-like vapors drifted up my nostrils, making my taste buds water. After the first lick, I swirled the sweet, creamy substance around the inside of my mouth while chomping on the bits of coconut. The smell and taste reminded me of my childhood days. No worries. No boys. No nuns . . . Now, I enjoyed each bite while I replayed the words from the book in my head.

Later that evening, Gramps met me on the front porch with a cigar in one hand and a glass of bourbon in the other. He sat down in a wicker rocker. I grabbed the Adirondack chair, faced it toward him, and plopped down.

"How's my sweet girl this evening?" He exhaled a plume of cigar smoke. "You want to hear a story?"

Usually, I enjoyed his stories, but at that moment, I wasn't interested. I couldn't stop thinking about the book. For a minute, I considered confessing to Gramps that I'd stolen it just to make it easy on myself and find out if I was barking up the wrong tree. Then, I opted against it. Even Gramps would have an issue with my stealing Mother Superior's book, no matter what it contained. Anyhow, I didn't want to abandon him. My mother had reminded me how fortunate I was to still have my grandfather. Both her grandparents had died when she was young, and Gramps seemed to be slowing down lately.

"Sure, Gramps," I said. "Tell me about the time you saved a girl during the war."

"Okay, okay." His eyes looked off into the corner of his mind, and he began speaking in a soft tone. "She had hair like you, Ivy—sandy blond curls that cascaded down her shoulders—and eyes the color of aquamarine. She'd sit on the front stoop of her house in Frankfurt and wave to me as I passed by, dressed in my Navy uniform. I'd tip my hat and offer a gentle smile so as not to frighten her. After many weeks, I asked her name and who her parents might be."

"What was her name?" I asked.

"Ella." His tongue held out the letter *l*. I wasn't sure whether this was intentional or due to the glass of bourbon.

"Was she always by herself?"

"Yes, Ivy, and I worried about her." He puffed on his cigar and blew out a miniature cloud of smoke, which veiled my vision. With his hand, he fanned the smoke away, but behind the cloud, his face re-emerged with tear-filled eyes, as he had many times before when he spoke about the war. However, this was the first time he mentioned the girl by name.

"Where were her parents?" I moved in closer to see if Gramps would share more about the story than he had the last time.

"One day, on my way to town for coffee and cigars, I noticed her missing from the stoop. The front windows of her house were wide open. A white lace curtain fluttered in the wind, reaching out as if the house were sending a signal for help."

Gramps seemed to be in a trance. He'd never gotten so detailed while sharing a story. His eyes were glazed over. If I had waved my hand in front of his face, I doubted he'd see it.

"When I approached the front steps, I could see inside and noticed a man lying on the floor and Ella curled up in the corner with her hands wrapped around her knees. Her hair clung to her face, hiding those pretty eyes as she sat shivering. A wheelchair flipped on its side lay next to the man with a gun beside his hand. A pool of blood surrounded his . . ."

"His what?" I asked. My deadpan expression must have brought Gramps back to his memories of the war.

"This is not a part of the story you need to hear," he said, and laid his cigar in the ashtray. "You're too young to have these visions in your head—what was I thinking?" He picked the cigar up and puffed it back to life.

"I'm not a kid anymore, Gramps!" I placed my hand on his shoulder. "I feel as if I know Ella, too. Please, finish the story."

He got up from the chair, dabbed out his cigar in the tray, and staggered inside the house, his hands trembling. "No."

Time after time, I had pushed Gramps to tell the whole story. This was the most he'd ever shared. His inability to continue intrigued me even more.

Optimistic he'd return, I stayed seated on the porch and grabbed a copy of *Reader's Digest* from a basket next to the table and read while I waited. What was he going to say next? Would it be about the girl? The man who got shot? Or, perhaps he'd tell me about himself. Maybe something completely different. On the edge of my seat, I waited to hear more about . . . *Ella.*

Gramps returned about fifteen minutes later, his eyes no longer sad, but gleaming like two blue marbles floating on a sparkling lake. He carried a cigar box that contained his coin collection. He set it down on the round wooden table next to the bucket of sea glass. We had started a collection the previous summer, planning to transform the old table into a mosaic work of art. One of us had lost interest in the project. Gamps would have suggested it was me, and he'd probably have been right. He re-lit the remainder of his now thumb-sized cigar, then laid it in the notch in the rim of the ashtray. Next, he picked up the box of coins. "You wanted to hear about the coins, right?"

He seemed confused, but I went with it. "Sure."

Before opening the box, he shook it as if he were clearing the ghosts left inside. He removed the top and collected several handfuls of change that lay on the thin layer of balsa wood.

"I leave these here in case a thief stumbles on them—thieves are always in a hurry." He winked. "They'd snatch up this change without ever knowing the real treasure that lies beneath."

I sat pensively and nodded. His hand shook as he removed a small coin from the insert and began to tell me what he'd already shared many times.

"This is my first. It's from Italy." He displayed the coin in his open palm.

"I thought you were in Germany, Gramps?" I asked, confused.

"Indeed, I was," he said, "but I also went to Italy. I traveled throughout Europe, Italy, France, England, Austria, and Germany— my parents were born there."

I nodded, already knowing this. "Is that why it's your favorite?" I asked, to goad him into more conversation.

"Yes, Ivy." He nodded with his eyes closed. "And I was one of the fortunate not to have been wounded, or worse." He glanced away. "So many lives were lost."

Gramps told me about his travels and how he began collecting two coins of each denomination from every country he had frequented.

"Like Noah!" I said, trying to lighten the moment.

Gramps laughed. "Not really. But having two of something is smart. If you lose one, you always have a backup, or you might want to give one away to somebody special."

"I wish I had two pairs of white shoes for every summer," I joked.

After our chat, Gramps fell asleep in the rocking chair as he often did, and his cigar sizzled out in the ashtray. I picked up the box, figuring

I'd take it back to his room. My room was at the top right of the stairs. The evening air had grown cool, so I stopped to grab a sweater. My thoughts were running rampant, and I wasn't paying good attention.

Without thinking, I placed the box in the crook of my arm and grabbed the doorknob. My grip slipped, and the box crashed to the wooden floor. A thin rectangle of balsa wood, like the one beneath the scattered change, fell out from the bottom of the box. An old, worn envelope fluttered to the throw rug next to my bed.

Most of the coins remained intact in the thick plastic sleeve. However, several were scattered on the floor. I picked up the cigar box and set it on my bed. Before collecting the missing coins, I removed the sand-colored page from its age-darkened envelope, merely addressed, *Francis*.

Dear Francis,

I will be eternally grateful to you for taking me out of Germany, but had I known you were only bringing me here to leave me, I would not have come. The family you left me with is sending me away, and I can't bear to never see you again. Being cold and hungry in Germany was less painful. Please return for me, I promise I'll keep our secret if I can only be near you.

Eternally yours,

Ella

My hands shook as I re-folded the letter. Pieces crumbled like Saltine crackers onto my powder blue bedspread. This is a *love letter*, I thought, shocked. Why would Gramps have a love letter? It made no sense to me because it was dated 1919, a year after the Great War had ended.

Gramps had already been married, and my mother was a baby. He told me how difficult it had been for him to leave his family, fearing he might never see them again.

Was this the girl that Gramps had spoken about with tears in his eyes so many times? Was this Ella—the person I thought was a *little* girl? She didn't sound little. What had I found? My stomach churned more at the thought that my grandfather had been involved in something immoral—even more than the possible atrocities of the head nun. How could it be possible? How could I have stumbled upon *two* mysteries in one day? Only one provoked me to prove someone's character was dishonorable, and the other, to prove it *couldn't* be.

CHAPTER EIGHT

Sherlock Holmes said, "When you have eliminated the impossible, whatever remains, *however improbable*, must be the truth." Therefore, if I wanted to find the truth about what Mother Superior was up to and what Gramps *had* been up to, this was the thought process I needed to follow.

One by one, I grabbed the coins and placed them back in their matching slots. First, Italy, then France, and Spain. When I got to Germany, I couldn't find the matching coin. I lifted the throw rug from the oak floor and ran my hand beneath it. For the second time in one day, my heart pulsed frantically. I reached beneath my bed as far back as my hand would go, my fingers grasping dust balls. If Gramps decided to pull out the collection again and see it missing, he might know I'd discovered the letter.

"Ivy, please come down and set the table," my mother called.

There was nothing more I could do at that moment, so I brought the box back to Gramps' room and laid it on his desk. I knew he kept a flashlight in his drawer, so I grabbed it in another attempt to find the coin. It had to be somewhere. My mother hollered my name this time.

"Coming!" I shouted.

I needed to keep my composure. Mata Hari had to dance half-naked in front of men while gathering information. *I could not react until I knew all the facts. One mystery at a time.* I had to keep my focus on its original course, put my latest discovery on hold, and devise a plan to approach Stella.

Different scenarios played out in my head. Maybe I'd say, "Stella, I know about your mom. I see her all the time leaving Cafferty's Bar. You know I live down the street. It's not like I'm spying." Even though I was. "I just want you to know, I've never told anyone. That's why I want to share a secret with you—one you can't share with anyone either." Or, perhaps I'd say, "Stella, wouldn't you like to see that rotten Mother Superior get hers? I know a way we can do it, but I need your help."

Then she'd probably say, "Why in the world would you need my help?"

* * *

My mother grimaced when I strolled into the kitchen, but she handed me a basket of warm rolls. The table was mostly set, except for glassware, which I took from the cupboard. I filled each glass with lemonade. Gramps sat down in his regular seat, leaving an empty chair between us, and my mother and I sat to his right.

"Let's say grace," my mother said, folding her hands and bowing her head. We did the same. She thanked God for all we had and prayed for what we didn't. *My father.* He seemed to be gone more often than not.

"Anything new today?" she asked and glanced toward Gramps and me.

For once, I had an entire diary's worth of *newness*, but I couldn't share any of it.

"Nothing here," I said.

Gramps commented, "Same dance, different song."

Afterwards, my mother directed me to wash *and* dry the dishes. When I finished, I rushed back to my bedroom and made another attempt to look for the coin with the flashlight. I shone it in every dark corner of my bedroom, but I couldn't find it. A similar incident happened with a pair of Mom's gold earrings I had borrowed without asking. After a week of searching, I finally gave up and spilled my guts. A few days later, I stepped on it inside my slipper. This time, I decided to wait; I believed it would appear just as the earring had.

In the meantime, I grabbed the black book and held it close to my chest, feeling its rapid heartbeat, while keeping a detective's mindset. All those years of reading spy novels would not leave my psyche alone. No doubt, Edith Cavell would have stolen the book if she thought it was for the greater good.

When Edith was sent to prison during the Great War, she didn't try to defend herself. She knew she was helping people in need. I was doing the same . . . for the girls at St. Teresa's. Not to mention, Edith's father was a priest. If she had discovered a nun as despicable as Mother Superior in her father's church, she would have exposed her, too. However, my ulterior motive for stealing the book in the first place was not quite as admirable. In any event, I believed Mother Superior did not deserve to run the girls' school.

As far as what I had just learned about Gramps, I had to keep that secret hidden in its own box. The figurative one in the back of my mind. It would be impossible to focus on both matters at once. I forced myself to believe there was more to this story than I could understand. When the time was right, I had to believe Gramps would explain everything and make sense of it all.

* * *

Saturday morning, I pulled on a pair of clam diggers, tied my hair in a ponytail, and rushed to the phone. My mother had gone out shopping, and Gramps was out back painting the door to his shed. It was the perfect time to call Stella. The phone rang several times before she picked up. "Hi Stella, it's Ivy.

"Uuh . . . Hi, Ivy. Why are you calling—and how did you get my number?"

"I got it from Laura. She still had it from our Girl Scout days."

"Girl Scouts?" she laughed. "That was a long time ago."

"Yeah, well, Laura's a saver. Anyhow, Stella, I was wondering if we could talk about something. It's not bad—it's something I think you could help me with."

"Like what?"

"Well, it would be better if we could talk in person. Can you meet me on the boards outside Convention Hall—first bench?"

The line was quiet for a second. "What could you possibly need my help for?"

"It's complicated. That's why I want to meet."

After another moment of silence, she asked, "Is this some kind of prank or set-up?"

"I know girls in school have hurt you, but I would never. Really. After we meet, you'll believe me—honest."

"Okay, why not? I don't have anything else to do."

"Can you meet in half an hour?"

"Half an hour?" I could hear her tapping on the receiver. "Yeah . . . I guess."

"Thanks," I said. "See ya later."

* * *

I waited outside Convention Hall. The ornate structure, reminiscent of Grand Central Station. Even more so, a Gothic museum. Its monstrous, Palladian windows, detailed with carvings of baroque creatures, were a highlight of our beach town boardwalk. The concert hall was inside the ornamental limestone-and-concrete façade building.

My parents wouldn't dream of allowing me to attend any of the rock concerts held there. After Frankie Lymon & The Teenagers' show at Convention Hall ended in a bloody riot two years prior, that was the end of that. Mother told me that Asbury Park's city officials almost indefinitely banned rock 'n' roll altogether. Dad said they should have. So, each summer, I lived vicariously through the teenagers who rushed into Mr. Fudge, Saltwater & Taffy, where I had worked, and eavesdropped on their conversations. Bill Haley and His Comets were scheduled to play at the end of June, but I had to pick my battles, and leaving St. Teresa's was more important.

The wind whipped my hair in all directions. Mothers struggled to keep their skirts down with one hand while holding their children with the other. A group of college-aged boys wearing Ivy League cardigans strolled past me and whistled. I hunched over and stared at my feet, hoping they wouldn't return and attempt to talk to me; my nerves rattled.

A beach ball flew over my head from behind and bounced on the boards. I flinched and reached down, picked it up, then tossed it back over the railing. When I looked up, I saw Stella sauntering toward me from the south end, past the empty Bubble Bouncer. In another week or two, the place would be packed with people. I glanced at the silver watch on my wrist, the one Gramps bought me on my sixteenth birthday. Perfect timing—a good trait for an assistant.

Stella wore blue jeans that cinched tightly at her tiny waist, paired with a white sleeveless midriff shirt tied at the bottom. Maybe she didn't have a perfect home life, but she had a perfect body. Her wavy wheat-colored hair was tied back with a blue ribbon, and her bangs curled under, low enough to offset her wide forehead, but not hide the perfectly penciled brows arched above her green eyes.

I waved and patted the bench for her to sit down. "Thanks for meeting me."

She eased onto the bench, crossing her long, shapely legs. Her full lips pressed tightly without a smile, and the faint smell of cigarette smoke rolled off her.

"So, what's this all about, Ivy?"

"You have to cross your heart, hope to die, and promise that what I tell you will never leave your lips. Not to anyone!" I stared deeply into her eyes, brandishing the most serious expression I could dredge up.

An ocean wave crashed, and I moved in closer to hear her response.

"Why should I keep a secret for you? It's not as if we're friends. You barely talk to me in school."

"I'm sorry, Stella. It's not that I don't like you—I do. And, I never say anything bad about you. We just have different friends."

"Why do you suddenly care about me now?" The wind blew her bangs to the side of her face, and her lips relaxed into a pretty pout. I'd never noticed just how attractive Stella was, and despite her low standing in society, a twinge of jealousy pricked me.

"Good question." I thought about mentioning what I knew about her mother, but that might sound like blackmail. A good detective wouldn't be so obvious. It might make her angry instead of wanting to help. I hoped she'd be willing, based on the simple, shocking truth of what I was about to say

"Stella, I'm going to confide in you because I think we can help each other." Out of habit, I wrapped my ponytail around my index finger, counting one, two, three, and letting it unravel on four, and repeated this several times. "I've done something bad, actually— unfathomable—seriously.

She arched her right eyebrow. Those cat-like eyes turned to a fresh grassy green color as the sun hit them.

"Well?" She tapped one foot on the boards. "Spill."

"You know the rumor about Mother Superior's 'Book of Ill Repute?'"

She nodded. "Ugh, yeah—were you not in class the other day?" She peered down her nose at me. "No one knows if it's true—I suppose you know something different?"

"Not exactly—not yet. But I found a book in Mother Superior's office closet."

Her jaw dropped. "You went into her office—her closet? Have you flipped your lid? Why?"

"Well, I got in a little trouble at the dance, and I wanted to see if there really was a book, and if I was in it."

"What did you find? If it's not the book about the students 'dirty deeds,' what is it?"

After releasing a deep breath, I clasped my hands and cracked my knuckles. "A book of men's names!" I hissed in her ear in case some passerby might hear and know what I was talking about.

"Huh?" Stella blinked several times and leaned away, and scratched her head. "That's weird. Aren't all nuns celibate?" Stella showed a smidge of a grin.

"Imagine if Mother Superior is a complete hypocrite and doing all the things she forbids us to do!" My heart raced with excitement. Could you imagine the possibility that I may have opened a case that no one would ever have known? We may have the power to make sure she never whacks anyone again!"

"She's an old woman! That's ludicrous!" Stella spoke with her hands, just as Laura did. "So, where's this book, and what do I have to do with it?"

"You don't have anything to do with it . . . but I need help confirming my suspicions."

Stella scrunched her eyebrows. "And what do you think?"

I dug it out from my knapsack and handed it over. "Before I tell you, I want to hear what you think. And if it is the same as me, we can work together to take Mother Superior down."

Stella turned to the first page, then the next. She began flipping through all the pages quickly, looking more shocked with each turn.

My heart pulsed quickly. I couldn't believe that I was sharing this with a girl who wasn't already a friend. Fear and doubt, a pile of rocks sat on my chest. Nevertheless, I trusted her more than my best friend, Laura.

* * *

Stella closed the book and looked up at me. "It looks like a list of men who seem to be clients—Men who Mother Superior supplies with . . . women!"

"That is exactly what I thought," I lied.

"Can you imagine Mother Superior having sex for money?" I laughed out loud. "And 'pretends' to be a nun during the day? This is lunacy!"

"Not her, stupid. She's too old." Stella shook her head. "She's in charge of them—the Madam! This really is 'The Book of Ill-Repute!'"

I felt like an idiot. Of course, she was the *Madam.* At least I was on the right track.

"We have to get more proof," Stella said. "I think we should follow her to see what she does when she's not in school–where she goes— and who she has working for her."

At that moment, Stella seemed to have more of a detective or spy quality than I did. I suppressed a scowl. This was *my* mystery to solve. If it achieved the outcome I'd set, it would be worth all the time and energy. If I could prove the nun was a liar, my original plan would solve itself. My parents wouldn't want me in a school led by a nun breeding prostitutes. Then again, what if I were wrong?

"Okay. We'll follow her until we find evidence. Are you in—I mean, really in? Like, we're partners?" I asked.

She thrust out her hand. Her creamy skin had turned red and purple across the knuckles, a reminder of the wrath of Mother Superior. "I'm in."

We shook on it.

"What should we do first?" she asked. "We need to calculate a plan."

"Code names, too," I said.

"Code names, really?" Stella raised an eyebrow as if I had said something stupid, again.

The screeching cry of seagulls interfered with my thoughts. I closed my eyes for a moment. "Who's your favorite actress?"

She shrugged. "Elizabeth Taylor, I guess."

"Perfect! Makes me think of Elizabeth Van Lew. She was the greatest secret agent of the Civil War."

"Who?"

"Elizabeth Van Lew," I repeated.

"What did she do?"

"Oh my gosh! What didn't she do?" I shook my head. "First of all, she spent years fighting slavery, hiding slaves, using the Underground Railroad, and she was especially outspoken—kind of like you." I grinned. "She even hung the first Union flag to wave over Richmond."

"What is this, history class?" Stella dropped her chin and rolled her eyes. "I don't remember learning this stuff."

"We didn't learn it in school." Maybe we would have in *public* school. "I learned from reading books."

Stella shrugged. "I prefer magazines."

"Maybe you should be Virginia?" I continued.

"Like, Virginia Grey?"

"Yes."

"Why Virginia?"

"Virginia *Hall* was a spy in World War II. She had a limp because of a wooden leg. And she could still fake people out. Or maybe Josephine Baker?"

"Who was she?" Stella asked. "A spy who snuck knives in a cake?" She asked sarcastically.

"Really? I can't believe you don't know of her!"

"Josephine was a singer and a French resistance spy in World War II. And she used her music to infiltrate intelligence—even hid documents in her underwear!"

Stella raised her hands as if to say she'd had enough. "Fine. I'll go with Jo. What about you? And please don't say, Marilyn," she said with an annoyed twist of her mouth.

"Let me think," I said. "It has to be one I'll remember to respond to."

Even though I suggested actress names, I couldn't find one I connected with. I closed my eyes and let my mind run through the alphabet. Audrey, Bette, Marlene, Susan . . .

"Vivien—Vivien Leigh!" I nodded with satisfaction. "I don't really like her, but the letters in her name will remind me it's *me*. You know." I said it out loud, "*V-I-V*—like a combination of Vivian and Ivy." Three letters; that's a good omen.

"You are an odd duck, Viv."

"It's a start, *Jo*."

We both laughed. For a moment, it all seemed to be fun and games. But it wouldn't be for long, especially if we got caught. We had to plan smart and strategically. Everyone knew nuns had eyes in the back of their heads. Following one around secretly would not be easy.

CHAPTER NINE

As I walked through the front door, I was struck by the blasts of the TV. A beautiful Audrey Hepburn filled the screen. She smiled at the interviewer, displaying a set of teeth as perfect as on the magazine covers. Her eyes grew wide, and her perfectly drawn eyeliner tilted upward like a feisty kitten. The TV host asked her questions about her new movie coming out next summer, "A Nun's Story."

"The book is based on the life of Marie Louise Habets, a Belgian nurse who similarly spent time as a nun," Audrey said in her velvety-toned voice.

I plopped down on the couch in front of the TV, hoping to gain insight into *my* nun's story. But I couldn't find any remote similarities. Then, the phone rang, startling me. I jumped up and grabbed the receiver from its cradle.

"Ivy, it's Mother."

"It is? Whose mother are you?"

"Stop the silliness," she huffed. "Don't forget to stir the stew in the pressure cooker and fix a salad."

"I won't—it's on my list." I grabbed a pen and wrote on the inside of my hand. "See you at six." I lifted the cover from the pot, stirred, and brought a spoonful to my lips.

After blowing on it several times, I shoved the savory contents into my mouth. Beef smothered in bouillon mixed with onions, peas, and carrots, one of my favorites. Soon, dinners would consist of summer foods—hamburgers, hot dogs, potatoes, and macaroni salads. Memorial Day weekend was only a week away. Then school would be out in three weeks.

If Stella and I didn't begin tailing Mother Superior right away, we could miss the opportunity. She'd be leaving for the nuns' summer retreat, or perhaps a family visit. Or she could just be pretending to do those things, but really working at her *other* job. Funny enough, I was reminded that I needed to get *my* job back at Mr. Fudge, Saltwater & Taffy for the summer.

With all this in mind, I grabbed my mother's recipe notebook from a drawer, ripped out an empty page from the back, and began writing a to-do list. I couldn't wait to start spying on Mother Superior. Wearing disguises seemed somewhat juvenile, but I didn't know any other way to go unnoticed. I decided it might be a good idea for Stella and me to dress like boys. However, I didn't have any boy clothes.

Gramps was only a few inches taller than me, and I remembered he had a trunk full of old clothes in the cellar that he refused to throw out. The clothes might be outdated, but it was worth looking at. Dressing like boys did have its drawbacks. We'd have to tape down Stella's chest with an ace bandage; for me, that was a non-issue. Stella could slick her hair back, tuck it beneath a baseball cap, pull on a pair of dungarees, and slap on a pair of sunglasses. She'd resemble a tall, attractive young man. Standing next to her, I'd be the short one. Together, we'd look just like the comic strip duo "Mutt and Jeff." No one would question us in Asbury Park; with all sorts of characters wandering those streets, we'd blend right in. I made a note to add men's sunglasses to our list.

* * *

The next morning, Stella and I met in the choir loft. The scent of wax from the melting candles permeated the air. I sneezed like I did every Mass. After sliding from the mahogany pew to kneel, I caught a glimpse of Mother Superior on her knees further down the row—black rosary beads in hand. Instead of closing my eyes to pray, I examined her face, committing the individual features to memory since I'd need to recognize her without the habit.

Her eyes were closed, but that cold, crystalline stare was embedded in my mind. I noted a small, crescent moon-shaped scar above her left cheek. Her nose was as perfect as a Revlon model, straight and narrow, and her chin strong—strong enough to grow that small, unfashionable patch of whiskers. No mistaking those tight lips, or her gray bottom teeth, which appeared when she bit down on her top lip during a fiery outburst. The top row of teeth hid behind a thin slice of a smile that only parted when she shared tales about animals from the local shelter where she volunteered on Saturdays.

It's strange how a person can maintain two faces. Was she the psychopath who lived two different lives? When she looked in the mirror, did she see the godly woman she portrayed, or a complicated imposter? Perhaps she *did* have a conscience and met regularly with Father Joe for confession. Naah—he would recognize her voice—unless . . . unless she disguised it! I imagined her raising the pitch to sound like Minnie Mouse with her confession, saying, "Forgive me, Father, for I have sinned."

"What is your sin, my child?"

"I am coordinating the meetings between young women and older men for profitable sex."

"Say a thousand Hail Mary's while kneeling upon a beach-bucket's worth of sand pebbles."

"Yes, Father," she'd squeak, and rush off to obey.

But now, Father Joe was concluding Mass with "In nomine Patris."

Sister Florinda appeared at the bottom of the steps, waving at us. We followed in a single file down the stairs.

"You have five minutes to change before we leave to do our volunteer work in Ocean Grove." She clapped sharply. "Chop, chop!"

We bustled into the locker room and changed into our navy culottes and white sneakers. As each of us exited, Sister Florinda slapped a pair of yellow gardening gloves in our hands.

"What are these for?" Stella asked, wrinkling her nose.

"Were you sleeping in class yesterday?" Sister handed her a large brown paper bag as well. "We're pulling weeds and picking up trash!"

Stella huffed in annoyance, grabbed the bag, and followed the nun out; I followed Stella.

We walked from Grand Avenue to Cookman, then down to Ocean. The concrete ramp led us up to the boardwalk, at the entrance, where the miniature golf place stood on the left and Mr. Fudge, Saltwater & Taffy on the right. The sun-bleached planks creaked and moaned as the group stomped along. The humid air reeked of fish. It smelled like Friday.

Halfway into the Casino that separated Asbury Park from Ocean Grove, Laura yanked at my hand, pulling me from the line. "Since when have you become buddies with Stella?"

I peeled her hand off of me.

She folded her arms across her chest and gave me a squinted stare. "What's going on with you, Ivy?"

Stella glanced back at us over her shoulder but didn't utter a word.

"We'll talk later," I said.

Laura grunted.

We got back in line and continued toward our destination, dodging a few puddles as we emerged from the tunnel-like structure that connected Ocean Grove and Asbury Park. It was jam-packed with resting bumper cars and Wheels of Fortune. In just a week, laughter and squeals would echo through the tunnel as it would be filled with people.

Chatter amongst the girls was suddenly interrupted by the faint buzz of a baseball game. Each of us surveyed one another seeking the source. I moved closer to the sound. It emanated from Sister Evelyn's habit. Her face blushed as everyone's eyes fell upon her. A few of us knew she carried a transistor radio during baseball season.

"What's that?" one of the girls asked no one in particular.

Sister Evelyn turned around and pressed a finger to her lips. "It's Dodgers versus St. Louis Cardinals. St. Louis is my hometown," she said and smiled proudly.

The girls giggled and gathered around to listen to the game while we pulled weeds, picked up candy wrappers, soda bottles, and empty cigarette packs from the ground. After collecting several bags of trash, I bent down one last time to grab an empty pack of Pall Mall. A black boot stepped on it, just missing my fingers.

"Hey!" I let go and stood up.

"Here ya go." Donned in a motorcycle jacket even though it was at least seventy degrees, Denny bent down and handed it to me.

I frowned and tossed it in the trash. "What're you doing here?"

Dark stubble shadowed his jawline. His eyes, like two glassy Coke bottles, glared at me, but I didn't feel he actually saw me. His pupils were so large that the brown of his iris was a thin eclipse.

"Hey, it's Ivy and the Penguin Brigade."

I scrunched my face at his rude remark. Though I wanted to move on from Catholic School, I still had respect for the nuns—at least the younger ones.

"Why aren't you in school, mister?"

"School is for fools," he said and puffed out his chest. "I got a job." His voice sounded lazy, almost slurred, but I didn't smell any alcohol.

"Oh, really?" I propped my hands on my hips. "Where at?"

"That's for me to know and you to find out." He ran his tongue across his bottom lip and winked. "See ya 'round."

Before he had a chance to take off, Sister Evelyn marched over. "Back to work, Ivy!" she pointed at the ground. "Young man, you don't look old enough to be roaming the streets," she told Denny. "If you're cutting school, I suggest you leave this instance before I call over a police officer to escort you."

Sweat trickled down my face, and I tore out another clump of weeds from the ground and wiped my forehead on my sleeve, unsure whether the sweat came from the work and warm weather or because Denny had flustered me, once again. Why did I allow him to get to me? Even if we became an item, I was certain my parents would hate him. Clearly, Denny was headed toward trouble; yet, something about him stirred my insides into cotton candy.

* * *

After the Ocean Grove excursion, we trudged back to school and changed into our uniforms to finish out the day with one last class. Sewing, my least favorite, happened to be with Laura. Trying to pin the McCall's skirt pattern to the fabric while devising a plan to dress like a boy seemed sort of twisted. Nevertheless, I pictured Stella and me strolling down the beach town streets doing just that. The corners of my mouth curled as I laughed in my mind at the absurdity of it all.

"What's so funny?" Laura asked with a deadpan face.

"Can you hand me those scissors?" My smile disappeared. "Nothing. Just remembering a joke Gramps told me."

"Are you going to tell me what you were doing with Stella?" She slammed a pair of scissors on the table.

I flinched. "Nothing, really. I'm just being nice to her because I feel bad—you know—about how Mother Superior whacked her hand

and all." I traced the pattern with a piece of chalk, then picked up the scissors. The chalk rolled onto the floor.

"It's not exactly the first time." Laura picked up the chalk and handed it to me. "She's a real closet case."

"So, I can't be nice to her?" I traced the other piece of the pattern where I needed to trim the waist to add buttons.

"I guess." She pressed the edge of the thin tracing paper against the material, holding the pattern still while I pinned it.

"Did you get the invitation to my birthday barbecue next weekend. My twin cousins will be there." She bumped my right shoulder with hers in a playful way. "They both like you. You can have your pick." She giggled. "They're like chocolates in a candy box; they look the same, but their insides are different. One's sweeter than the other." She grinned.

I faked a smile. "I know. I can't wait." My stomach churned at the thought of her twin cousins with their arrogant attitudes. The less attractive one seemed to think he could have his way with any girl because his dad owned a Cadillac dealership. The philosophical one had bad breath and never let anyone get a word in a conversation.

"Good." She grabbed my hand. "It's gonna be a great summer. I'm not supposed to tell, but . . . I gotta tell someone. My dad bought me a car for my birthday," she whispered. "My mother doesn't even know yet."

My face grew warm with jealousy. I forced a smile so it wouldn't show. "Really! What kind?" I gasped.

"A T-bird!" She grabbed my shoulders and shook me. "Baby blue!"

"Wow, that's so boss. I'm really happy for you."

"Be happy for both of us!" she said. "You're my best friend, after all. The passenger seat has your name on it, Ivy."

"Girls!" the sewing teacher snapped. "Stop all the chitchat and get to work."

"Yes, Sister," Laura and I murmured simultaneously.

I went back to my project, trying not to hate my best friend for her advantages and trying not to hate myself for lying to her.

* * *

After school, Stella met me a block away on Springwood Avenue just as I'd told her to. I was afraid Laura would see us together. Hiding from my best friend didn't feel right, but as much as I wanted to, I couldn't risk her telling everything. She might slip and tell her mother. Then her mother might spread it all over town. Not the part about what the nun might be doing—the fact that I stole the book.

I spotted Stella leaning against the street sign, one leg bent at the knee, her sandal hitched up on the pole. Dirt smudged the rim of her white Peter Pan collar. The bottom button of the blouse was missing. A triangle of creamy skin peeked through above the waistband of her hunter green skirt, which was shorter than her fingertips, a dress code no-no. It may not have been her intention. Unlike me, her growth spurt didn't coincide with the Catholic school dress code.

She stepped away to meet me halfway up the sidewalk. "So, you got any new ideas?"

By the azalea bushes, I swatted a bee that had been following me since I turned the corner. "Yep. We have to disguise ourselves."

"I'm not too sure about that, Ivy." Stella scrunched her eyebrows. "Don't you think people will recognize us?" She pulled a magazine from her gym bag, *True Detective*. "We should read this if you're serious. It shows what real investigators do."

"Where did you get this?"

"My sister has subscriptions to some magazines. Sometimes free ones come in the mail."

"How convenient for us." I rubbed my hands together.

She nodded. "If we're gonna do this, we have to do it right."

"I hope to God we *are* right. If not, and we get caught, we'll end up in reform school!"

"We aren't going to tell anyone. If we *are* wrong, no one will ever know. For God's sake, Ivy! You're the one who started this. Are you turning chicken?"

I rolled the magazine, whacked the bee, then hit the palm of my hand the way I'd seen cops do with their nightsticks on TV just before they close in on a criminal. "No! It's just, well—I expected to find a list of students' misconduct. Not some weird book filled with men's names."

Stella nodded. "Yeah, it's crazy. More than crazy—insane—actually. But you *did* find it. We can't stop now."

"Aren't you afraid—even a little?"

"No, not at all! I'm sick of all the double standards in the church and school." Stella crossed her arms. "No one is righteous, Ivy. No one! Not me. Not you. And most definitely not old Mother Superior." She pulled out a half-filled pack of *cigarettes* from her purse and tapped it against her palm until one cigarette slid out. Then, she dug into a pocket in her skirt and pulled out a book of matches. Striking one, then cupping her hands around the flame from the wind, she lit it.

"You'd better find a new spot for those, Stella, before you get another whack!"

Stella blew a plume of smoke into the air. "Yeah, well, I usually keep 'em in here." She bent and tugged at her right knee sock, which had no elastic left. "I need a new pair." She shrugged nonchalantly and stuffed the pack into the other sock.

Unlike Laura, new clothes didn't enter our closets weekly, and neither of us would be receiving a car on our birthday. But I'd never had to worry about a good pair of socks or clean clothes. My mother took care of all of that; I quietly empathized with Stella.

"See ya tomorrow," I said.

"By the way, can we meet at your house?" She blew a smoke ring and poked one finger through it.

"Usually, that'd be fine, but my dad just came home from a business trip. I'm not allowed to have friends over on those days."

"That's weird."

"Well, it's just that— he's away a lot. My mother wants us to have time alone—as a family."

Embarrassed, I shrugged matter-of-factly to move away from the topic.

"My mother will be half in the bag, and my sister will be busy with my niece. But you're welcome to come to my place if you want." Her voice dropped an octave, sounding sarcastic.

Feeling even more awkward, I blurted, "Sure—if that's okay. I'll bring some things we can use for disguises."

Stella's comment, "half in the bag," seemed an odd way to describe her mom. Also, Stella made no mention of her dad. With no idea what to expect, I said, "Okei dokie, artichoke."

She blew another perfect smoke ring. "Later, alligator."

I turned away, glancing toward the sky, thinking what an unusual friendship we had developed. Stella went right on Main Street, and I turned left. Both headed toward our very different homes, but with the same outlandish mission on our minds.

CHAPTER TEN

I laid my uniform neatly across the chair in front of my white desk and turned on my record player. Excited to use my new forty-five adapter on the spindle, I placed several records in the queue to automatically release onto the turntable after each song. First up, Elvis Presley. *Since my baby left me . . .*

Books and music allowed me to escape when my mind needed a break from my never-ending thoughts. However, oftentimes, both inspired me to think. I grabbed a copy of *Life Magazine* off my nightstand. I thumbed through a sobering article about a fifteen-year-old girl sentenced to life imprisonment for helping her boyfriend on a spree of killings, while my mother sat downstairs watching *How to Marry a Millionaire.* A shiver ran over my body. How and why would a girl like that do something so horrific? Perhaps she went to Catholic school and went mad. Mother would most likely say she went to public school and had no repercussions for poor behavior, and parents who didn't care.

I earmarked the page and went back to foraging through my dresser drawers. Sleeveless sweater tops, blue polka dots, stripes, and paisley. I held each one up and viewed myself in the mirror, turning from side to side, then tossing each one onto the bed. By the time I made a choice, the last record dropped. I plopped on the bed, my mind returning to thoughts of my next move.

* * *

The telephone rang, and my mother shouted upstairs, "Laura is on the phone!"

I groaned. "Tell her I'll call her later." I got up and fingered through another stack of records. How long could I keep her at bay? It had been a long time since she'd betrayed my trust. We weren't kids anymore, and her alliance with Mother Superior was one-sided. Maybe I could trust her now. Perhaps I'd test her with a secret I didn't really care about. I'd make up something just to see if she'd slip.

Suppertime had arrived, but I still hadn't finished my homework. Dad was due home from his business trip, and Mom was dolled up in a grape-colored polka dot dress. The sweetness of the peach pie baking in the oven filled the house, calming me. I knew it would make Dad happy, too. He always seemed to be wound tight after business trips. My mother worked hard to loosen him up. Gramps, on the other hand, often did the opposite.

"How can you be so blind. This world is going to Hell in a handbasket." Dad often hollered at Gramps when it came to statements about society and the government.

"Are you kidding me! The government is pulling the wool over your eyes. Are you blind?" He'd respond.

"The truth is always somewhere in the middle," Mom would interject, though most times, both Dad and Gramps were too heated to listen. These disputes would end with my mother turning up the music or slamming down a plate, which would alert them to end their discussion. However, these techniques had not been working as well as they once had.

"Ivy! Set the table," My mother hollered, always on me to help around the house, though it barely got messy. I grabbed four plates from the cupboard and placed them on the table. Mom didn't work outside our home. She spent the days cleaning, cooking, and volunteering. When I'd complain about having to help, she'd remind me that I needed to learn these domestic skills so I could be a good wife one day.

"I was very lucky to have met your father so late in life," she'd remind me. "Gramps could not take care of my ill mother by himself. All my friends were getting married, and I stayed home to help him until she passed. I was twenty-six by the time I finally left home. If the owner of the boarding house where I had moved hadn't introduced me to your father, I might have become an old maid like my aunt. After caring for her sick mother, she was never lucky enough to find a husband and have children of her own. At least I had you. Though I always hoped you'd have a sister or brother," she hung her head.

Those comments only annoyed me. Just because she wanted to be a wife and mother didn't mean that I did. Though I couldn't deny my attraction to boys, marriage was far off my radar. Crafting silk floral arrangements and preparing four-food-group meals every night enchanted me less. Perhaps one day I'd marry someone who saw me as an equal. Until then, my goals and dreams remained focused on an education that would lead to more meaningful work, such as investigating and solving crimes. Gramps understood this. That's why I preferred his company at home.

At 5:30, Gramps showed up in his color-stained, white painter's pants, with his happy-go-lucky smile. Music emanated from his pocket just like Sister Evelyn's, but he sang songs from the likes of Frank Sinatra and Bing Crosby. His posture was weak because of the constant ache in his back, but he still managed to glide into the room like a celebrity prepared to give a speech.

"How is my princess today?" Gramps patted my cheek with both hands, rough with dried paint. Then he kissed my mother's forehead.

Mom sashayed around the living room to *Strangers in the Night* dusting, straightening, and primping anything not perfect to her eye. Then, the hum of Dad's car sounded from the driveway. A minute later, he appeared at the front door. Dressed in a gray suit, tie undone, and briefcase in hand, he removed his hat. His disheveled blond hair revealed patches of gray spreading from his ears down to the stubble across his chin. My mother sauntered to the foyer and greeted him with a kiss—something I hadn't seen her do in a while. I turned away, embarrassed.

"Now, that's the way all men should be greeted after work," Gramps stated.

Both my parents blushed. Gramps's statement had been out of character. Dad kissed the top of my head, patted Gramps on the back, and handed his suit jacket and hat to Mother, who hung them in the hall closet.

"Go wash up," she instructed. "Dinner is just about ready."

Dad returned and took his place at the head of the table. We ate and talked about his travels. He complimented Mom on her delicious rice-stuffed chicken and peach pie. Despite my disdain for rice after having spent half my childhood kneeling on it—uncooked—I enjoyed the chicken. I was also glad my dad had returned home. We were a picture-perfect family.

After supper, Gramps stood up, tossed his napkin on his plate, and proclaimed, "I've made a decision."

We all turned toward him and waited to hear what he had to say. He never spoke much at dinner when Dad was home, let alone stand up to make a speech. Slightly hunched, he appeared shorter than usual. His white hair needed a trim; it was curling wildly at the collar of his red flannel shirt. Patches of sun-kissed skin peeked out from behind his white mustache and bearded face.

"I've supported a family, served my country, and now I'm goin' fishing."

"Well, isn't that wonderful!" Dad began clapping, then Mom clapped too, and I followed.

I wasn't sure if our accolades were meant to be real or sarcastic. My father often enjoyed poking fun at Gramps.

"Hope you catch a big one, Gramps," I said and shoveled another bite of peach pie into my mouth.

He laughed. "I don't think you understand what I'm saying."

Mom gingerly wiped the corners of her mouth. "You said you are going fishing, Dad. If you're not going fishing, what is it you *are* trying to say?"

His thick, white brows furrowed, creating two straight lines at the bridge of his nose. "Delores, I'm retiring."

With that last statement, Gramps stood up from the table and tightened the rope that held up his pants and said, "Who wants to come with me?"

"Puleeze, Father," my mother groaned. "I don't fish, and Richard has no time for fishing."

"Ivy, how 'bout you? Will you come fishing with me on my first day of retirement?"

"I'll have to get back to you on that, Gramps." I shrugged and glanced at the ceiling.

Growing up, in the summers, Gramps had taken me along on the big boats that sailed off early in the morning from Belmar to catch Bluefish. My mother would pack us a lunch of peanut butter and jam sandwiches, Charlie's chips, green grapes, and a big jug of water. On our way there, we'd stop at Foley's Diner. I'd order a pile of silver dollar pancakes, and Gramps would get two eggs over easy, several strips of bacon, and dip his rye toast into the broken yolks.

Fishing with Gramps would be a good opportunity to ask him about the letter. Though I didn't want to commit yet. Too much was going on, and I couldn't spread myself thin. A statement I learned from my mother, who often said those words to my father, and he'd respond with, "Would you prefer we sell your car and move near the train station?" She would drop the subject, and Dad would nod.

Before I could answer Gramps, he said, "I think I'll take a nap!" He grabbed his radio from the counter and disappeared.

After dinner, I cleaned up so my parents could spend time alone. Later, we all sat together to watch *Ozzy and Harriet* on TV. Gramps sat on his ugly, lime green recliner, and I sat on the couch with my feet curled to the side. Despite the comforts of home, a stirring inside my gut reminded me this moment could take a turn once I brought the letter to Gramps's attention.

When the show ended, I rushed back to my room and propped myself up in bed with Stella's copy of *True Detective*. I thumbed through the table of contents and some advertisements. The headline of the first story startled me. A photo of a blond-haired, blue-eyed woman with blood dripping down her perfectly chiseled cheeks plastered the opposite page, and the title MURDER glared at me. I quickly flipped through the pages and found more articles about horrific deaths, mostly of pretty females. This was not what I had expected.

After reading several paragraphs about a private eye who'd discovered a woman who had been murdered by the neighbor's husband, I shoved the magazine into my bottom bureau drawer and turned out the light. Goosebumps trailed down my arms. Though I thought detective work could be an occupation to follow, I hoped I'd never encounter something as sinister as what I'd just seen.

✳✳✳

My parents left for a drive after breakfast. While they were gone, I snuck into their bedroom and perused Mom's side of the closet. A pair of slim black cigarette pants hung in the back. She hadn't fit into them for some time and probably wouldn't notice them missing. A black shell top hung next to the pants. *Spies always wear black, right? Perfect.* I grabbed them from the hanger. Lastly, I snatched her big cat-eye sunglasses from the top drawer. Those I'd need to get back quickly.

I flipped the cellar light switch on and tiptoed to the bottom of the steps. Shivering from the temperature change, I pulled my sweater tight and glanced around for Gramps's trunk. A muddled baseball game blared from the living room upstairs. Attempting not to sneeze from the mildew that permeated the air, I rummaged through several boxes. In the corner near the far wall, a black trunk lined with brass studs and stickers from several foreign countries sat on the floor.

With a quick press from my thumb, I released the thick brass latch. A strong mothball scent rushed up my nostrils. Heavy, dark-blue woolen uniforms were neatly folded and stacked. Small piles of letters, covered in faded blue ink and bearing multiple foreign stamps, lay among the clothing. The time capsule intrigued me; it brought Gramps's stories to life.

Just as I pulled out a pile of letters wrapped in a red rubber band, the lights went out. I shrieked.

"That you, Ivy?" Gramps said.

"Yes, I'm down here doing laundry," I lied.

"Sorry 'bout that." He flicked the light back on. "Just trying to save on electricity." The floorboards creaked a distance from the steps.

I let out a sigh of relief and turned back to the stack of letters. The return address on the first envelope was from a town in the same county where Mom had grown up. I knew I was trespassing on Gramps's privacy, but I couldn't stop myself. With careful hands, I opened the fragile envelope and began to read.

Dear Francis:

   Due to unforeseen circumstances, we can no longer care for Ella.
   We have found a suitable home for her, and feel it's best we all move on.
   We shall keep our records confidential in honor of your service.
   Regards,
   Robert

In complete shock, I couldn't believe what I was reading. The letter was connected to the one I'd found in Gramp's coin box. Who was this man? Where did he send Ella? What happened to her? Confused and curious, I desperately needed to speak with Gramps despite his unwillingness to share more of Ella's story. If I told him what I had found, he would have to fess up. Working to solve two separate mysteries was a challenge I hadn't expected. Each one needed to be placed in a separate compartment in my mind, just like the coins in the box. Without pondering, I slipped the letter into my back pocket and continued to rummage through the clothing in the trunk.

Several white Navy caps and ties were mixed in with the uniforms, along with belts and heavy black work boots. A sudden memory of the time I borrowed the boy next door's clothes to paint with Gramps sparked an idea. Bunching up the clothes, I also grabbed two caps and shoved them all into a Sears bag I'd found in a cabinet beneath the kitchen sink. I'd bring everything to Stella, and we'd figure out how we could make outfits ourselves.

CHAPTER ELEVEN

Stella lived across Main Street on Springwood Avenue. A rusty tricycle turned on its side greeted me on the sandy grass in front of the house. Scattered toys lay in disarray leading up to the front porch. The black screen on the upper half of the storm door was torn and detached from its hinge. I turned the knob, but it was locked, so I knocked on the bottom half.

A child's voice shouted, "Coming."

The storm door opened, but no one appeared in the gap. Then, I heard a scraping across the floor, and a toddler suddenly appeared standing on top of a chair.

"Hi," she grinned, showing tiny, pearled teeth, cheeks smeared with dried chocolate, and a mess of ginger curls that needed combing.

Stella appeared behind her. "Come on in," she said matter-of-factly. "Go play, Molly," she said to the toddler.

I held my gasp as I scanned the home's appearance. My mother would rather kill herself than allow our home to be in a state resembling this. Our house smelled like fresh flowers, baked goods, or a stew brewing on the stove. Sometimes it reeked of perfume on evenings Mom hosted Avon parties. Stella's house reeked of cigarettes and cat urine. A full litter box was tucked behind a ratty armchair in the corner of the living room. Mother would never have allowed a litterbox in our home. We once had a cat who was never allowed inside. Toys and clothes were scattered everywhere, and dirty dishes filled the kitchen sink. I forced myself to act as if none of this was new to me.

"Come on in." Stella led me to her bedroom. "Let's see what you got."

Her bedroom followed the rest of the home décor—sheets as curtains, an unmade bed, and piles of clothes and magazines everywhere.

I opened the bag and pulled out the black slacks, top, and sunglasses.

She nodded. "Tried any of it on yet?"

"No, I had to sneak everything out of the house. I couldn't take anything until my parents went out. Couldn't risk my mom catching me with stuff I took without asking."

Stella rolled her eyes. "Put it on."

Uncomfortable removing my clothes in front of her, I stood there without response. She took my cue and pointed to the bathroom in the hallway. "Let's see the spy version of Ivy Munroe—the one Mother Superior won't recognize," she said with a sideways glance and a gleam in her eyes, as if she didn't think my idea had much merit.

Without a word, I marched into the bathroom, changed into Mom's black pants, shirt, and her slingback shoes. When I re-entered Stella's bedroom, she bent over and howled.

"Seriously? All you need is a mask and some felt ears, and you'd look like Catwoman from the Batman comics."

I glanced at myself and tilted my head, "Meow."

Mom's slacks fit me much more snugly than they ever did her.

"You would certainly draw attention to us rather than away," Stella said.

"You have anything better?" I asked and pointed toward the pile of clothes next to her bed.

"What else is in there?" she pointed to the bag.

I dumped the Navy clothing onto the floor.

Stella made a face and looked down her nose at me.

"We don't have to dress like boys," I said, dragging out the word *have*. "We can dress like old women."

Stella put her palm to her forehead. "Sure, that'll work." She rummaged through the pile, and I cleared a space for myself and sat down on her bed. Molly toddled in, with Stella's mother following behind.

"Who are you?" she asked. A cigarette hung from her lips. She removed it with two yellow-stained fingers, flicked the ashes into her left hand, and dumped them into the front pocket of her housecoat. Her skeleton-frame and ashen skin gave me the willies.

"This is Ivy, Mom," she answered for me. "She's from school. We're doing a project together."

Her mother bent and picked up a dime that had fallen from a hole in her pocket onto the floor. A silver patch seeped out from the roots of her wiry, orange-colored hair. When she stood, her eyes glared at me suspiciously. Her face had a grayish tint, and her mud-brown eyes stood in a pool of yellow. I swallowed hard, trying to hide my discomfort.

"Maybe she can help you clean your room, too." She huffed and walked out, leaving the door open.

Stella slammed the door shut. "Don't mind her. She worked the late shift last night; she's cranky."

I nodded without meeting Stella's eyes.

The pile of clothes next to her bed extended to the wall near the window. I wasn't sure whether the clothes were dirty or clean, and had never been put away. Stella kneeled on the floor and started digging through the pile again. She tossed several items onto her bed.

"I've been looking for that," she said each time she discovered something hidden in the pile. After about five minutes, she pulled out a pair of black slacks like the ones I had brought as well as a man's blue button-down shirt. She pulled off the dungarees she was wearing and threw them onto her bed with the rest of her clothing. Her bare legs were long, thin, and the color of tea with skim milk. I envied them, but I didn't envy Stella. Her life in the messy house with a mom "half-in-the-bag" reminded me how fortunate I was. Stella slipped on the slacks, shoved her arms into the shirt sleeves, rolled them up, and tucked the shirt into the waist of the pants.

"Is that your dad's?" I asked.

"Why would you think that?"

"Ugh, because it's a man's shirt." I grabbed a few hairs from my ponytail, twirled them around my finger four times, and stared down at my shoes.

"No, my dad is dead."

"I—I—I'm sorry. I didn't know."

"Why would you?" she shrugged. "He died a long time ago." Stella wrapped her arms around her body as if she were trying to comfort herself. "That's if you want to call it 'dying?'"

"Not sure what you mean." Wide-eyed as the plastic doll that lay in the pile of clothes, I asked. "Did he get killed in the war?"

Stella cleared her throat. "Not exactly—he killed himself—right in the garage." She pointed outside. "Yup, I guess he figured two kids were one too many. He did it right after I was born."

I gasped.

"One night, he turned on his car engine while parked in the garage, closed the door, and poof, that was the end of him," she said. "That's the story my mother tells." Stella scratched her head and turned away.

"Oh, my gosh." I put my hand to my mouth. "Stella, I'm so sorry."

"It's okay," she said. "I never knew him; you can't miss what you never had, right?" She released a subdued grin and walked over toward the mirror. "What do you think?" She spun around and stopped to face me, striking several poses like a model. The outfit she'd put together from the mountain of clothing she'd swiped from the bedroom floor looked nice. Anything would have looked good on her. I envied Stella once again, for just a moment. But none of these outfits would constitute a disguise.

"Think about this," I said, and grabbed the white cap from the pile next to the Sears bag. I stood in front of her bureau mirror, wrapped my ponytail around my hand, shoved it inside, and placed it on my head. Then, I put on the long-sleeved polo, grabbed the white tie, and continued to dress myself like a sailor. "Voila, what do you think, now?"

"Hmm, maybe you have something." Then she pointed at my feet. "But those shoes—I don't think so. What else you got in there?" She pointed to the bag.

I pulled out the work boots. "I'm sure they're going to be too big, but we could wear extra socks." My feet slipped easily into the boots. Then I slapped on the sunglasses, put on the peacoat, and stood tall.

"This could work," Stella said and picked up the second set of clothing, and tried them on.

The pants hung loosely on her, but the top stretched tightly across her breasts.

"Do you have another pair of boots?"

"Not with me, but I'm sure I can find a pair in my grandfather's closet." The two of us stood side-by-side and stared into the mirror above her messy bureau. "I think we could pull this off."

She turned toward me and nodded. "Let's give it a shot. The cat-eyed glasses won't cut it, though," she said. "We definitely need men's sunglasses. Here, stick this in your mouth." Stella handed me a cigarette.

I placed it between my lips and let it hang, the way sailors on the Asbury Park boardwalk let their cigarettes hang. Please don't ask me to light it, I thought. Though I couldn't help but be curious. Suddenly, I was on the brink of doing all kinds of things I shouldn't be doing, and the thought of smoking cigarettes, too, made my stomach churn. I needed to go to confession soon, just for my thoughts alone.

I handed the cigarette back to Stella. "You keep it 'til tomorrow," I said. "How 'bout we go to the boardwalk and get the sunglasses, now? I'll buy them." Before she could answer, I pointed at her, "Give me back the clothes. I'm going to iron 'em."

"Sure," she said. "Never seen a wrinkled sailor. We'd be spotted for sure." She stepped out of the clothing pile, handed them back to me, and put her pants and blouse back on.

"After school, we will change behind the green trash bins that face the woods. Wait for Mother Superior to leave, and we'll nonchalantly follow her."

"What if someone sees us?" she said.

"I'll look out for you, and you'll look out for me," I said.

Stella nodded. "Swell."

On the way out, we passed Molly, sitting on the floor in only a diaper. Her tight ringlets stuck to her cheeks while she stared at the small black and white television, eating Cheerios from a coffee cup. Stella's mother babbled on the phone, ignoring her. Stella bent down and kissed the top of her head.

Molly grabbed onto her leg and began to sob. "No go, Ant Tel."

"Sorry, Molly. I'll be back soon, I promise."

"No! No go!" Tears streamed down her face. Her tiny chest heaved, panting, then she flipped herself onto the floor, kicking and screaming.

Stella picked the toddler up and looked into her eyes, then kissed her on the forehead. "I'll see you after nap time," she said and placed her back on the floor.

Molly's pudgy fingers grabbed hold of Stella's ankle.

"I'll bring you back a lollipop—a red one."

Molly sniffled, and her bottom lip quivered. I could barely contain myself. Stella pried Molly's fingers loose and directed her back in front of the television, and we escaped out the door.

CHAPTER TWELVE

Stella and I stepped onto Main Street. Filled with weekend tourists, the sidewalks buzzed with chatter, and cars slogged up and down the street. An unseasonable warm breeze kissed my face as I inhaled the fresh spring air. The sunshine reminded me that I needed to head to the boardwalk and see about getting my old job back at Mr. Fudge & Saltwater Taffy—later.

Shuffling in and out of several stores, I had no luck finding sunglasses at a price I could afford. We turned down Cookman Avenue toward Steinback's. Out of the corner of my eye, I saw Mother Superior step out of a phone booth, hands clasped, head down as if exiting a confessional. The blackness of her habit stood out like a cow among parakeets since most of the women on the street were adorned in bright-colored spring dresses and pastel pillbox hats.

"Can you believe it?" I whispered to Stella. "What're the chances?" I cocked my head to the right and pointed with my chin.

Stella's eyes grew. "Holy Moley! Here's our chance to follow her."

"But we're not disguised."

"So, what. There are a ton of people around. If we keep our distance, she won't notice."

I paid close attention to Mother Superior's body language. A trait I had learned from reading detective magazines. Fixated on her every step, I shadowed her like a thin thread through a needle hemming an ugly skirt. When Mother Superior veered away from the phone booth, she slowed down and began walking with the meek demeanor . . . the way she did in school when she wasn't reprimanding a student. Then, she sped up again. She began marching at a fast pace as if she were trying to catch up to someone *or* to get away. Could she have seen us? Even if she had, there was no reason for her to run away. It wasn't like we saw her doing anything, *yet.*

"She must be going back to the rectory," Stella said.

After a block or so, she turned the corner and disappeared from our sight. Stella and I turned around to go back. We noticed a crowd had formed in front of an appliance store. The group was glued to live news footage on a television in the store window. A black man was raising his fist in the air, hollering into a crowd of other people of color. The door was open, and the sound from the television spilled out onto the sidewalk. "Each time one of our churches goes down in the south, we need to put one back up, right here!"

The crowd on the television cheered, and the man continued. "We need to support our brothers and sisters in Alabama and Mississippi."

Middle-aged men stopped in their tracks in front of the store and tucked their newspapers beneath their arms. Women huddled close to their husbands as they listened with curiosity. They whispered back and forth. A tension filled the seaside community, which seemed to be in an altered state. Even the buildings lining the streets seemed to understand that change was in the air.

Mostly oblivious to the political climate, I had only recently learned that civil rights issues were growing. At home, I'd often sit with Gramps when a news segment would appear on TV, and he would add to the commentary.

"You know, Ivy," he'd shake his head, perplexed and say, "it's not right to separate people—to treat them differently because of the color of their skin—no different from what Hitler did. Mark my words, there's gonna be lots of change coming, young lady. Pay attention."

Up until then, the only change I had been seeking was for myself. Soon after, my naivety and narrow mind began to shift. So did the world around me. It had only recently occurred to me that no colored girls lived on my side of town, or went to my church, or shopped at our grocery store. They were not even allowed to frequent the same side of the beach as us. I had never even spoken to a person of color. Gramps and Dad didn't agree on any topics regarding change, except for Dad's suggestion that Gramps change his liberal ideas to conservative ones.

Each step toward my mission led me further away from my lily-white comfort zone.

"Everything is fine the way it is. They're comfortable among themselves. Just some troublemakers stirring the pot," Dad said one night at dinner.

"They're comfortable?" Gramps' voice escalated. "I'm the old man, but you—you're the one who can't see it's time for change—actually, it's long overdue! Don't you watch the news? Read the papers?" Gramps' face turned crimson as the words tumbled from his mouth, huffing and puffing. "Has your sales job taken you so far off the road that you aren't even in your own country anymore?"

"I read the same paper as you," Dad said. "Only you see it through rose-colored glasses and half a brain."

Discussions like this made dinners uncomfortable. Eventually, Mom forbade Gramps from talking politics when Dad was home. Once he left town again, though, Gramps sang out his opinions like a canary. Mom listened but made little commentary.

As Stella and I looked around the street, it was obvious the disagreement went beyond our dinner table. Stella and I stood amidst a sea of people, some grumbling and agitated, while others grinned with satisfaction as cigars and cigarette smoke wafted through the air.

I stood on tiptoe one last time, trying to find Mother Superior amongst the crowd. I only saw small children clutching melting ice cream cones. They grasped their mothers' skirts with their free hand, fearful of being lost in a forest of legs.

"Forget it." Stella glanced down at her watch. "She's gone, and I have to get home to take care of Molly."

"You didn't mention that before." I shifted the Sears bag of disguises to my other hand. "We never got the sunglasses."

She shrugged and glanced away. Clearly, this wasn't going to be as easy as we'd thought. A week ago, neither of us would've imagined we'd be sneaking around town looking for proof that an old nun was a madame to our local prostitutes. It was all beginning to seem rather silly. Does it even matter? We'd be graduating next year, anyhow. Plus, my original goal had been to get the heck out of St. Teresa's and spend my last year in the public school. Maybe it didn't matter after all. Maybe the transformation that was beginning in our world would lead to change for my future as well.

I couldn't speak for Stella, but my mission had begun for the mere purpose of fighting against a future of expectations set by my parents. If I succeeded, Mother Superior would become a long-lost memory. On the other hand, the opportunity to develop sleuthing skills would be valuable training for my future profession. Then again, maybe we were completely off base about the book. Maybe our wild imaginations had sent us on a distorted goose chase. But a sense of intuition nagged at my gut, saying, *stay the course.*

"Maybe," I said, drawing out the word, "she makes the calls from this phone booth. It's the only one close to the rectory," I twisted the wrapper from a piece of gum around my forefinger while I looked toward the sky, seeking answers.

"Why wouldn't she just use the phone in the rectory?"

"Because—because she *is* hiding something!" I said, no different from Sister Florinda's asking Stella if she'd been asleep in class. "She can't speak openly about something she's hiding!"

"True. It does seem fishy," Stella admitted.

Spending time with Stella to solve this mystery had me questioning my sanity. Did I really need her at all? At that moment, I decided, *yes*.

"I'll hunt down sunglasses over the weekend and bring them to school on Monday along with the clothes."

Stella wandered over to the candy shop and purchased a cherry lollipop.

"You're definitely still in?" I asked once more.

"Sure." She grabbed a pack of cigarettes from her purse and smacked them against her palm. One slid out, and she pulled it with her long, thin fingers toward her mouth. She slipped the pack back into her purse and grabbed her matchbook, lit the cigarette, and took in a deep drag.

I looked around nervously. "Aren't you afraid someone might see you smoking?"

"What do I care?" She smiled, blew a puff of smoke in my face, and turned the corner.

* * *

The evocative sound of the harmonica greeted me before I reached my house, courtesy of Gramps. He sat on the porch, wheezing in and out of the tiny metal soundbox. A sound I'd grown accustomed to hearing throughout my childhood. I waved hello, hurried inside, and slid the Sears bag under my bed.

Next, I pulled out a yellow sundress from the closet. Still a chill in the spring air, I grabbed my white cardigan and slipped on my favorite yellow leather flats. Turning from side to side, I admired myself in the mirror. Confident I'd get my old job back, I rushed back out the door with hopes maybe I'd run into Denny, too.

85

CHAPTER THIRTEEN

The church bells rang six times, and the pipe organ swelled with the evening hymn. Even over thrashing branches and squawking gulls, I recognized the melody—"Blessed Assurance." I'd heard it hundreds of times before.

By Sunset Lake, a family of geese halted traffic, and I tiptoed around the mess they left behind. When I reached the boardwalk, anticipation for the coming Memorial Day weekend stirred. Purple, blue, red, and amber lights flickered from the carousel as it spun, its grinding calliope music casting the eerie, familiar sound of summer.

Wooden horses bridled and saddled in colors of turquoise blue, yellow, and burgundy, slid up and down brass poles. The calliope music forced them along in a perpetual motion. Children, mothers, fathers, and sweethearts sat astride the painted ponies, displaying wide grins and laughter that traveled like funhouse voices through a wind tunnel. Pinball machines pinged and dinged. Its players slapped the buttons on the sides of the contraptions, shaking and rocking them into submission to keep the silver ball in play.

Rows of boardwalk stands, with pimply-faced teenage workers, lined the stretch of weathered gray planks built above the sand. They shouted to all those passing by to take a chance and win a large stuffed animal. Most who attempted left with a booby prize. And the scents of deep-fried zeppoles drenched in powdered sugar, pizza, and candied apples wafted through the salt-laden air.

I scanned the crowd and recognized several familiar faces. Sitting on a bench across from Madam Marie's fortune-telling booth with a guitar in his lap was none other than Denny Carson. He was strumming "Jailhouse Rock." I hid behind a streetlamp so he wouldn't see me. He stared at his fingers as they slid up and down the guitar neck, while he hummed the melody. I teetered toward him, trying not to bring attention to myself until I was standing in front of him, admiring his skill as he plucked the strings. When he finished, he glanced up as if he felt my presence. Squinting, he blocked the sun with his right hand.

"Ivy! I was hoping you'd stroll by."

"Oh, really?" I tossed a nickel into his open guitar case. It landed among several other coins, a quarter being the highest in value. He glanced up and smiled.

"Is this your new job?" I asked. "Playing guitar for tips from strangers. *This* is what you quit school for?" I pointed toward the guitar case. "Looks like you're on your way to fame and fortune."

He picked up his guitar again and raced his finger up and down the neck. "No, this is just to pass time. But why not make money while it's passing?" He grinned, showing a pair of slightly crooked teeth that added something cute to his smile. Then, he laid his guitar on the ground. "Come." He patted the bench. "Have a seat."

"I'm not a dog." I propped my hands on my hips. "Are you drunk?"

He seemed more lucid than his usual self. Denny had more personalities than the Good Humor man had ice cream flavors. Trying to pin the real Denny down seemed as much a mystery to me as the Mother Superior's list of men and the letter I'd found in the box of Gramps's coin collection. But Denny's behavior kept me intrigued on a different level.

"No, I am not. Please sit down next to me. You know how I feel about you." He slipped one hand inside his leather jacket and thumped on his chest, mimicking a heartbeat.

"Don't bother. You won't fool me again, Denny Carson." I squinted at him, trying to hold back a smile. "I refuse to be some wild card in your deck. That apple butter you cook up isn't going to sweeten me this time." I wasn't sure whether I meant what I said or just said it to elicit a response. And which Denny would the response come from?

"Aw, come on, Ivy. What are you sayin'?" His charisma muddled my emotions again, and I tossed my anger into the ocean breeze.

"You know what I mean, Denny. You left me at the dance, wondering what happened to you." I gave him the side-eye. "Everyone knows you're sweet on lots of girls." I kicked a sand pebble off the boardwalk. It dropped several feet onto the beach. "You're a player . . . once you get what you want, you'll fade out of sight." I had to show him I was not the gullible girl he may have thought I was.

He reached out and grabbed my hand. My body warmed at the touch of his calloused musician's fingers. I turned my head and looked away, keeping my chin straight and eyes forward.

"Sit down, would ya?" He threw an arm around my neck, playfully pulling me into a headlock, drawing me close enough to kiss my cheek. His scent, cigarettes, citrus, and vanilla brought me back to the night of the dance. My heart sped up, and I pulled away, refusing to be sucked into his passionate lure. I was a magnet, and he was a coin attempting to slip into my shoe.

"Why don't you dance while he sings, honey?" A guy shouted at us as he strutted by with a group of hoodlums. Each one mimicking as if they were doing their own dance, shoulders rocking from side to side, acting like fools, thinking they were cool. To me, they were thugs with nothing better to do.

Denny's eyes narrowed, and nostrils flared. He stood up.

"Don't!" I jumped in front to block him, fearing he'd get into a fight.

The guys flicked their cigarettes into the wind and strutted away, mocking us.

Denny sat back down and reached for my hand again. "Come on, Ivy. I thought we had something—before that rotten nun threw me out of the dance."

"So, it's true?" I grinned. "She really threw you out?" I was glad he fessed up. A small part of me wasn't sure whether Laura had made up the story because she didn't like Denny. She had warned me about getting involved with him.

"Yeah!" I was waiting for you right outside the bathroom door!" He appeared sincere.

I folded my arms. "I'm not some stupid girl, Denny. I mean—how can I trust you?"

"Yeah, I guess you're just too good for me." He flipped his guitar pick into his case. "You live in a nice house with your mom and dad, and I live—I don't need to tell you that. You already know, right?" He slumped, not looking so confident anymore. "You need some square from the football team or the debate club. Why'd I ever think you'd be interested in me?"

Surprised by his words, I softened my tone. "That's not true. I never thought badly of you. You just—just—you know— move too fast."

He pulled me even closer. "Ivy, when we were makin' out that night of the dance, you didn't seem to mind how fast I was moving."

"Oh, really. That's what you think!" My face was suddenly flaming. "If that were true, why would I run off to the bathroom?" I backed away from him and wrapped my finger around a dollar bill inside my pocket. Full circle again, Denny had brought me from anger to acceptance and back to anger. He'd given me a free ticket to an emotional roller coaster ride. I wanted to hand it back, but I stood there with lead in my shoes.

He reached out with both hands and pleaded. "I'm sorry. Really! I didn't mean any disrespect. I just thought you liked me as much as I liked you." His dark eyes bore into mine as if I were a piece of fudge he was about to bite.

Uneasy, I turned away from his stare, refusing to let him blur my focus despite the fact that my entire body was tingling from the touch of his hand. "I have to go," I said. "I need to get my summer job back at Mr. Fudge."

He shoved his fists inside the pockets of his dungarees and cocked his head, and half smiled. "See you around, then." He bent down, picked up the guitar, and continued to play.

* * *

Before making my way to the fudge and taffy store, I stepped off the boardwalk and onto the sand, shuffling along, daydreaming about Denny. His eyes burned a picture in my memory that I couldn't shake. My gut told me he was not right for me. But I couldn't stop the flutter of excitement that continued to rumble in my chest. As far as I was concerned, Denny was full of hot air, but a part of me thought maybe he really did care about me. Just a little. But I had a mission to complete. A good detective wouldn't let Denny, or any other boy, get in her way.

When I finally reached the store, I yanked the heavy glass door open, setting the bell over it to jingle. I stepped inside, removed the gum from my mouth, and tossed it into the tall silver trash can.

"Hello—Mr. Fotopoulos," I shouted to the air in the store.

The owner, Mr. Fotopoulos, had changed the name of his store after its first season on the boardwalk. Prior to that, it was a joke around our dinner table and a few others in the neighborhood. No one could pronounce *Fotopoulos* Fudge, Saltwater & Taffy, and they created several humorous versions.

Mr. Fotopoulos, whom we referred to as Mr. Fudge amongst ourselves, was a stocky man with eyebrows so thick he could have pulled them down on sunny days to shade the sun. His five o'clock shadow showed up at least by two each afternoon, despite being clean-shaven every morning. And his hair, a thick, wiry black mass of curls mixed with streaks of silver, spread above his ears. He was stern, but kind, and he loved his store and the people of Asbury Park. Not to mention, Mrs. Vanessa Fotopoulos a.k.a. Mrs. Vanilla Fudge, kept his wandering eye in check. He kept her in expensive clothes and jewelry, apparently to keep both of them happy.

When the store first opened, Dad commented, "What does this guy know about running a boardwalk fudge and taffy store? Greeks own diners and restaurants. I give him one summer, and there will l be a sign on that door saying, 'Closed for business.'"

Gramps, on the other hand, said, "If this guy can make fudge as good as spinach pie, his store will be a winner. Not long after, the store sign changed. Instead of "Closed for Business" as Dad had predicted, it read "Mr. Fudge & Saltwater Taffy." After that, everyone flocked to it each season.

"Ivy, so glad to see you." He bent down, hugged me, and kissed each side of my face. His late afternoon stubble chafed my cheeks. Not wanting to embarrass him, I held back a wince. "You back to work for me this summer?" he asked with his Greek accent and held up a sign. "I was just about to put this in the window." The sign read, "Help Wanted."

I straightened my posture and smiled.

"I need one more summer worker." He pointed to the back room. "If it's you, Ivy, I put the sign away," he said and waved it in the air. "I like to hire back good workers."

"Yes, I would love to work for you, again, this summer," I said.

"Kala—kala," he said, which I had learned meant 'good' in Greek.

We chatted for several minutes, and then Denny sauntered up to the glass counter from the back of the store, wearing his old grin and a new blue Mr. Fudge t-shirt.

"You remember Denny, right?" Mr. Fotopoulous placed the sign down, reached into a drawer under the counter, and pulled out a sheet of paper. "He's a back, too!" Mr. Fudge clapped his hands. "Fill this form out for the government like you did last year and bring it back." He handed it to me. "We're closing now."

I glanced at my watch, surprised it was already eight o'clock. Through the big plate-glass window, the sun attempted to abandon the day, leaving streams of lavender, periwinkle, and pink hues as the sky slowly swallowed it up.

"Thank you, Sir," I said and folded the paper.

Denny winked at me from the back of the store. The paper slipped from my hand and fluttered to the floor. He rushed toward me and bent down to pick it up.

"Here ya go." He held it out. "If you wait up, I'll walk you home."

The roller coaster ride had not ended. On its second loop, Denny was as intent on getting me to respond to him as I was determined to hold my ground.

"Thanks, maybe another time," I said and left him standing. The bell above the door jingled as I opened it to leave the store. I wanted to say *yes* so badly, but my gut screamed, "NO." It wouldn't be easy working with Denny, but I had to remain focused on solving the two mysteries in my life instead of the one temptation that gnawed at me relentlessly. Besides, the pretty yellow shoes that had called my name hours earlier, now shouted at me to rip them off.

CHAPTER FOURTEEN

A fter lunch, the next day, Gramps approached me. "So, are you going fishing with me or what?"

"Gramps, I never catch anything."

He looked at me through hopeful eyes. "Come on! Spend a little time with your Gramps. It's not always about catching the fish, you know."

I didn't feel like going back to the boardwalk, and it would probably be a good idea to get together with Laura soon so she wouldn't be suspicious about my spending time with Stella. My best friend had been bugging me to check out her new summer wardrobe; she'd gotten it compliments of *Bettie's by the Sea,* the boardwalk store that her mother owned. These days, she worked there more often than her mother, whose time revolved around Laura's late-in-life twin brothers. As much as I wanted to see the new clothing, I knew I'd feel jealous even though Laura had always offered me her hand-me-downs the following season.

Also, going out with Gramps might give me an opportunity to question him about the letter. Aside from that, a nagging thought often played in my head. Laura's grandpa had died right before Easter. I feared the same could happen to Gramps since he was getting older, too. I loved him dearly. If I didn't go with him and such a horrific incident occurred, I'd never know the answers to what I had found in the letter. It would haunt me forever, and I'd hate myself for making that a priority. Shoving all the crazy thoughts aside, I believed I could accomplish both tasks.

"But fishing? Do we have to go fishing?" I asked.

He scrunched his face and looked upwards like he was thinking hard. "How 'bout we continue our search for sea glass and finish that table this summer?" Then, he grinned so wide I saw the gaps on either side of his three forlorn bottom teeth.

I clapped. "Yes! Can I bring your binoculars?"

"The distance from your head to the sand is not that far." He raised one furry brow.

"I know. I like combing the waves from time to time for ships."

He grinned, then pointed to the ceiling. "They're on my dresser."

"Thanks!" I rushed upstairs to his bedroom. A large brass anchor was mounted above the headboard. Several photos of Gramps in a Navy uniform hung on the light-blue walls to the left of the bed. An oval-shaped, wooden frame with Gramps and Gram's wedding photo hung above the dresser. Stacks of old and new magazines sat on top: *Look, National Geographic, and Reader's Digest.* No binoculars. I didn't see them in the top drawer, nor in the second or the third.

He must've meant his nightstand. So, I dug around inside its drawers and finally found them buried beneath several pairs of white socks and t-shirts. When I lifted them, the strap had gotten tangled with several tablespoons. Beneath the spoons, three small, clear plastic bags of what seemed to be sugar appeared.

I thought it odd that Gramps kept sugar in his bedroom. Maybe he feared another depression and worried about a shortage for his daily cup of coffee. He had a serious sweet tooth and was known to carry a pack of rock candy in his pocket or chomp on long sticks of strawberry licorice. I was surprised he had teeth at all. After Laura's grandpa passed, the family found hundreds of dollars beneath his mattress rolled in handkerchiefs. So, I didn't think twice about my find. I tucked the spoons and sugar back beneath his things and closed the bedroom door.

"Got 'em," I yelled as I strung the binoculars around my neck and galloped down the stairs, hopping over a book Mom left for me to put back on my shelf.

Gramps and I grabbed a bucket and left for the beach. Though it was only several blocks from home, my parents didn't spend much time there anymore. Gramps, on the other hand, loved the ocean. "It's why I joined the Navy and not another branch of the armed services," he told me. Before moving into our family home, he had lived in the house where he'd raised Mom after my grandmother had died in North Jersey. However, a fall from a ladder laid him up for many months. Mom took care of him at our house, and he never left.

We trucked several blocks to the path that took us to our regular spot. Sea grass reached out of the dunes, grazing my bare legs. Pebbly sand slipped between my toes and sandals, crunching with every step as sharp edges pinched my skin. I removed the shoes and continued barefoot. Gramps trudged over the sand several steps ahead, bending, picking up sea glass, examining, then tossing most of it back.

"See the surfers, Ivy?" He pointed at the group of guys to the left of the jetty. "Those new suits keep them warm all year long—winter, spring, summer, and fall."

I lifted the binoculars. "Yep, I've seen them a couple of times."

Tan-faced teenage boys with broad shoulders dressed in shiny black wetsuits dragged their surfboards into the ocean. They hopped onto their boards, legs dangling in the water, and paddled away from the shore. Once past the small waves, they turned onto their bellies and intermingled with the foamy water. One by one, they disappeared behind the ripples and returned, balanced on their feet as they rode inside the barreling swirl. The waves surged, plunged, and spilled them onto the shore. They looked like skinny dolphins frolicking in the wake of a ship. They climbed back on their boards and repeated the rhythm. Their perseverance reminded me to stay the course to achieve my goal, no matter what got in my way.

"You should see the waves on the South China Sea?" Gramps said. "I rode them myself."

With a quick turnabout, I stopped in my tracks. "You were a surfer too?" I joked.

"Nooo," he said, drawing out the word. "I rode those waves on a Navy destroyer." He winked.

I shook my head and continued alongside him away from the surfers, toward the jetty. The scent of seaweed and salt hung in the air. Rocks of all sizes fit together like a giant puzzle, creating one long arm beckoning ocean lovers and fishermen out to sea. Up close, the rocks varied in size and color: greenish-brown, topaz, and slate gray. I tiptoed across one, stepping carefully on the slick stone so as not to fall. The next group resembled a cracked tombstone toppled on its back. When Laura and I were young, we pretended that an old pirate was buried beneath.

Gramps waved me back to shore. "Get back here," he yelled. "I'm getting too old to run out and save you if you take a spill."

I carefully placed my foot on each rock and returned to the beach. Both Gramps and I bent down and rolled up our pants higher as the tide rose.

"Look at this, Ivy!" He opened his arms wide, facing the ocean as if to embrace it. The late-afternoon sun illuminated the symphony of waves as if they were a hidden treasure.

"It sparkles like fine crystal filled with a thousand bottles of champagne. One of God's greatest gifts."

"Do you miss being out there?" I asked, referring to his time on

Navy ships.

He nodded. "There are things I miss, and some I don't." He huffed a bit as he trudged up ahead of me and raised the binoculars again to watch several sailboats in the distance. I could see their white sails flickering gracefully like angels in white dresses dancing on the ocean.

"Ivy, over here!" Gramps yelled above the shrieking gulls.

I trampled over a mound of broken shells and cracked carcasses of tiny sea creatures.

In his hand, Gramps held the largest sand dollar I'd ever seen. He dipped it into the ocean to wash away the sandy particles, then took my hand in his and rubbed my thumb across its shallow indents and smooth surfaces.

"Know why sand dollars are so special?" he asked.

"Because they're so hard to find." I shrugged.

"It's more than that! They represent the birth, crucifixion, and resurrection of Jesus."

Hmmm, the nuns had never taught us that in Catholic school. Was Gramps as crazy as Dad indicated, often mumbling under his breath? Or did he have more knowledge than anyone I'd ever known?

He held out his hand. I gave him back the sand dollar.

"See this?" He tapped the dome of the shell. "The Star of Bethlehem." His thumb caressed it. "Around its edges is the Easter lily, a sign of His resurrection. The tips of the star are the four holes." He pointed to each. "And in the center, another, where the wounds were inflicted upon Christ when they placed the nails through His hands and feet while placing Him on the cross."

I'd never have thought about these markings, and never would have if Gramps hadn't shown me.

He gave me the sand dollar, and I shoved it in the pocket of my sweatshirt.

The light in the attic of my spy-brain flicked back on. The holes in the sand dollar were like clues. Each one led to the next, connected by fine lines on the surface until you reached the center, which held the answer. In the mystery of Mother Superior's book, I had only found the first clue. Once Stella and I got into our disguises, we'd have the freedom to find the next. The only obstacle I could foresee would be keeping Laura out of our business.

"We should head back," Gramps said. "It's getting chilly."

Shivering now, I agreed, but I had to ask him about the letter. Biding time, I glanced through the binoculars. This time, I used them as a voyeur, watching people up close as they strolled the boardwalk. It was entertaining to see their faces so clearly, some opening their mouths like animals scoffing down pizza. Others, sucking in cigarette fumes and women yapping to one another. But when I lifted the binoculars above the horizon, I saw a young couple locked in an embrace on the skyline ride. I re-adjusted the dials to get a clear view. My hands began to tremble. My chest tightened. *No.* It couldn't be. *No,* I heard myself say softly.

Stella and Denny were kissing high in the air above me. The wind caught her hair, and Denny brushed it behind her ear the same way he had done it to me the night of the dance. My body stiffened, my legs became heavy, and my arms limp. Suddenly, each step through the sand weighed a hundred pounds. Even though the sight of them caused my stomach to cramp, I couldn't turn away. I was *jealous* of Stella. The girl who lived in an unkempt house with an unwed sister, a fatherless toddler, and a mother who spoke to her like a stray dog who'd slipped into the house. The girl who had no one home baking pot roast and peach pie on Sunday. The girl with a dead father who'd chosen to kill himself rather than stick around to love and support his family.

Now, Stella did have something I didn't.

Gramps peered at me with a furrowed brow. "Looks like you just saw a ghost."

"Just one of my friends," I said. "I think I'll go up to the boardwalk. Tell Mom I'll be back for dinner." I handed him my bucket, which had only a handful of sea glass at the bottom.

He grabbed the meager bunch and let it sift through his fingers. Each piece landed on the plastic bottom like tiny muffled wind chimes. "Next time we'll have to get out here first thing in the morning."

I nodded and started toward the boardwalk.

Stella didn't know about Denny and me. How could I be angry with her, though I couldn't imagine how I could stand being around her, now. And I was seething with anger toward him. My mind reeled, working hard to figure out my next step.

* * *

Once on the boardwalk, I slowed my pace. What was I thinking? Why in the world did I want to take a chance running into Denny and Stella? If I confronted him while they were together, it could ruin my relationship with Stella. There would be no way of knowing if she'd turn on me; everything could fall apart. So instead, I turned in the opposite direction of where I'd seen them, toward *Bettie's*.

And, of course, there stood Laura, glaring at me with a furry cone of pink cotton candy in one hand. "Ivy!" she exclaimed! "Where've you been?" She shoved a wad into her mouth, hoping for an answer.

I released the strap from the binoculars, which had been twisted so tightly around my hand that it had stopped the circulation in my fingers. My hand, cold and numb as my heart. I didn't want to let Laura know what I'd just witnessed, of course.

"I—I've just been busy—spent the day with Gramps."

"I waited half the day for you to come by; I finally gave up. What're you doing up here by yourself, now?" She glanced down toward my sandy feet. "Were you on the beach?"

"Yes." I took the sand dollar out of my pocket. "Gramps found this and gave it to me," I said, almost in a trance, going through the motions.

"Cool beans," she said nonchalantly. "You'll never guess who I saw!"

I knew what she was going to say.

She smirked, narrowed her eyes, and blurted. "Denny and Stella!" She stared at me, waiting for my reaction.

"Yeah, so." I shrugged, pretending that I was not affected at all by her words.

"Aren't you glad you didn't get involved with that cad? Good thing Mother Superior tossed him out of the dance." She flipped her ponytail in a 'know-it-all' fashion. "I saw him standing outside the arcade smoking a cigarette when Stella sauntered up all cat-like. They talked for a few minutes, then he grabbed her hand, and they took off toward the Ferris wheel . . . and then, I saw them . . ."

I raised a hand. "Ugh, no details, please. I don't care about Stella. And I certainly don't care about Denny." The anger rising in me made it easier to hold back my tears.

"Good. I'm glad." She shoved another wad of cotton candy into her mouth. "So you want to see the new summer collection?"

Nothing could have been further from my interest. Just as I was about to say *no*, I heard a familiar voice nearby. A short, frail man with gray hair strolled past us with a woman at his side. He wore black trousers and a gray collared shirt that matched his hair. No lines or dark spots like Gramps appeared on his face. This led me to believe he wasn't as old as his hair suggested.

"What makes you think this will work?" the woman asked him.

I worked hard to hear their conversation without getting too close while Laura tagged my heels.

The woman had salt-and-pepper-colored bangs that sat perfectly straight above her long face. Dressed in a simple, pleated navy colored skirt, her white blouse was buttoned to the neck. The square heels of her black Mary Janes clanked like the percussion sound of a woodblock. I sped up, and Laura picked up her pace to keep up with me.

"I guess that means, yes," Laura said.

"To what?"

"You want to see the new summer collection!"

"Sure, let's just walk a bit first. I guess I'm a little upset about Denny and Stella." That fact was true, but eavesdropping on this couple's conversation redirected my thoughts. I had a hunch I finally hit pay dirt.

I couldn't make out the first part of the gray-haired man's answer; all I heard was, "Having you at my side will make them trust me."

"This is very risky," the woman said. "We're treading on territory neither of us has been on before."

Her voice sounded close to cracking. But I knew without a doubt that the voice was coming from Mother Superior, without her habit.

"Whatever it takes," he said. They turned off the boardwalk toward Kingsley Street.

"Come on, it's getting late," Laura whined.

Strange, she hadn't recognized the nun as well.

"I'm sorry, Laura—I'm really tired," I said. "Gramps and I have been on the beach for hours, and I feel gritty. Can I have a rain check?"

"Seriously?" She squinted and curled her upper lip. "Sure, I guess."

I rushed toward Kingsley to follow them, but they were gone. A shiver ran down my arms, thinking that a nun and a priest could be involved in something so perverse. Not just a nun, my nun—Mother Superior. Despite my discovery of Denny and Stella, I needed her more than ever. At the moment, all I had was circumstantial evidence. Without pictures, no one would believe me.

But how could I stand being around Stella, now, knowing she'd been kissing Denny? Did he breathe on her neck, too, warming it the way he did mine? Did he say to her all the same words that had made me feel special? I agonized over these questions as the sea breeze grew colder, reverting spring to late winter. Waves crashed against the shore as bonfires crackled and burned, releasing salt, smoke, cedar, and the sweet scent of marshmallows into the night air. All alone with no one to confide in, I wandered off the boardwalk.

Counting steps prevented the thoughts in my head from multiplying into outlandish scenarios until I saw two girls not much older than me standing in front of the Empress Hotel. Skirts, inching above their knees with spiked heels. They stole attention from Tillie, the huge painted mural on the side of the Palace Amusement building. The taller girl had on a candy-apple red dress. Her legs, two cinnamon sticks covered in black net stockings.

The shorter girl wore a ponytail sprouting a plume of wheat- colored hair from the top of her head. Dime-store eyelashes accentuated their eyes. Crimson lipstick covered their pouty lips. I had never seen girls like this in *my* neighborhood before. Once, on a trip to New York City, Dad made a wrong turn, and I saw a group of girls similar to this. My mother covered my eyes and told me to look away. Now, I couldn't help but stare and speculate.

* * *

Twisted like a pile of wet socks at the bottom of a washing machine, my emotions didn't know which way to run. I sobbed heavily into my pillow. After the tears subsided, I grabbed my yearbook from the drawer of my nightstand. I flipped through several pages to my photo, but zoomed in on Stella, whose picture was next to mine. Just as in class, the alphabetical order of our names kept us side-by-side for most of my school life. I examined her face, then mine.

Who was I, really? Black and white eyes stared back, though mine were blue with specks of amber. They drooped slightly at the corners like a Basset Hound's. My front teeth, straight, were bracketed by two pointed incisors like Dracula's. My nose wasn't big, but the end was rounder than I'd wished. My bottom lip was plumper than the top because of a fall I'd taken from my bicycle in third grade.

Was I as pretty as my mother said? Did I have that something special in my eyes and smile, as Gramps had always told me? Or did I lack that *something* I heard sung about in songs—a quality that made a boy like Denny want a girl like Stella, instead of me?

I slammed the album down and grabbed a copy of *Look magazine* instead. Bing Crosby and his new wife, thirty years younger, graced the front page. After flipping through a few more pages, checking out new fashions and diet plans that I didn't need, I placed it down and picked up *True Story*. I thumbed through it and dog-eared several pages about a woman who had been cleaning her husband's car and found several matchbooks from restaurants. She'd discovered her husband had been having an affair with a waitress, and the woman used the matchbooks to set the bed on fire while her husband slept. That's how people mess up. They leave evidence behind—evidence that reveals the truth when people don't—or won't.

CHAPTER FIFTEEN

After school on Monday, Stella and I met behind a giant green garbage bin behind the school building. Flies buzzed around the smelly trash baking in the afternoon sun, adding extra tension as we changed into our disguises. Swatting them with the cap, I tried not to freak out. After we both tucked our hair beneath the sailor caps, I tucked away thoughts about Stella and Denny, too.

"Here." I handed Stella a pair of men's sunglasses I'd found in the garage and put on a pair I'd snatched from Dad's nightstand.

"You make a cute boy," Stella said.

"Thanks . . . I guess."

Normally, I would have cracked a smile, but I could only bury my thoughts and emotions so deep.

"What's wrong with you today?" Stella asked, her hand propped on her hip. "You've barely said a word."

Focusing on the back door of the school rather than looking at Stella, I answered. "I'm just not in a good mood. That's all."

A good sleuth had to present an inscrutable face to the world. I decided to view this as a test, imposed on myself to prepare for my future.

"Do you want to call it quits?"

"No," I said. "Are you crazy? Why would I do that?"

"I didn't mean for good—just for today."

"No, we're going through with it!" I stepped closer to Stella and eyed her closely, then pointed to her chest. I scratched my head, trying to figure out the best way to mention that the shirt wasn't designed for her robust female features. "You—um—need to stretch the shirt or strap them down." Certainly, that was part of what allured Denny toward her. I dug into the Sears bag and handed her the Ace bandage I had anticipated needing.

She batted her eyes in a shy but proud way. Then, she turned around and pulled her arms loose from her blouse and wrapped the beige elastic around her breasts. Heat rushed over my face. Did Denny try to touch them, too? *Shut up. Shut up. Shut up.* She put on the sunglasses and hat.

"You look much better." I pulled the camera from the bag I'd taken from Mom's dresser. "Let's test it—say cheese."

Stella didn't smile, but I pressed the shutter anyway. The photo slid out of the camera, and I held it in my hand for several minutes until it appeared into being.

"Just in case I need to identify you one day," I said.

"Geez, that's morbid," Stella said. "And who would recognize me? Isn't that the purpose of this whole get-up?" She grabbed the picture, and a perplexed look appeared on her face.

"What's the matter?"

She handed it back to me. "I look like my dad."

Not knowing how to respond, I blew on the photo and slipped it into my knapsack. "You go around to the right side of the school in case she leaves from the side door. I'll stay back here in case she comes from the gym."

"I hope this pays off and we find something today," Stella said.

"Me too," I said, emphasizing the word me. "Though it may take time." I cleared my throat and stood tall. In my mind, I was a young, male sailor, and everyone who saw me would agree.

At last, our joint effort to spy on Mother Superior was firmly in place. Soon we'd be gum on her shoe. Though, I hadn't thought far enough ahead about how we would react when we did catch the head nun in the brothel, we believed she was running.

Stella touched my arm. "Oh, by the way, did you return the book?" She looked concerned.

"No, it's still underneath my bed." I tugged at a string that hung from the bottom of the coat, yanked it free, and wrapped it around my finger. One. Two. Three times. "Darn, what if she knows it's missing?"

"Maybe she does," Stella said. "Did you see her face this morning?"

"How could I miss it?" I unwound the string and dug my hands into the pockets of my dungarees, feeling around for the pack of cinnamon gum I had shoved in earlier. "She looked even more miserable than usual." I pulled out a stick, unwrapped it, and shoved it in my mouth. The spicy, sharp taste stung my tongue. "You want some?" I held the pack toward Stella.

She unwrapped it and shoved a piece into her mouth, as well.

Now we really looked like sailors.

"She looked different today," Stella said.

"How?"

"That little patch of whiskers on her chin was gone." Stella rubbed her thumb over the same spot on her own chin. "I see it every day, and it's revolting," she sneered. "Maybe she does have—you know, men in her life—that's why she shaved it."

I thought about the man she'd been walking with on the boardwalk. They hadn't appeared to be together in *that way*. But if they were, I couldn't imagine they'd risk displaying public affection. They must've been on their way somewhere private. It still surprised me she'd even risk being seen in public with a man. I couldn't even imagine Mother

Superior making out with a man *at all.* Nor did I want to. The thought was repulsive; I suppressed a shudder.

"Look!" Stella said. "There she is."

The nun rushed out the side door of the school. We followed from about half a block behind, keeping her black habit in sight. She didn't turn or look back to see if anyone was following her, so that was good. We stayed on her heels for two blocks, toward the northeast end of town. There, she got into a blue and white car that pulled up to the curb. The man she had been with on the boardwalk was driving.

Stella threw up her hands. "Now what're we going to do?"

"Hold on. I have to figure this out," I said. "Okay, so this is turning out to be a little more difficult than I'd thought. But we're on the right track." I turned to Stella. "I saw Mother Superior on the boardwalk last night with a man."

"Why didn't you tell me?" She stepped back and crossed both arms over her flattened chest, sulking. "I thought we were in this together."

"I wasn't sure it was her," I lied. "She wasn't wearing her habit."

"Then how do you know now that it was?"

"Because that was the same guy, the one who just picked her up," I said with an irritated tone. "Plus, I know that voice!"

"Holy cow." Stella gasped, "He must be a . . . John," she said with a devilish grin.

*　*　*

I wrote down the license plate, make, and model of the old, blue Chevy with the whitewall tires.

Stella snickered.   "And what are you going to do with that information—go to the police? Geez."

I frowned. Stella was right.

"There's nothing else we can do today," I said. "I need to get home.

My dad is home from work. Dinner will be at six o'clock sharp.

"I can't remember the last time my mother cooked dinner."

I felt sorry for her, again. And really, why should I be upset with her because of Denny? She didn't know about us. We weren't *real* friends before all this. Just classmates who were cordial to one another. We barely knew anything about each other.

"Maybe you can come over and eat dinner with us sometime." I glanced over and gave her a half smile, but I was already thinking. *Why did I say that?*

She didn't respond to the invitation. "You really should get that book back, Ivy."

"You're right. I'll sneak it into her closet tomorrow. See ya."

We parted ways. I headed back to my small, loving family, and Stella to her small, broken one. The street was void of all the weekend tourists, only locals on their way home from work and mothers rushing by with children at their sides. Pink cherry blossom petals were scattered across the sidewalks.

I slid in and out of store doorways, trying not to be exposed. Without Stella at my side, I didn't have the same confidence. Though being dressed like a boy made it easier to blend in with the few people out and about. Just before I turned the corner toward my house, I ripped off the cap and sunglasses and stuffed them back into the Sears bag.

* * *

I tossed the evidence of my covert lifestyle under my bed, then went downstairs, where the scent of celery and onions filled the air. My mother stood at the stove stirring a large pot. Wearing her rooster-covered apron, hair pulled back in a bun at the nape of her neck. No make-up. No smile. No interrogation about my day.

"Mr. Fotopoulos called while you were out, she said."

"What did he say?"

"He asked if you could work tonight. It's busier than expected, he said." She wiped her hands on the apron.

The table wasn't set for four as usual. There was a beige tablecloth with geometric shapes in green, yellow, and orange, and a bowl, spoon, and napkin on a yellow plastic placemat in front of my chair. Mom stirred the pot again, then turned off the flame. "Make yourself a bowl of stew before you go."

"Where is everyone? What happened to Dad?"

"He'll be late, and Gramps is napping." She wiped down the counter, then washed a couple of sharp knives in the sink. Carefully, she removed one knife at a time, gently rubbing the towel up and down the flat end before replacing it into the wood block. "Are you on top of your homework?"

"Yes, I did it during study hour."

My mother removed her apron, hung it on a hook inside the pantry door, and meandered into the living room. She sat down, turned on the evening news, and folded handkerchiefs at the coffee table. With all the time my mother had on her hands, it baffled me that she had no opinion on anything outside of this house—or in. Was she really as clueless as she seemed?

CHAPTER SIXTEEN

The scent of peanut butter, vanilla, chocolate, and maple walnut greeted me as I opened the door to the fudge and taffy boardwalk store. The air, sticky with its sugary vapors, tickled my nose and probably made everyone who entered mouth's water. A line of people stretched out the door and down the boardwalk for about a block. It was half-price fudge on Tuesday, which attracted many local folks, though it was still only May.

Mr. Fotopoulos himself stood behind the counter, catering to customers by adding or removing fudge on the scale.

"A half pound of vanilla and a half pound of chocolate, please." An elderly woman asked as she dug into her purse for money.

"Can I have a half-pound of butter pecan, a quarter pound of chocolate walnut, a quarter of lemon saltwater taffy—no, wait—make that three-quarters of a pound of chocolate walnut and a pound of butter pecan. Add a quarter pound of vanilla, too, please," said a younger woman with two children.

"Thank God you are here, Ivy." Mr. Fudge, as I often referred to him, waved me in. He stepped away from the scale and moved to the register.

"Miss! Miss! Do you have a bathroom?" asked another woman holding a little girl's hand whose short legs were crossed. Both mother and child's large, brown eyes pleaded with me to hurry.

"I'm sorry, ma'am. No, we don't," I said with compassion in my voice. "But there is one out on the boardwalk." I pointed toward the door. "It's not far." I smiled awkwardly.

I hated refusing people the use of the bathroom, especially children. The terrible day I had wet my own pants when I was five on a New York City bus remained embedded in my memory. But Mr. Fudge always said, "If we let one in, we'll have to let 'em all, and the antique plumbing can't handle it."

Denny rushed in behind me, filling the case with more fudge. Each time, he grazed my shoulder with his as he made his way past me in the narrow space behind the counter. I ignored him. He didn't know I'd seen him with Stella, but I hadn't given him any indication I'd go out with him the last time we'd spoken. Therefore, he had no reason to suspect I knew he was a duplicitous cad.

At 8:30, I turned the OPEN sign around to CLOSED and locked the door. Denny rolled out the large tin bucket filled with bleach and water and mopped up, while I wiped down the counters. Mr. Fudge counted the money in the register. He locked up and said goodnight. Denny and I took off in opposite directions. Only a minute later, I heard footsteps behind me, then Denny's voice. "You want to go out for a burger or something?"

I didn't turn around or answer right away.

"Come on, Ivy. Let's celebrate our first night of work for the season." He grabbed my hand and drew me in, so I was facing him. I pulled away, but his crooked smile pulled me back. *Picture him kissing Stella,* I told myself.

"It's a school night," I said. "Oh, but not for you, right? You quit." I folded my arms.

"Why do you have to be like that, Ivy?" Now, he delivered the sad puppy-dog eyes.

I couldn't believe I was allowing him to charm me again. Why didn't I ask about Stella? Why did I find his cajoling demeanor so irresistible? Perhaps being stuck in a girls' school all day was the cause. All the more reason to solve the mystery of the crooked nun and get out before my senior year.

Ultimately, I reasoned that one hamburger couldn't cause much harm. Since Denny and I were not exclusive, I had no right to be angry with him. Nor did Stella confide in me, or me in her. Denny appeared to be a secret we both shared alone.

"If my mom wants me home, then it will have to be a 'no,'" I said, my voice conveying a superior attitude. "If she says, 'yes,' I'll go with you, but only for a hamburger." I held my palm out. "Got a dime?"

He dug into his pocket and handed me one. I shoved it into the payphone slot and dialed home.

Mom was in an exceptionally good mood when I called. She agreed to my request. I figured Dad had made it home.

"Yes!" I held my arms up in victory, but dropped them quickly. I didn't want Denny to think I was too excited. Regaining my composure, I said, "I've got to be home by ten."

He grabbed my hand, pulled me close, and kissed my cheek. I could feel his desire for me, but I could also tell he was moving more slowly than last time, which made me feel better about myself and about him. Why couldn't I just blurt out *I saw you with Stella?* Maybe it was better not to hear his excuses for the moment. After all, we weren't an item, and I knew what I was in for if I got involved with a boy like him.

* * *

White clouds spread out like icebergs melting across the midnight blue and periwinkle sky. A mere thumbprint of the sun remained in the distance as we walked down Cookman Avenue. The smell of salt and the charred meat of greasy burgers and fries filled the air. Streetlamps flickered on and off, as if they couldn't decide whether it was evening or daytime. I tried not to let Denny know how much I enjoyed strolling with him, but a grin remained plastered across my face for two or three blocks.

"Hi Denny," two girls cooed at the same time.

"Who are they?" I whispered.

"Aw, just some girls from my neighborhood." He reached for my hand again, but I shoved it deep into my cardigan pocket.

He didn't stop to talk with them. "Come on, Ivy, what's wrong now?" He shot me the puppy-dog face again, but I refused to fall for it this time. "If you think I dated them, you're wrong."

"I really don't care who you date or dated," I said snidely and reached for a tall clump of sea grass growing at the curb. With a quick reach, I yanked one blade off and wrapped it around my finger while I kept my gaze on the sidewalk, avoiding Denny's eyes.

"I don't live on your side of town, you know," he pointed out. "There's lots of people over there you wouldn't see normally. But I do. Anyhow, girls like that are everywhere."

"Oh, really?" I glanced back. "Why are they suddenly on my side of town?"

"You know what, Ivy?" Denny said. "You're stuck up. Always worried about what everyone else thinks. You gotta step outside of your little square seaside bubble. Relax and have fun. Like the girl I kissed the night of the dance." He ran his hand over the back of his neck. "Oh, hell. Why am I wasting my time?"

My heart was stung by his words. I'd tested him by acting standoffish, and it had worked all too well. Now he didn't care anymore.

"I don't worry about what everyone else thinks." I dropped the strand of sea grass. It unraveled and fluttered to the ground. "All that matters to me is that you don't take advantage of my good nature."

"Just cut loose, Ivy. Show me more of that good nature you're talking about." He cocked his head and winked. "How 'bout I take you on a real date?"

"Where would you like to take me?"

"You like flicks?"

"Of course, I like movies—I mean, flicks—who doesn't?"

"How about next Saturday night?"

I paused. "What about your other girlfriends? How would they feel if they saw us together?"

"What other girlfriends?" He closed his eyes and shook his head.

"Could you please stop playing me for a fool already?!"

"Sure, I see other girls, but I don't take them on dates," he adamantly stated.

Hmm, so Stella wasn't his girlfriend. Suddenly, guilt thrust itself on me. If she saw me out with Denny, it might cause a problem between us. I forced the thought from my mind. Stella and I really weren't friends; we were working together to solve a mystery. More like . . . colleagues at an office.

"Okay, I'd love to go on a real date," I said with surety. "But that means you have to come to my house and meet my parents."

"You got it," he said.

Denny grabbed my hand, and we rushed across the street, beating the red light. Once we reached the sidewalk, he pulled me close and kissed my lips. My pulse beat in my ears like bongo drums. I didn't want to spoil the evening. I put everything else out of my mind, including Stella.

The sun set, and the temperature dropped as it had the night before. I pulled the sleeves of my sweater over my hands. Denny took off his leather jacket and draped it over my shoulders. I liked the way it felt on me. The leathery scent smelled like him. He stopped at a newspaper stand and slipped a coin into the metal box. He grabbed the paper and tucked it into the back pocket of his dungarees.

"What's that for?" I asked.

"To check out what flicks are playing. You said you wanted a real date, right?"

He pulled out an empty chair from the sidewalk café, and I sat down. A girl about my age wearing a pinstriped dress and white apron rushed over with a pad and pen in her hand.

"What can I get you?" she asked.

"Two burgers, an order of fries, and one Coke—and two straws." Denny glanced over at me for approval.

I smiled. "Two straws, please."

He shrugged. "Whatever the lady wants."

We chatted about music, movies, and made-up stories about the people strolling by. Denny pointed to a pale-yellow Cadillac convertible parked next to the curb. "I'm gonna have one just like it one day," he boasted. "Only newer."

"I'd prefer a Mustang, myself," I admitted. "Maybe blue."

As he stared at me, I admired his face. "I can see you in a blue Mustang," he said.

Denny took a bite of a French fry and handed me the other half. I slipped it into my mouth. Next, he leaned across the table, kissed me softly, and let it linger. Our date felt as real as any official date. However, having him come to my door like a respectable young man would be even better. Denny held my gaze for a very long time. Lost in his deep brown eyes, I had to force myself to pull away. A smart girl never lets a boy know how much she likes him; I read that in a magazine. I inhaled a satisfied breath and looked off to the street, letting our cat-like gaze dissipate with the wind.

We chatted and smiled at one another for awhile. Then, an older man, dressed in a fancy suit and wearing spectator shoes, approached our table.

Denny stood up abruptly. "Wait here. I'll be right back."

I had no idea why he'd be talking to this man. He looked to me like an undercover policeman. Perhaps he was in some trouble and didn't want me to hear. My eyes stayed glued to them while I struggled to make out their conversation.

Denny pulled the newspaper from his back pocket and exchanged it for one that the man handed him. "Just give the stuff to him when he meets you," the guy told him. "He'll be in the phone booth outside Convention Hall. When he sees you, he'll come out. Then, you go in. On your way, pass him the stuff like we just did."

This didn't sound good. It reminded me of a day I'd gone to the racetrack with Gramps many years ago.

* * *

It was the day after my thirteenth birthday. The air stank of horse manure and cigarette smoke. We sat down on the bleachers, and Gramps set a racing program on his knee to use as a table.

"It's like this, Ivy," he said. "You check the names of the horses and the jockey. I got my favorites—everyone does. Check the last three races, the odds, and what they pay. Let's say we want to bet on Gypsy Wind. She has a two-dollar win. We take those odds and multiply the first number by two, then divide by the second number, and then add two more. Simple as that!"

"I don't get it. You know math isn't my favorite subject."

"Okay, okay, I'll make it simpler," he said. "The greater the odds, the more you win, but it's risky. The horses most likely to win pay less, but if you triple your bet, you'll win more."

"So, which is better?" I was still confused. "Bet less on a long shot to win more, or bet more and increase your chances?"

"All depends on how lucky you're feeling." He kissed my forehead.

I scrunched my nose and turned away from his cigar breath. "Are you feeling lucky?"

"You betcha. That's why we're here."

That day, he'd won the long shot, and later treated me to a burger, fries, and an ice cream sundae. On our way out, his eyes turned to follow a man I'd never seen before. "Wait here just a minute," he said.

Tickets, stubs, and programs littered the ground. Frowns accompanied the faces of the crowd of people heading toward the exit signs. Others grinned, heads held high while waiting in line for their winnings.

I stood in place as Gramps had instructed, but kept my eyes on him. Gramps handed his program to the man in the spectator shoes. Then he took the program that the man had handed him. When he came back, I asked him why he had given the man his program. Gramps laughed and said, "Cause it was his lucky day, too."

* * *

Denny sauntered back to the table, the other newspaper in his back pocket. I glanced around, looking for the guy with the dapper shoes, but he had gone. Instead, I spotted a man who looked like the priest who had been walking with Mother Superior the other evening, dressed in street clothes. He seemed to be eyeing Denny.

"Better get going," Denny said. "I don't want you to get into trouble." He grabbed my hand.

"Who was that man?"

"Nobody," he said. His voice sounded flat, almost dead.

A rumble in my gut told me I was treading on shaky ground, setting my sights on Denny. Whenever I started to feel good about him, he did something that had me questioning my judgment. My heart and my head couldn't seem to meet. Obviously, Denny had something to hide.

Thin threads were connecting moments in my mind, and Denny always seemed to be in the center of a tangle. I had no idea what the exchange of papers meant between Gramps and that man at the racetrack years ago, and I didn't know what it meant when Denny did the same. Maybe the exchange had no importance regarding my concern. Maybe my constant inquiries came off as nosy. I really needed to stop analyzing every single situation. But I couldn't help myself.

CHAPTER SEVENTEEN

The next morning at school, Stella was not in her seat. Maybe she overslept. The room was stuffy, so Sister Florinda opened the window near my desk. The scent of late spring wafted into the classroom. The familiar scent of blooming azaleas and dogwood trees reminded me that school would be out soon. Denny and I would be holding hands in a movie theater, sharing buttered popcorn. Maybe, we'd even be kissing on a lifeguard stand under a full moon while the stars twinkled above.

Following roll call, Laura rushed my way, practically tripping over her own feet. She clutched her books to her chest as if someone might snatch them away.

"Did you hear about Stella?" she whispered.

"No, what happened?" I didn't want to seem too concerned, because she still didn't know Stella and me were palling around. She'd think we were friends, and I'd be forced to lie and say we were, for the sake of my covert mission.

"My neighbor works at the police department. He told my mom a scuffle of some sort sent the cops to Stella's house last night."

"Oh, my gosh! Is she alright?"

"Not sure." Laura squeezed her books even closer. "I bet it has something to do with the riffraff that's been hanging around town.

My parents are never going to let me out of the house this summer."

"I hope she's okay." Guilt weighed on me like wet sand on a beach blanket as I thought about how I'd been with Denny the night before. A stupid thought because she couldn't have known I'd been with Denny prior to her being with him.

After the bell rang, I sat down in first-period class and grabbed my textbook from my knapsack. And there was the black book, like a grenade staring at me. I knew I'd better get it back before it blew up my life, and I haven't even had the chance to live the best part of it yet.

I placed it on the rack beneath my seat. Sister Florinda began writing on the board; I did my best to pay attention.

Mother Superior marched into the classroom. "Good morning, girls."

"Good morning, Mother Superior," we responded in unison.

"It's a glorious day."

"Indeed, it is." We responded again. Sister Florinda beamed. Unlike the other nuns, she seemed happy with her life in the convent. I'd often wondered what inspired her to become a nun. Though the habit only showed a part of her face, it was obvious she was pretty—much prettier than the others. Long eyelashes and high cheekbones peeked out from the habit headpiece. She also spoke with more refinement than the others. Sister Florinda reminded me of Elizabeth Taylor. Not as stern as Mother Superior, but she had a strong command over the girls. All the girls respected her.

"Just because it is near the end of the school year doesn't mean I will be any lighter on our weekly practices." Mother Superior counted students with her eyes. "I do not take joy in this ritual. However, you must remember how easy it is for sin to sneak in. Even to good girls like you. Satan is always on the prowl."

Gosh, she sounded like a broken record. How could I ever take anything she said to heart again now that I knew about her, or at least what I believed to be true? I bit my lip, so not to show a face of disgust.

"You will all be seniors soon, and I have decided corporal punishment will only be used in severe cases. If I should find something that is not appropriate, we will discuss it in my office. Penalty will be issued on a case-by-case basis."

Why hadn't I put the book back sooner? The minute she found it, my life would be over. No doubt, this would be considered a severe case. The ruler would come crashing down on *my* knuckles for sure. I longed to run like a cockroach that had been exposed to light in the middle of the night. Maybe I'd pretend to faint from a fictitious illness and disrupt the search. Maybe I could rush to the girls' room, claiming I had a sudden case of diarrhea? I had to figure out a way *not* to get caught.

Mother Superior first approached Laura. Her desk was two rows to the left of mine, so I had a clear view of her face. Damp with sweat, her chestnut bangs were pushed to one side of her forehead like a clump of wet leaves. The nun tapped the ruler on Laura's desk and repeated the words of the weekly ritual. Laura emptied the contents of her purse in front of her. Mother knocked off a tube of red lipstick as if it were a hockey puck. She caught it in her right hand.

"Laura—respectful young ladies should not be wearing lipstick— especially *this* color." The nun raised an eyebrow, which disappeared behind the habit headdress. She opened the tube and held the red cylinder up like a model in a TV advertisement, but with no smile.

Laura sank lower in her seat. Mother Superior shoved the lipstick into her pocket and moved on to the next desk and the next girl. On and on, not finding anything else of interest. Trembling, I anticipated my turn to reveal my belongings on the desk. If I could just slip the book out of my knapsack and under my seat, I could toss my sweater on top. If she would just turn around for a few seconds, maybe . . . The classroom door squeaked open on its ancient hinges, and Sister

Agnes barged in.

"Excuse me, Mother. Father Michael McVee is here to see you."

Mother Superior dropped the ruler on the floor. The sound of the copper tip caused me to flinch. Laura, always ready to kiss Mother Superior's rear end, jumped from her seat, picked it up, and handed it back.

"As you were, girls." With perfect posture, she glided from the classroom after Sister Agnes.

Sister Florinda took over again. "Take out your algebra books."

I had just dodged a barreling bus plunging down a steep hill by the tip of one pinky nail.

"May I go to the girls' room?" I asked.

"Go ahead," Sister Florinda said. I grabbed my knapsack and whisked out the door. Looking both ways to make sure no one was around, I charged into Mother's office and right before I opened the closet to return the book, Laura appeared in the doorway.

"Ivy! What in the world are you doing in here?"

Panic-stricken, I held the book close to my chest, pretending it was my own, and said nothing. I rushed past Laura as if she were a stranger and made a beeline to the bathroom, where I busted into the stall and lost my lunch.

I knew I'd owe Laura an explanation, but for now, I trusted she would keep our meeting in Mother Superior's office to herself. On the way back to class, I peeked inside the front office. Mother Superior stood with the same man I saw the night before, now wearing a priest's collar. My mind reeled with confusion. A nun who was a madam with a priest who was a John? How crazy did that sound? It didn't make sense. Unless . . . maybe they were having an affair. But that wouldn't explain the book. Nothing made sense. Everything had two sides, and like a coin, each secret came with a price—some worth a silver dollar—others a penny. I had to figure out which was worth investing my time and efforts. Would not knowing about something that could change everything be better than knowing the truth? I'd often heard my mother say, "What you don't know can't hurt you." The statement suddenly intrigued me like never before.

CHAPTER EIGHTEEN

After suffering through the school day, the bell finally rang. I shot out the door and headed toward Stella's house. More new faces appeared on the beach town's streets now that the weather had warmed up. Strange men stared openly at me as they passed by. My skirt hem, an inch shorter than it had been at the beginning of the school year, drew attention. Mother Superior *must* have been preoccupied not to notice the infringement. Self-conscious of the stares, I tugged the elastic waist toward my hips, trying to *add* inches to my skirt, and pulled my blouse to cover everything.

I crossed the tracks and turned up Springwood Avenue. Though only several blocks across Main Street, it seemed as if I had walked into another town. A man with a scruffy beard, wearing clothes that looked slept in, held out his palm. "Hey Sistah, can you spare a dime?"

Without answering, I turned away and picked up the pace. I wished I were still dressed like a sailor. Finally, I made it to Stella's house and knocked several times, but not too loudly. After a minute or so, I knocked again, this time with more force. No cars were parked in the driveway in front of the house. I was relieved her mother wasn't home, but it didn't appear Stella was either. Persistent, I knocked a third time. The wooden door opened, and a black-eyed Stella stood in front of me. Her hair was tangled, and she was dressed in the same wrinkled blouse as the last time I'd seen her. Dark purple skin surrounded her right eye. The swelling continued on the side of her cheek. She pulled the rugged door back, inviting me in without words, then forced it shut with her foot.

"Oh my God, Stella."

I followed her through the living room, stepping carefully across a minefield of scattered toys. A naked doll with ratty hair and googly eyes startled me. I stumbled over a pile of wooden blocks.

Stale coffee and cigarette smoke hung heavy in the air along with the reminiscent odor of cat urine. Stella led the way to the kitchen. I sat down on a wobbly chair at the dinette table. She avoided making eye contact with me. I glanced away and noted the sink filled with dirty dishes. Were they the same batch left from my last visit?

The kitchen held no similarities to mine at home. No curtains furnished the one window in the room. Only rusty Venetian blinds bent at the bottom hung raggedly. No knick-knacks on shelves or a China cabinet displaying patterned dishes and teacups. No colored dish towels or ceramic bowls filled with fruit on the countertops.

An old washing machine with four legs and a double rolling pin ringer stood in one corner like a dirty white monster waiting to be fed. A horrible vision of little Molly's hand lodged between the pins ran through my head. The thought of the sweet little girl living in the neglected home saddened me.

Silence roared as I waited for Stella to speak, so I finally asked, "Who did this to you?"

"Who do you think?" she snapped. "A couple of debs from the riding academy?"

"Huh?"

"I have no idea. Someone came at me from behind."

She avoided my eyes again and shook her head fast as if to shake it free from my question and all the information she held inside. It frightened me to think someone in our town could do such a thing.

Stella propped her right elbow on the counter, rested her cheek on that hand, and rubbed the back of her neck with the other. "I was at the wrong place at the wrong time—I'll be fine," she said nonchalantly.

I didn't want to ask any more questions after that, and I didn't know what to do to console her. Though she didn't appear to need consoling.

"Why'd you come here, Ivy?"

"Wouldn't you do the same if it'd happened to me?"

"How did you even know anything happened to me?" Stella asked with annoyance.

"I–I just wanted to make sure you were okay because you weren't in school," I lied, and stood up from the wobbly chair. "Call me when you feel up to talking."

"You should probably put ice or a bag of peas on it." I pointed to her face.

"I'll be fine," she murmured.

"See ya."

Stella closed the door behind me, and I heard the sound of two clicks as the locks slid into place.

* * *

The tomato-ey smell of stuffed peppers baking in the oven greeted me as I opened our front door. Our home hugged me like an extension of my mother's unemotional, but loving arms. Stella may never have experienced something I had taken for granted. End tables were covered with photographs of family and friends in decorative frames. Comfy pillows were strewn across the cushy sofa. Paintings of sunsets and oceans plastered the walls. A custom beadboard chair rail surrounded our oval dining table and chairs, where we gathered every holiday. An etched glass chandelier shaped like a flying saucer hung above it as if it were in the center of our pretty universe. Our square, little seaside bubble, as Denny had put it.

Even the Hummel figurines that filled the China cabinet seemed content. Years ago, Gramps had sent them to Gram from Germany. I remembered him telling me the chubby-faced porcelain children were inspired by the drawings of a nun. I opened the cabinet and carefully picked up my favorite. Two little girls with scarves wrapped around their heads, one blonde and one light brunette, wearing similar dresses. The rosy-cheeked blonde leaned toward the other, sharing a secret. Just like Stella and me. Except unlike the figurines, Stella's hem would need mending, and her dress would be a hand-me-down.

I used one sleeve to wipe the dust off the girls, then returned them to the shelf. *A place for everything, and everything in its place.* That was my mother's mantra. Keeping order filled her soul. Keeping peace gave her joy. Keeping quiet put a frown on her face, yet she complied to keep everything status quo, most of the time.

CHAPTER NINETEEN

The following day, Stella still didn't return to school. Mother Superior hadn't been there either. Afterwards, I went straight home to help around the house and mentally prepare to begin work at the fudge and taffy shop. Preoccupied with the first barbecue of the season, my mother rushed around dusting everything in sight, even though the party would be outside.

"Please set the table after you get changed, Ivy," she called from the kitchen. Her tone was direct, but kind. Not the way Stella's mom spoke to her. Usually, Mother's commands annoyed me. Not today.

I rushed to my bedroom, slipped into my Mr. Fudge t-shirt, brushed my hair, and washed up. After spending time at Stella's, I couldn't help but feel sorry for her. Nothing about her house resembled mine. In the center of the gray speckled Formica counter stood a bouquet of pink roses. It reminded me that my father loved my mother–another thing Stella didn't have.

Red and white gingham curtains patterned with assorted fruits were pulled back with yellow ribbon ties above the sink. The sunlight streamed through the open window, letting in the cool air. My home, located two blocks from the beach, sometimes presented a fishy scent. Compared to the cat litter box at Stella's house, I found the scent welcoming. Today, the air smelled saltier than usual. Some days, the air was so fresh you'd never know the ocean was around the corner. On the salty-air days, I took in extra breaths, attempting to breathe summer right into my soul.

Mom's collection of ceramic roosters lined the shelf above the pink cabinets with the silver knobs. The Noah's Ark cookie jar, never empty, stood at the end. I lifted the top and pulled out an oatmeal raisin.

"Only one." Mom grabbed the roof of the Ark. "Don't ruin your appetite."

"You've said that a million times, and I can honestly say, it never has." I took a bite and licked my lips.

Staring sternly down her nose at me with a half-smile, she covered the cookies. "Daddy is back on the road. Don't set a place for him."

That explained the flowers.

"I'm running out after supper, so I need you to clean up."

Normally, I'd protest, but not today. "Okay."

"I have to prepare for the weekend," she said. "Dad's co-workers are coming by for a barbecue. I'll need your help."

"I know. You have mentioned this several times." I set the napkins and holders in the center of the table.

Mom disappeared into the laundry room while I placed the dishes on the table. With a quick turn of the dial, I searched for music on the radio. Dad always left it set on the news. But this time, Johnny Cash sang out:

When you go through the tollgate
Well, you don't have to pay the man no toll

Funny. Dad was always complaining about tolls. I bet he'd like this song if he'd just listen to music once in a while. A burst of static took over, and the music disappeared. I turned the dial, but only found news. I clicked it off.

Gramps strolled in. "How's my beautiful girl today?" He pinched my cheek with his chalky fingers. Johnny Cash returned from Gramps's transistor. Though he had proclaimed retirement only a few days ago, he still wore his splattered painter's pants. Now, he was working for free for the widows and women with "bums for husbands," my dad had commented.

I had taken a break from thinking about the letter, but I hadn't forgotten. Considering I accidentally came across it and it *was* hidden, I had to be careful about how I approached him. He may very well have forgotten about it—or wanted to. But I couldn't rest until I learned the truth.

"You want to go fishing this weekend?" he asked.

Bopping across the kitchen floor to the music on the radio, I answered, "It's Memorial Day Weekend—gotta work—and go to Laura's birthday party. I'll be around afterwards."

"Sure, Princess. You can keep me company out in the shed as you used to when you had time for your old Gramps. I promised Mrs. Correll I'd paint her shutters and bookshelf on Saturday. She wants everything painted red."

"Oh my!" I laughed. "She is a colorful lady," I said. "Love her funny accent and the tiny dogs she carries around in the baby carriage. After work on Monday, you can count on it."

As I prepared supper, Mom said, "Before I head over to the grocery store, I'm going to drop off a container of stew for one of the shut-ins at church. And this evening, I'll be watching that new couple's baby so they can have a night out. I won't be home till late."

"Sure thing." I welcomed the chance to catch up on reading the new *True Detective*. Maybe I'd get some insight.

Gramps rubbed his belly. "I'm going to the park to play shuffleboard with the old geezers. I might as well be productive now that I'm retired."

"Retired, my elbow!" Mom grabbed her purse and rushed out the door.

Gramps snickered and trudged up the steps to his room.

After clearing the table, the phone rang, and I grabbed the receiver. "Ivy, it's Mr. Fotopoulos. No come to work tonight," he said in broken English. "My wife—she come to help and reorganize. Sorry."

Though I could have used the $ 1.00-per-hour pay, I welcomed the idea of having the house and the evening to myself—a rare occasion.

* * *

After washing the dinner dishes, I collapsed on my bed. Propping myself up with pillows, I pulled *The Maltese Falcon* from the pile of books off my nightstand. As I read, I checked the storyline for similarities to my own mystery. Then, I ran water in the tub for a bubble bath. Right before I dropped my terrycloth robe on the bathroom floor, I heard a knock on the front door.

I gripped the robe tight and peeked through the blinds. Stella was standing on my front porch. She had never come to my home uninvited. Actually, she had never come to my house. Could she be in trouble again? I stood still for several minutes, hoping she might decide to go away.

I didn't get many opportunities to enjoy the freedom of being home alone. I waited a couple of minutes and cracked the blinds again. Stella was pacing. If I didn't open the door, she wouldn't know I wasn't home. If I did open it, I feared I might be sorry. If I didn't open the door, I wouldn't have a peaceful bath or sleep or *any* peace at all. I'd be wondering what Stella wanted and feel sorry for her all over again.

After a deep breath, I trampled down the steps and opened the door. "Stella! What's going on? What're you doing here?"

Her eyes darted back and forth as if she thought she was being followed. "Are your parents at home?"

"No. You want to come in?"

"Yeah."

I opened the door wider, holding my robe at the neck, and rushed in front of her, leading her to the kitchen.

"Sit down." I pointed to the table and slid into the seat across from her.

Stella glanced around my kitchen for a moment. "You are not going to believe what I saw," she said, as if she had just seen a crime or even worse—a murder.

"What?" I touched her wrist, concerned. It was hard to tell if she was excited or scared.

"Well, I wasn't going to let what happened keep me stuck in the house—you know," she said matter-of-factly. "So, I went out with some friends—no one you know," she added.

Oddly, I had never seen Stella with anyone, whether I knew them or not.

"We got sodas at Woolworth's, but I still wanted to get home before dark, so I left early. My friend walked with me most of the way. I took a different route this time—around Deal Lake. Near one of those huge houses. An older woman and a man were talking to a couple of girls."

"Really?" My heart raced. "What did the woman look like?"

"She had silver hair, but it was straight; her bangs so long they almost covered her eyes. Everything about her was plain. It didn't make sense why she would be speaking to someone like them."

"And?" My hand began to throb from my nervous habit of wrapping things around my fingers—the belt to my robe this time. I switched it to the finger on my other hand. "Do you know who she was?"

"I didn't at first. But the closer I got, the better I could hear. Who could forget that voice?" Stella clasped her hands together, inverted them, and cracked her knuckles. She stared into my eyes. With a deep voice and staccato tone, she said, "Mother Superior."

"Oh, my gosh! Um . . . what did you do?"

"I watched from across the street, following while keeping enough distance behind parked vehicles so they wouldn't spot me. She disappeared into a big house on the lake."

"No, kidding!"

"It's true." She nodded with complete assurance. "It was that one with the huge wrap-around porch. You know, the big mint-green house with the pillars and pink shutters."

"The one with the glass doors to the porch?"

"Yes! There's even a third floor, with a smaller porch and a balcony around the back. Fog covered the lake, and I couldn't see clearly. But all the lights were on. We've walked past this house many times before. I've even imagined what it would be like to *live* there. Now, I wonder what sort of house it really is?"

I unwrapped the belt, my hand throbbing. "This is big!"

Stella brushed her bangs from her eyes with a tired stroke of her hand. "You know what kind of house it is, Ivy." She said with a gleam in her eyes.

"I know what you're going to say."

"That's right." She slapped the table. "It's one of them high-class whorehouses. You know, a brothel. Only those girls didn't look very classy."

"Hmm, maybe that's where Mother Superior takes the girls to meet the men whose names are in the book? Or, maybe she takes them there to class 'em up." I smirked.

As more thoughts ran through my mind, I began to speak more quickly. "That man you saw with her—maybe that's his house? Or, maybe he's her partner. This is all so crazy. It's hard to know for sure."

"We have to get inside," Stella said.

"Are you batty?"

Stella closed her eyes tightly for a second. "Bring that camera again.

We'll take pictures of anyone entering or leaving. Then, we'll figure out how to get inside." She grinned for the first time since she'd arrived. "We can't give up now."

"You're right," I said, though the thought of sneaking inside made my stomach drop. "Great work, Stella." I shook her hand. One sleuth sealing a secret pact with the other.

I was intrigued by her discovery, sure. But, it also felt like we were getting in over our heads. And now, I needed to sneak Mom's camera out of the house again. Between work at Mr. Fudge's, school, helping Mom, and digging for the truth about Gramps, our tiny mission had ballooned into something huge.

Stella got up from the table. "See you tomorrow. Don't forget the camera."

I shut the door behind her and returned to my bath. The water had turned cold, and all the bubbles had dissolved. I drained out a few inches, released some of Mom's lavender bath beads into the water, and ran the hot tap. I dropped my robe to the floor and stepped in. My mind was a TV flipping from channel to channel. A romance. A mystery. A love triangle. I imagined the news at eleven with a story headline: *Two teenage girls discover a brothel in a suburban seaside neighborhood run by a nun.* Unable to relax, I cut the bath short. I had to get the camera before my parents came home.

After the bath, I slipped into my parents' bedroom, searching for Mom's Polaroid camera. My hands shook as I grabbed it from inside the nightstand drawer. This constant borrowing without asking was becoming risky. But Stella and I needed to get pictures in the next two days. If I'd asked, Mom would have wanted to know what the camera was for. She also might ask to see the photos, and I'd have to tell another lie. It seemed simpler to ask for forgiveness (should I get caught) than to ask for permission and be questioned. Just as I was leaving the bedroom, the car's headlights shone through the curtains.

CHAPTER TWENTY

The next day, after school, I had expected to meet up with Stella to discuss our next move. Instead—just my luck—I ran into Laura.

"Ivy! Are you coming by this weekend or what?" she whined.

I thought about it for a minute. I didn't want to be forced to make small talk with her twin cousins. However, it would be her birthday as well as the holiday weekend, so I had to make an exception. After all, she was my best friend, even though lately, I had been ditching her constantly.

"I'm working at Mr. Fudge, but I'll stop by," I said. "I also promised Gramps I'd help him out. Not to mention, I have to lend my mom a hand with the barbecue she's having for Dad's clients." I took in a deep breath. "It's a real busy weekend."

She curled her upper lip and looked away. "Every year is Memorial Day weekend, Ivy. But every year is not my seventeenth birthday."

"Of course not. I wouldn't miss your party! I just don't know exactly what time I'll get there." I shrugged, trying to look distraught. "Some of us have to work."

"Are you trying to say I don't?" Her face grew red. "Just because my parents own the store doesn't mean I'm not working when I'm there."

"Just joking around." I forced a smile to jolly her up. "What can I even get you?" I asked. "For a gift, I mean."

She perked back up. "Maybe something to hang from the mirror of my new car?"

I cocked my head to the right. "I like that idea."

"Ivy, I just want you to be there for me," she said, less the attitude. We hugged like the old friends we were.

"You got it," I told her. "I'll be there."

* * *

In the end, I never met up with Stella. When I walked past homeroom, I saw her with Sister Florinda cleaning the chalkboards, and I wasn't in the mood to sit around and wait. Laura had gone, so I headed home alone. My knapsack, close to me, fearful someone could grab it and run. While I strolled down the sidewalk, I hoped I wouldn't encounter any strangers, beggars, or looters. Now that the summer season had begun, in addition to a multitude of new families, it seemed as if all kinds of desperadoes were creeping into town. Though mostly locals, teens, and college kids worked the boardwalk stands. Transients also found their way to the boardwalk. Some with good intentions, some not.

The temperature had risen to ninety degrees. I took my navy cardigan off and tied the sleeves around my waist. As I crossed Main Street, I noticed a group of black teenage boys standing on the corner near Cuba's Spanish Tavern on Springwood Avenue. Dressed in black trousers with white shirts, red bow ties, and shiny black shoes, all four were singing in harmony. The lead singer's voice was as high-pitched as Frankie Lymon's, the guy who sang, *Why Do Fools Fall in Love?*

I stopped to lean against a telephone pole and listen for several minutes. The singer glanced over at me, then stepped closer and stared into my eyes while he sang. Heat rushed over me, and hives appeared under my chin. This happened frequently when I was excited or nervous. I smiled at him. He smiled back. What if my mother drove by? I turned away and began scratching like crazy. Then, I crossed the street in the middle so I wouldn't have to walk past the group.

My feet began to ache from all the walking. I needed to get back on my side of town. Earlier, on Cookman Avenue, I'd seen several sawhorses blocking the road, preparing to keep the cars out for the parade coming to town for the holiday weekend. Zigzagging through back streets and taking shortcuts, I ended near the police station on Bangs.

Just outside the double glass doors stood the blonde with the high ponytail. The one who seemed to be everywhere lately. This time, no red lipstick or flashy clothes. She drifted over to a bench at the bus stop. I couldn't take my eyes off her. Her nose kept running, and she used the back of her hand as a tissue each time before scratching her arm over and over. Then, the priest who'd been with Mother Superior appeared and sat beside her. This time, wearing his collar. I edged closer, trying to catch what he was saying to her.

"I can see you're sick."

"You got that right, Father," she answered. Her face was peaked, and her hair scraggly.

"Don't you want to get well?" he asked. "For good this time."

She continued scratching her arm as if mosquitoes were biting it. Sweat trickled down her face. "I'm real tired, Father. I've gotta get off the street. So, yeah, whatever you say—I'll do it—I'll do anything this time!"

"I'm glad to hear that," he said. "Wait here while I make a phone call." He walked across the street and entered a payphone booth.

Ironically, this time, the girl didn't look like someone who could attract a man. Worn out and ragged, the only remnants of makeup on her face were dark smears of mascara beneath her eyes. Her ponytail was loose, lank, and unwashed.

Pretending to be waiting for the bus, I stood several feet away from the bench. The priest returned and sat down next to the girl, again.

"I want you to get on the next bus," he said. "A woman will be waiting for you when you get off. She's going to take you to a hospital where they will help you." He handed her a piece of paper. "Her name is written here. Tell her Father McVee sent you." He pulled money from his wallet, and she opened her hand again. "Promise me you will be wise this time."

"I will, Father, I swear it." She opened her purse and shoved the money inside.

"I'll come check on you in a couple of days."

"Thank you so much."

I got up, walked past them, and turned the corner, then peered around the building. A city bus pulled up, and she stepped on. The doors closed behind her.

Stella and Denny were right, I was a square who lived in a bubble. After seeing the priest and hearing his conversation, I realized how off-base I was. Did I want to leave Catholic school so badly that my mind conjured up the insane scenario? A nun palling around with a priest? Obviously, Mother Superior was *helping* the priest with the prostitutes, not acting as a madam. I felt like such a fool. Had my parents sheltered me so much that I had become delusional? Still, something didn't sit right. And I couldn't forget what I'd heard the nun say to the priest that night on the boardwalk: *I'll help you if you help me*. What did she need him to help her with?

CHAPTER TWENTY-ONE

I picked up the phone and dialed Stella, but no one answered. If I didn't get to her soon, she might go off on her own to follow Mother Superior, and it might be all for nothing. What if she got caught and spilled the beans? The nun would certainly call my parents, or maybe worse.

"Ivy," Mom hollered from the kitchen. "Telephone."

I took the handset and waved her out of the kitchen. "Hello."

Stella was on the other end. "You are not going to believe what I saw today," I told her everything. She listened without interruption while I wrapped the chord around my finger.

"So now what?" she asked.

Her tone gave me the impression that it began with a roll of the eyes. Her mother's scratchy voice shouted in the background. I didn't know whether Stella was annoyed by the new information or irritated by her mother's voice. From my perspective, Stella needed a sense of purpose as much as I did. But in retrospect, I think she wanted vengeance.

"Listen, we'll talk more in person tomorrow. I have to work tonight." I glanced over my shoulder to see if my mom was lurking around the corner, listening. "Then I'll explain everything."

"Fine," she said.

"Great. Now, don't do anything until I see you."

* * *

After supper, the rain began, and the temperature dropped. It seemed like winter made an unwanted encore. The ocean winds left the beach town ten degrees cooler than the inland areas. A bonus during the dog days of summer, not so much in the winter and spring. By the time I was ready to make the fifteen-minute walk to Mr. Fudge's, the rain was lashing sideways.

I rushed into the living room. My mother glanced up from the TV guide in her hand. "I didn't know you were working tonight." She laid the guide on the end table and snatched up the car keys. "By the time you get there, you'll be drenched and in no shape to serve customers. Not that I imagine there will be any tonight."

"I still get paid either way." I shoved a pack of gum and a dime inside my change purse. My mother always warned me to never leave the house without some "mad" money to call home in an emergency. I'd used the dime on many occasions, but fortunately, none had been for emergencies.

We left by the kitchen door, the shortest route to the driveway where our ugly, wood-panel DeSoto Station Wagon was parked. Mom drove to Ocean Avenue and pulled up behind the entrance to the fudge and taffy store. "Don't forget, I need you to help straighten up after school tomorrow. God-willing, the rain will stop. Your father will be back late Friday evening."

I nodded.

"Call me if it's still raining at the end of your shift." She pulled a plastic scarf from her purse and tied it beneath her chin. "The temperature is supposed to drop to forty tonight—don't want you catching a cold."

I gripped the door handle, trying not to roll my eyes while she spoke to me like a child. Had she known I was investigating a possible crime that might involve a nun and a priest and that I had discovered more about her father than she could ever imagine, worrying about me catching a cold would be the least of her problems.

She pulled away in the 'Woodie,' but hit the brakes and honked. Rolling down the window, she shoved a black umbrella into my hand. Despite wearing my yellow raincoat with the hood, I accepted it.

Using the umbrella instead of my hand, I waved goodbye, then sprinted up the wooden steps to the store entrance. The car backfired. I turned around in time to see the billowing smoke and smell the stink of gasoline. Still not a practiced driver, my mother must have forgotten to pull the choke. As much as I hated that car, I hoped my dad would let me drive it when I turned seventeen. It was better than nothing. My savings were not nearly enough to buy my own car. However, I was working on it. A sudden rush of envy toward Laura snuck up on me. I fought it, reminding myself that I was lucky to have a friend with a cool set of wheels.

A sweet rush of chocolate, vanilla, peanut butter, and everything sugar flooded my nostrils when I opened the door to Mr. Fudge & Saltwater Taffy. Denny stood behind the counter. His slicked-back hair made it difficult to tell whether he'd gotten rained on or had just doused it with too much Vitalis hair tonic.

"Ivy's here, Mr. F.," Denny hollered. "No need to call her now." He put a tray of fudge down on the counter, then rubbed his hands together and licked his lips. I knew it wasn't the tray of fudge that warranted his salacious stare.

I squinted, confused by his comment, and hung my raincoat on the rack in the corner.

Mr. Fotopoulos appeared from the back in a white t-shirt and pants. A rainbow of stains covered his light blue apron, with *Mr. Fudge*

& Saltwater Taffy printed in block letters. His salt-and-pepper hair was curled tighter than usual. Thumb-sized pockets of flesh drooped beneath his eyes. A testament to years spent soaking up the morning sun before crafting his tasty treats.

"I was just about to call you and say no come. Since you here, start moving fudge from back of trays to front. Neh?"

"Neh."

Neh, meant *yes* in Greek. I'd learned that the hard way after a discussion that sounded similar to Abbot and Costello's comedy skit *Who's on First.* If it weren't for the help of Mrs. Fudge, I would have quit the first week, confused and in tears.

"If rain don't stop and business pick up, we make a few batches of taffy, then you go home early." He disappeared behind the curtain at the back of the store.

Denny brushed up behind me and whispered in my ear, "If he lets us out early, maybe we can hang out for a while."

"And where are we gonna go in this monsoon?" I slipped on a pair of plastic gloves, reached inside the glass cabinet, removed two stale-looking pieces of fudge, then tossed them in the trash.

He licked his bottom lip just like before. "No worries. I have a car tonight."

"What?" I stepped back and glared at him. "Where'd you get a car?"

He winked. "A good friend lent it to me for doing him a favor."

"What kind of favor?" I grabbed a bottle of glass cleaner, sprayed, and wiped down the smudged panels of the fudge display case.

The bell above the door jingled. A gentleman about Dad's age, wearing a gray trench coat and a matching fedora, rushed in from the rain. He removed his hat and shook it out. Droplets hit the glass case. I groaned beneath my breath; thanks a lot. Just as I set down the bottle and walked over to assist the guy, Denny stepped in front of me.

"Can I help you?" he asked.

I backed up and scowled at him. He ignored me and continued to assist the customer. I continued checking the fudge, removing the dried-out pieces, while inconspicuously keeping an eye on Denny and the gentleman. He wrapped several pieces of peanut butter fudge in wax paper and placed them in one of the little white candy bags. Then he reached inside his own pocket and shoved a wad of money inside, too.

"Thank you, sir," Denny said. "Keep dry."

The man nodded. Placing his hat back on, he left with the bag.

"Why did you do that?" I asked.

Denny frowned. "Do what?"

"You know what." I squinted at him, like one of the cops I'd seen on Dragnet.

He grabbed a towel and wiped some sugary crumbs off the counter. "I don't know what you're talking about."

I know I didn't imagine what I saw. It reminded me of what he'd done the other night with a different man and a newspaper. Was Denny gaslighting me? His attitude flip-flopped from day to day, sometimes minute to minute. Sometimes I found him skittish and aloof, other times, charming and charismatic.

Apparently, Denny was involved in something shady. I was insanely attracted to him fifty percent of the time, but whatever he was doing the other fifty percent began to weigh on me. Why was he lying? Could my brain be on overload from all the suspicions I had with practically everyone in my life? Probably best to play it cool and observe him more closely before I asked questions.

By the time seven o'clock rolled around, only a handful of customers had come into the store. Mr. Fudge instructed Denny and me to go to the kitchen and make a batch of blueberry taffy for the morning. We were running low.

Denny stood in front of the taffy-wrapping machine, covered in confectionery sugar, after tending to the fudge. The loud noise of what sounded like an oversized sewing machine made a thump after each fold. First, I grabbed a measuring cup, added vanilla extract, and dumped it into the pot. Next, I added the syrup and the blue coloring and began stirring. After several stirs with the wooden spoon, I turned off the flame and covered the pot. Then I moved on to the hot box, a warm refrigerator that cools the taffy while keeping it warm.

I opened the large metal door, grabbed a bundle of taffy, and plopped it down on the steel cooling table. Denny's warm hands grazed mine as he clutched the gooey mass of sugary clay and stretched it across. Now facing me, he thrust his fists into the mound and began to knead. I did the same. Next, we pulled the taffy. Our eyes locked. Denny tugged harder. I matched his force. He folded his portion. A slow surrender as the taffy yielded to movement, and I folded mine over his in a rhythmic motion. His triceps bulged as he pushed down on the thick mass. Together, we repeated this action much longer than needed.

The warm taffy and being so close to Denny overwhelmed my senses. Space and time had disappeared. For a moment, I saw and heard nothing—only images in my mind: being lip-locked with Denny, our breaths mingling, his passionate eyes—until the bells hanging over the front door jingled, and a customer's voice called for Mr. Fudge.

"So, you gonna stick around?" Denny asked. "We can play pinball or something. I'll come get you when I'm done here." He stared deep into my eyes the way he always did when trying to charm me. If I were a piece of taffy, I believed he'd sink his teeth right into my flesh.

"I don't know, Denny. I still have homework, and my mom's expecting to pick me up. She won't be too keen on you driving me home, having never met you."

I feared that if I went out with him, we'd be playing backseat bingo in that car instead of pinball. However, Denny's shady antics began to raise doubts. My Catholic school upbringing gave me faith that I would be able to abstain from his advances. With a mixed bag of emotions, my mind reeled. Denny seemed to be playing me like a yo-yo, and I didn't like it. Only, I couldn't seem to cut the string.

"Sure enough," he said.

I pulled off my apron and plastic gloves and tossed them in the trash. "You can meet my parents on Saturday when you pick me up."

"Yeah . . . okay." He raised his chin a little. "Maybe I'll borrow my friend's car again, and we'll go to the drive-in."

The thought of going to the drive-in with him sent butterflies and apprehension to my gut. However, that didn't mean I would allow my hormones to direct my brain, despite its overthrowing temptation regularly. Though I didn't trust Denny, I trusted myself. My boundaries were in place, and if Denny crossed them, we'd be done.

Denny began refilling the napkin holder. "I saw the schedule. You're working Saturday afternoon, and I'm on Saturday night."

He clicked the napkin dispenser shut and brushed up behind me. His warm breath was soft on my neck. He took my hand and squeezed it lightly. The same magnetic pull that had ensnared me the night of the dance threatened to take my emotions hostage once more. That warning flare telling me I might be falling for him despite myself blared through me.

"That's fine. Give me a bell, okay?" I said, trying to sound cool.

"You're becoming a real hipster, Ivy." His eyes twinkled.

I grinned. Never had I referred to a phone call this way. I sauntered to the back of the store, slipped my dime in the payphone, and called my mother for a ride home.

"Goodnight, Ivy." Mr. Fudge waved without glancing back.

****

On my way out the door, Denny pinched my cheek. "Give you a bell—later, gator."

I cracked a smile, grabbed my purse, and left through the front door, facing the boardwalk and the ocean. The rain had settled down, but the wind still whipped hard enough to knock the signs against the glass. Mom would be waiting for me around the back, where I had entered earlier. Denny had flustered me so much that I rushed out.

The rain started again, and I opened my umbrella, only for the wind to flip it inside out. I turned it back into place and, rounding the corner onto the street, paused to lean against the wall. As I waited, my thoughts corralled the growing mysteries that had piled up since I decided to leave Catholic school: Gramps, Mother Superior, and now Denny. How could I possibly make sense of all this on my own?

CHAPTER TWENTY-TWO

Mom sat in the front seat, the kerchief covering her head. The news from the radio filled the silence on the quick ride home. I figured Mom had a lot on her mind, planning for the holiday weekend. She rarely did anything for herself. Always bringing food to the sick, mending clothes, helping new moms with their babies, cleaning, and cooking. My mother was more of a saint than anyone I'd known. The thought of disappointing her tugged at me, but I deserved more freedom, I told myself.

I broke the silence and nervously blurted, "Denny asked me on a date to the drive-in movies on Saturday; can I go?"

She turned toward me with scrunched eyebrows. "You are only sixteen. Boys and cars at your age are not good companions."

My voice elevated. "All the girls I know have been to the drive-in—all but me!"

"We don't even know this . . . *Denny*."

She pulled into the driveway, and I continued my argument. "You'll meet him when he picks me up—please—we have worked together since last summer." I dropped my shoulders and gazed up at her, hoping to pull her heartstrings.

"I'll talk to your father and see what he thinks."

At least she hadn't responded with a definitive no. However, I didn't have complete faith that my father would give me the answer I wanted.

"Thank you." I planted a kiss on her cheek and ran inside the house.

*   *   *

I tossed my coat on the kitchen chair and began to remove my shoes.

Mom hung her coat in the closet. "Oh, shucks—I left my purse in the car. Ivy, please run out and get it?"

"Sure." I threw my coat back on and trudged outside. While opening the car door, I caught sight of Stella's mother staggering out of Cafferty's. She stopped after a few steps and attempted to light a cigarette. The wind and rain kept blowing out the matchstick's flame. A thin gentleman wearing a blue work jacket embroidered with the name Esso in red on the front right corner stepped up behind her. He flicked open a silver Zippo. She moved in close and leaned into the flame with the cigarette hanging from her orange lipstick-caked mouth.

I couldn't hear anything they were saying. She inhaled, removed the cigarette, and held it in the air. Dancing around the rain pellets, she laughed and followed him as he waved her toward his car. She stumbled into a puddle. "Damn!" she hollered.

He opened the passenger side door, and she climbed into his red Chevy Coupe. The man drove away, running up the curb before he got back onto the road. They disappeared around the bend. Did she plan to bring him back to her house? If so, was this something she did regularly? Maybe she wouldn't go home at all. Seedy images raced through my mind, and I suddenly understood Stella a little better.

After I grabbed Mom's purse from the back seat of the car, I brought it inside and laid it next to mine on the kitchen table. This time, I hung my coat in the closet. Standing next to the black telephone, she whisper-yelled into the receiver. I assumed she was speaking to my father. Gramps sat half asleep, struggling to watch *Dragnet*. His cigar still burning solo in the ashtray.

"Hi, Gramps." I bent to kiss his cheek. His eyes were slightly open, and I could see the whites. Startled, I gasped. "Gramps, you okay?"

He shook his head and gazed up at me. "Yes, Ivy. How's work, dear?"

"Slow." I shrugged. "Came home early. You sure you're okay?"

His face was pale and clammy, and his speech slurred. He braced himself on the arm of the chair and sat more upright. "Yes—yes, I'm fine, dear."

Though he was getting old, sometimes it seemed as if he were on another planet. No alcohol on his breath or empty glass next to the ashtray. His age had to be affecting him in ways I couldn't know.

"Sit down and talk with me." He patted the arm of his ugly green chair.

The TV show's theme song signaled the end of the episode.

"I hear you might be going on a date Saturday night," he said. "I hope he's a good boy?"

Mom hung up the phone. Just as the speed of light, she must have leaped to the phone to call my dad while I was getting her purse from the car. Obviously, Gramps overheard the conversation.

I felt like saying, "Me too!" But I only grinned and nodded.

Gramps raked his mustache with his bottom teeth. "How'd you meet?"

"Met him last year at Mr. Fudge's." I picked up an abandoned rubber band from the end table and wrapped it around my forefinger. "He works there, too."

"What's his name?"

"Denny."

"You know his family?"

"Well . . . he doesn't exactly have a family." I began to sweat. "He lives in, um . . . Asbury Boys' Home. Not because he's a delinquent." I inhaled and exhaled. "At least that's what I've heard." Though now I was beginning to wonder. "It's because his dad left his mom when he was little, and she couldn't care for him."

Gramps bent to pick up his dull, glowing cigar stub and sucked life back into the red ember at its end. "What do you mean, 'that's what you heard?' Didn't he ever tell you about himself?"

"Well . . . nothing that personal. We haven't had a chance to get into a discussion like that." I wiped my forehead on the back of my hand. "Gramps, this is our first official date. If it goes well, I'll learn more about him in time. Anyhow, you sound like Dad." I placed my hands on my hips.

He put the cigar back in the ashtray and reached for my hand. "That's because I love you—so does your dad. We're both of the male species. We know how they think better than you do." He picked up his cigar again and took another puff.

"Well, if Dad says yes, you'll meet him tomorrow night. But please don't ask him personal questions like that." I squeezed Gramp's hand. "Okay?"

"Oh, don't you worry. I can size a fellow up by the tone of his voice and the way he stands."

My shoulders slumped, and I let go of his hand. "Whatever you size up, please don't share it with me until after the date." I brought my hands together in the prayer position. "After all, if things don't work out, I'll still have to see him at Mr. Fudge's all summer."

Gramps didn't argue. He just caught his mustache with his bottom lip and nodded pensively. My heart raced, fearful he planned to give Denny the third degree regardless of my request. I almost wished I'd never told Denny I wanted to go on an official date.

* * *

The next morning, after the school bell rang, Sister Florinda hurried us inside the classroom and closed the door. The girls were chattier than usual. Laura's ponytail danced the cha-cha from its pink ribbon as she sauntered over to my desk and slapped down an advertisement for a cruise ship.

"What's this?" I asked, confused.

"My mom and I are going on a cruise this summer. A Mother's Day gift to her!" she exclaimed. "Just the two of us." She grinned so wide I could see her tonsils. "My dad's agency is expanding from corporate to vacation travel. We get to go and report back on the amenities so he can share with potential customers."

"Cool beans," I said while I dug inside my purse for a file. I didn't want to show too much excitement because I'd be faking it. But I didn't want to be too disinterested because I'd appear jealous.

"We are going to Bermuda! I wish you were going with me, but I'll send you a postcard."

"Okay, thanks." Despite our friendship, I couldn't wait for the conversation to end.

Sister Florinda clapped her hands and announced, "Roll call."

Within a second, we were all seated and facing front. I instantly noticed Stella missing from her desk, yet again. Crazy thoughts ran through my head. What if the guy I saw with her mom killed their whole family? After reading the detective magazines Stella had given me, I was becoming paranoid. But I couldn't keep knocking on Stella's door as if I were her personal bodyguard.

After we performed our daily ritual, acknowledging our attendance and pledging to both flags, the next bell rang, signaling the start of our first period.

"Hey, wait up," Laura called. She sped up to catch me in the hallway. "Wanna come over to my house after school?"

Since Stella was MIA, and I needed to suppress Laura's suspicions, I thought I'd better; otherwise, she'd be upset with me and ask questions I didn't want to answer. Though my quest for truth about Mother Superior had suddenly fallen on the back burner of my to-do list, I was at a standstill without Stella.

"Sure," I told Laura. "I'm free today, and it's been a while."

She pulled me by the hand. "Sure has. We can listen to music—got a new Bobby Darin record."

"Sounds great! I'll meet you out front after school," I said and rushed off to Latin class while Laura went to typing.

At the end of the day, Laura waited for me in front of the school. We walked along chatting about Summer, boys, and of course, her car.

"Let's walk down Main Street. There's a car that looks just like mine."

I untied the white ribbon of my own ponytail and combed back the loose strands with my hands, and retied the ribbon to my finger.

"Don't you want me to see it for the first time on your birthday? If we go now, it'll ruin the surprise."

She shrugged. "It'll still be a surprise. The one on Main is white with a tan interior. "Mine is blue with white, but I guess you're right."

I was glad she took my suggestion. My motives were based on jealousy, not a sincere desire to be surprised on Laura's birthday. Now, she would have everything: a dream cruise and a car. Sometimes my face grew so hot when she talked about getting this or that. No worries about money or a future. Her parents had everything. However, I was surprised she was getting a car, considering they barely let her out of their sight unless she brought her brothers along. Maybe they were finally loosening the reins. So, I changed the subject.

"Has your dad given you driving lessons?"

She raised both eyebrows. "Oh, yeah, he started to, then he hired someone from a driving school to finish the job. He said my slamming on the brake wasn't good for his heart." She giggled. "I'm doing great now. You'll see."

I hoped she was telling the truth, considering I'd soon be a passenger in her car.

"Can't wait," I said and looked across the street.

A boy about our age crossed over and walked toward us. Our mouths dropped. "Oooh, he's cute. He might be the new guy I heard my neighbor talking about," Laura said.

"Naah, he's here on vacation."

"How do you know that?" She scrunched her eyebrows and glared, tilting her head sideways like a confused puppy.

"You can tell by the way he walks." I mimicked his tentative steps, staring from one side of the street to the other as he paid attention to every little thing he passed. "He wouldn't be doing that if he lived here."

"You're good, Ivy," she said. "Maybe one day you can figure out whether Mother Superior really keeps a secret book on us girls." She shot me a smug look. "I don't have to worry about being in it, of course," she said confidently. "But I'd sure love to see who is."

Her statement had me reeling. Was she dangling bait in front of me to see if I'd bite? Or was the remark purely honest and coincidental? We made a turn at Deal Lake toward her house, the largest on the street. Different from mine. Different from Stella's. A large stone fountain sat in front of the house, and of course, there was a statue of Mary in the garden that was bountiful with white azalea bushes and red roses. Heavy wood, double doors with brass knockers shaped like the letter C, for Capri, greeted the entire neighborhood.

She shoved her key in the lock and opened the right door. The shiny oak floors suggested I take off my shoes and slide across the foyer, as we'd done as kids. If the white velvet sofa in the living room could speak, it would have said, 'Don't you dare sit on me despite the hard plastic covering.'

A tall floor lamp with three globes sprouted from behind the half-moon sofa, and a hot pink love seat, in one corner, had round, silver lighting fixtures, like something you'd only see in Hollywood or on a spaceship. The largest wall was covered with a painting depicting what appeared to be a bunch of triangles wrestling. Laura's mother liked everything modern, and she didn't like clutter. Laura's younger brothers had a playroom all to themselves. They were forbidden to bring toys into any other part of the house. Not even a TV was allowed in the living room; even that had to be viewed in the basement.

On our way downstairs, we passed the kitchen, where wall-to-wall, mauve Formica cabinets hung on every inch of the pale pink walls. Nothing sat on the countertops except for a percolator and toaster, both covered with white appliance jackets. No room had any photographs of family members, anywhere. It seemed as if Laura's mom didn't want anyone to know they actually lived in the house. In a way, it was true. They mostly lived beneath it.

"Come on," Laura led me to the finished basement.

"I also got Connie Francis's new record, *Who's Sorry Now.*" She rushed to the cherry wood console stereo, pulled the record out of its sleeve, and set it up to play. "Sit down already!" She grabbed my arm again and pulled me over to the black leather couch. "What's up with you lately?" Laura stood over me with her hands on her hips.

"Okay, okay," I said and dropped down onto one cushion.

She stood over me, still with her hands on her hips, frowning. "Well."

"What are you talking about?"

"Is it Denny?" She tilted her head again. Honestly, she was starting to remind me of Lassie.

"What do you mean?"

"Don't give me that stuff." She sat down and turned toward me. "You're still upset about him and Stella, aren't you?" She leaned over and hugged me. "I know you liked that jerk, but I warned you. He's trouble; she is too."

It wasn't an easy task to keep quiet about all I'd gone through during the past couple of weeks, with Laura relentlessly badgering me. I was just about to crack and tell her everything when the door flew open, and the scent of fresh-baked pizza wafted into the room. Two rambunctious boys with olive skin, caramel eyes, and dirty blond crew cuts barreled down the steps. Her six-year-old twin brothers busted in like puppies chasing a ball. Both boys wore identical horizontal blue-and-white striped shirts, blue jeans, and white Keds sneakers.

"Mom!" Laura hollered. "Ivy is here. Can't we have a little privacy?"

The record dropped onto the turntable, and Connie Francis crooned. Laura's brothers showed up at the perfect time. Any moment, I was about to cave in and give her an earful. But I didn't want to reveal anything until I knew all the facts. Surely, Mother Superior couldn't be a real madam, but I wanted to find out exactly what she was involved in.

"Hello, stranger," Mrs. Capri directed her comment to me. A short, thin woman with the same chocolate-colored hair as Laura's but styled in a French twist. Her yellow-flowered dress swung as she chased the boys with a washcloth. Holding the cloth aloft, she hugged me lightly and kissed my forehead.

I stood in place. "Hi, Mrs. Capri."

"Oh, sit down. I'll take the boys back upstairs. Why don't you stay for pizza?"

I didn't sit again. "Thank you, but I really can't stay long. We're having company this weekend, and my mom needs my help."

"Just a slice, dear." She scooted the boys along with the back of her hand. "You have to eat, don't you?"

Laura batted her eyes and pouted her lips. "You can't be going already?"

"I'll have one slice, but I really do have to get home soon. My mother is counting on me."

"How 'bout the movies tomorrow night?" Laura blurted.

Oh, boy. I couldn't tell her I was already going with Denny. Then, I'd have to explain everything. Though now it wasn't only about my feelings for him. Curiosity lingered in the back of my mind so strong it seemed to direct every move I made. It was also getting tough to hold back all that was going on away from Laura. Soon, I feared, I would burst.

"Hmm, what's playing?" I asked, although I already knew.

"'*Gigi* or *Vertigo*?'" She dramatically laid both hands across her chest. "I can't make up my mind which one to see."

"I like Jimmy Stewart and Kim Novak better."

"Me, too. But Leslie Caron is all the rage as a dancer." Laura said as she swayed into a two-second cha-cha in front of me.

Laura's mom reappeared with two steaming pizza slices and two bottles of Coke. She set down everything on the bridge table next to the stereo. "Enjoy, girls."

"Thank you," I told Mrs. Capri. I took several quick bites from the pizza and a sip of soda. "Sorry, but I'll have to get back to you later about the movies. You know, the big social whirl at our house this weekend, and all."

"Okay." She walked over to the stereo, lifted the arm from the record, placed it in its cradle, and switched off the player. "If not, maybe we can go out later for a float or something?" She leaned an elbow on the table and propped her chin on her palm. "Bet there'll be tons of guys on the boardwalk." She smiled. "This is the big weekend!"

I nodded. Though my mission seemed to be taking more turns than a prima ballerina, it kept *me* on my toes. Nevertheless, I missed hanging out with Laura. It would be fun cruising in her new car this summer. After finishing the pizza and cola, I wiped my hands and mouth clean with the paper napkin and stood up. "I really have to go.

CHAPTER TWENTY-TWO

Sorry."

Just as I announced my leaving, Laura's brothers barreled back down the stairs and into our space.

"Boys!" she yelled.

"I'll call you later about the movie. Thanks for the pizza."

She followed me upstairs. I thanked Mrs. Capri again and left for home.

Ten minutes after I arrived, I phoned Laura and told her I'd have to pass on the movie, but I promised, again, to be there for her birthday party. She didn't seem upset. Why would she be? She was getting her first car!

CHAPTER TWENTY-THREE

ustomers lined the boardwalk in front of Mr. Fudge's store. Denny and I were running back and forth all day without much time for flirting. When I finally got home, I rushed to my closet to find an appropriate outfit for our date. I wanted to look swell, but the fear that Denny would think I was easy, again, played a role in my clothing choice. The signals between my brain and heart were miserably entangled. I feared I might make a mess of things if I couldn't keep control.

After ransacking the closet for the perfect outfit, I pulled out a red-and-white-striped dress with a sweetheart neckline. I held it up and stared in the mirror. Did I want Denny to want me, or did I want him to be tempted to take me? That was a serious question. I had not thought about it as in-depth as I should have. No way would I go all the way with him or anyone, for that matter. But I did like the feeling of being wrapped in his arms. I had to think carefully about how to handle the evening.

Did Mata Hari ever have a conflict between her mission and her emotions? The situation I'd found myself in had become more serious than I had ever expected. I traded the red dress for a pale-yellow one with a flared skirt and a hem that stopped just at my knees. Then, I covered my shoulders with a white cardigan.

When Denny appeared at our door, it was apparent he hadn't put as much thought into his appearance as I had. I wanted to run out to the car without my parents having to meet him, but that was the whole reason I'd arranged for him to pick me up. After having seen Denny act shady with the guy at Mr. Fudge's, everything had changed. Now, I questioned my decision to have him meet them. Had I just inadvertently asked for trouble without realizing it?

"Come on in." He stepped inside and stood with his hands in his pockets, gazing around the walls. His eyes followed the trail of photographs hanging on the wall along the staircase. Most of the framed photos were of me at various milestones in my life: a baby picture in a pink bonnet, a toothless photo from second grade, me in my Brownie uniform, and a headshot from eighth-grade graduation.

Denny's silence and introspective eyes had me believing he felt as awkward as a church mouse in a synagogue. It hadn't occurred to me that he might not have any photos of his childhood hanging anywhere. He might not have photos at all. Suddenly, my heart grew a compassion for him I hadn't had before.

"Mom, this is Denny Carson," I said, introducing the two.

She scanned him from head to toe, then back to head with a somewhat cross between a sneer and a grin. Finally, she held her hand out. "Hello, Denny, nice to meet you."

He reached out and shook it lightly. Then Dad appeared. Now, my stomach was flip-flopping and gurgling.

"Dad, this is Denny Carson."

Dad left Denny's hand hanging in the air without shaking it. "Have a seat, Denny," he said.

Denny sat down on Gramps's green recliner, and my father sat across from him on the couch. "So, where do you live in town, Denny?" He didn't smile. He didn't sneer. He held an intimidating stare.

Denny nodded. "Over on Bangs."

"Is that so?" Dad crossed his right leg over his left. "What does your father do?"

I clenched my jaw. Mom had known he lived at the boys' home, having no family. She must not have told Dad. Denny's right foot began tapping at a high speed, and luckily, Gramps strolled in from the kitchen.

"Gramps!" I stepped toward him, hoping to diffuse the awkwardness. "Denny, I'd like you to meet my gramps."

Suddenly, my grandfather's face turned pale, and he began coughing so hard that I thought a bug had flown down his throat.

"Excuse me." Gramps covered his mouth with one hand. Then he cleared his throat and reached out to shake Denny's hand, but started coughing again. He held up his palm as if he were signaling a car to stop. "Sorry, must be the pollen. Nice to meet you, Denny." He turned away and rushed up the stairs.

We all glared at Gramps, not knowing what to say. I always worried about his health because of his age, but he was acting so strangely now. I wasn't sure what to make of it. Denny looked mortified, and Dad sat there waiting for him to answer the question. Beads of sweat had formed on Denny's forehead. He swallowed hard. The tension between him and Gramps, even though they'd only met for a second, was odd and obvious. And the fact that he completely ignored my father's question had me rattled. So, I jumped into the conversation.

"Dad, Denny lives at the boys' home on Bangs. I already told Mom this." I gave him a pleading look, hoping he'd stop with the questions. We really need to get going. We don't want to be late for the movie."

My father stood up. "What are you going to see?"

"'Vertigo,'" I said, before Denny had a chance to answer. Quickly grabbing my purse from the chair, I wrapped the strap around my hand tightly, ready to run. I couldn't get out of there quickly enough.

"Now, Denny," Dad said, "make sure you bring Ivy home right after the movie. Her curfew is eleven o'clock. I'll be waiting up."

"Sure thing, sir." Denny hurried to open the front door, then I walked out and closed it firmly behind me.

* * *

Denny opened the passenger side door of a brand-new, turquoise Buick. The earthy scent of its black leather interior drifted in the air as I slid across the bench seat, which felt like a satin glove caressing my body. He shoved the key into the ignition, turned on the radio, and put his arm around my shoulders, pulling me close. His leather jacket smelled different from the car, but the combination electrified my senses in every way imaginable.

Being so near to him brought back the feelings I'd been trying to suppress. Darn it!

"Oh, my gosh, Denny! Where in the world did you get this car?" I grazed my hand along the seat.

He squeezed my shoulder. "Told you, a friend let me borrow it for doing him a favor."

I inched away to face him. "What kind of favor?"

He turned up the radio. Tony Bennett's song "Rags to Riches" blasted out of the rear speakers. Denny could not have planned that.

He put the car in gear and pulled away from the curb, staring through the windshield as if his life depended on it.

I patted the smooth seat and repositioned myself. Though I loved being inside the car, I had to know where it came from. It made no sense to me that someone would just lend a teenager a car like this. Seeing Denny at the wheel of a luxury sedan seemed unnatural. I wanted a reasonable answer, but I feared he couldn't give me one.

He stopped at the end of the block and turned toward me again. Then, he slid his arm from around my neck and twisted the knob to turn down the radio volume. "What? Are you writing a book? I picked you up for a *real* date, as you asked. I met your parents. What else do you want from me?" His eyes narrowed. "I don't do this for nobody." He tilted the rearview mirror toward himself and raked a hand through his slicked-back hair.

My heart sped up. Denny's irritation and slippery attitude confirmed my belief that he was involved in something shady. It was apparent he had no intention of answering my question. I'd never had a boy interested in me, so I had nothing to compare. But my instinct told me Denny's behavior was not normal. I constantly justified his excuses because of his background and lack of family support. Now, I was torn between wanting to enjoy our date and getting close enough to him to earn his trust. At the very least, I believed he liked me, and that would work toward my advantage either way.

"I don't mean to sound so hard," he added, still not meeting my eyes. "But first, the inquisition with your pop, and now you. I feel like I'm being interrogated by a couple of private eyes."

His comment made my blood run cold. I needed to work on a more subtle approach.

"Sorry, Denny. No more questions." I slid back to his side of the seat and turned up the volume on the radio.

CHAPTER TWENTY-FOUR

We drove for about ten minutes, listening to music and not talking. The bright lights of the drive-in movie shone out onto the highway. We pulled into the line of cars waiting to go in. Denny rolled down his window and reached for his wallet from the inside pocket of his leather jacket. He pulled some cash from a large wad of bills and paid the cashier at the glass booth. I held back commenting on the cash. Then, he followed the other cars into the lot and parked a few rows away from the snack bar. He released me, yanked the speaker from its stand, and hung it on the edge of the car window.

A thousand butterflies seemed to have emerged from chrysalises inside my belly. I was alone in a car. At a drive-in—with Denny! No matter what bad stuff he might be involved in, I couldn't turn off what I felt for him. I even tried reciting what Mother Superior had ingrained in my mind to remind me how important it was to control lustful desires: *One moment of pleasure can create a lifetime of pain.* But all I could think about was making out with Denny. Like a child told not to touch a hot stove, I allowed my curiosity about his mysterious ways to lure me.

Nevertheless, I still had some wits about me. I observed him closer than ever before. His eyes were narrow, and the irises one shade lighter than his pupils. What a handsome profile. His jawline was perfectly square, like James Dean's. He had the same contemplative look as the actor, too. His face was rough but soft at the same time. I didn't want to keep staring, but I was afraid that if I asked more questions, he'd get angry. It occurred to me that I had no idea of Denny's ethnic background. Dad was always making statements at the dinner table about this sort of thing. It made me wonder. I didn't think asking about *that* could make him mad.

I leaned against the passenger side door and stared into his eyes. "You know, I'm German on my mom's side, Irish on my dad's. What about you?"

He paused for a moment, seeming puzzled. "Italian on my mom's side, so I'm told. Don't know about my dad." He glanced down.

Maybe the rumor about his mother leaving him at Sacred Heart Orphanage for Boys and never returning was true.

"I bet you're part Indian," I said. "Maybe Lenape. That tribe's from New Jersey, you know."

He lifted a hand, palm out. "How."

I giggled. "You're funny."

He winked. "Want some popcorn and a soda?"

"Do you?"

He shook his head. "Why do girls always answer a question with a question? Can't you just say, 'yes' or 'no?'"

I nodded. "Sure. I'd *love* to *share* a tub of popcorn with you," I said enthusiastically.

"Good." He opened the car door. "Be right back!"

"You want me to come with you?"

"Naah." He leaned over and planted a quick, hard kiss on my cheek and took off.

My heart fluttered with excitement. Nevertheless, I still planned to take a minute and investigate the car. Once Denny was out of sight,

I opened the glove compartment and groped around inside. I was hunting for information, something with a name on it, like the car registration. Beneath the General Motors buyer's guide, I found a blue plastic square. An insurance card and registration were inside. Fearful of turning on the light, I squinted to read the name—Joseph Finetti—Newark, New Jersey.

Why would Denny know someone in Newark willing to lend him a swell car like this? The last name on the registration tugged at my memory until it clicked—I'd seen it in Mother Superior's book. Just then, the crunch of gravel signaled Denny's return. I slid the paper back into the compartment, only to spot a small bag of white powder like the one I'd once found in Gramps's drawer. The truth hit me hard: two grown men carrying sugar bags was no coincidence. I lifted it for a closer look, but Denny's footsteps were nearly upon me. Snapping the latch shut, I slipped the bag into the pocket of my cardigan.

"That was quick," I said, my heart pounding and a little breathless.

He handed me a bag of popcorn and a soda. "Yeah, we beat the rush—you alright?"

"Sure, just hungry," I said, and shoved a handful of popcorn into my mouth. I washed it down with a gulp of cola. About ten minutes into the movie, Denny inched closer to me. He placed his arm around my neck, then gently kissed my cheek. I could feel myself blush. My skin tingled, and my heart quickened just as it did the night he kissed me at the dance. The heat of his breath warmed me everywhere.

"This steering wheel is a pain in the ass," he whispered, as if someone might hear us. "Wanna sit in the back?"

"Oh—but—then we won't be able to see the movie," I tugged at the sleeve of my sweater, trying to twist it around my finger.

"Sure, we will. It'll be more comfortable."

"I . . . I . . . I don't think that's a good idea." Releasing my sleeve, I glanced down into my lap and began fiddling with the napkin. Wise enough to know that neither Denny nor any other guy wanted to hear that answer, I feared he'd get upset again.

"Aw, come on, "I'm not gonna try anything," he said with that Johnny Ray voice and proceeded to climb into the back seat. He reached for me and then guided me toward him. Despite the fact that I allowed him to lure me, I quickly turned around to face the front to watch the movie.

"Do you mind if I take off my boots?" he asked.

"Go ahead." I shrugged.

"My feet don't smell—promise," he said as he unlaced his boots. "You can take yours off, too. Unless you have smelly feet."

"No!" I cracked a smile.

Denny let his black engineer boots fall to the floor.

"Relax. Stay awhile." He tilted his head in that charming way.

I'd done it again, leading him to believe I could be easy. Saying no with my mouth, but yes with my actions. I removed my shoes and dropped them to the floor next to Denny's. He put an arm around me again.

"That's better. Isn't this nice?"

He didn't give me a chance to answer. He just began kissing my neck, my cheek, and then my mouth. Any moment, his hand would be reaching for something I wasn't ready to allow him to touch, despite my hormones. What had I gotten myself into? Why did I keep letting this happen? Fury burned through me, but it tangled with a wild passion that felt stronger than my own will—intoxicating, and impossible to resist. I returned Denny's kisses until we were both panting for breath. The car windows had completely fogged up. Denny rolled down the window to let in some air. I rested my head on his shoulder, and we got back to watching the movie.

The movie's character, Madeleine, had just awakened after Scottie had pulled her out of the San Francisco Bay. Her eyes were wild with questions and suspicion, caution, and desire. They seemed to convey all the emotions I felt toward Denny at that moment.

He stroked my hair and unclipped my barrette. This time, he pressed his mouth on mine harder, moving with more insistence until his body pushed mine down, pinning me on the seat. Once again, his hands crept beneath my blouse. I let them remain against my skin, but grabbed them before they reached their destination.

"Stop."

His mouth turned down, and he sat up. "Why are you such a tease?" He rapped the back of the front seat with the palm of his hand.

His action shook me. "I'm not a tease. You lied." I sat up, crossed my arms in front of my body and frowned. "You said you wouldn't try anything. Isn't kissing enough for you?"

"I'm sorry, Ivy. It's hard being this close to you."

Having the 'Holy Ghost in the middle' began to make all the sense in the world to me. "If you can't control yourself, maybe we should watch the movie up front."

"Fine." He threw the jacket over the back of the front seat and hopped over, spilling the popcorn. "Damn!"

"I'm sorry." I got out, opened the passenger-side door, then swept the popcorn back into the bag. When I handed it to him, he tossed it out the window.

"You didn't have to do that!"

He clenched his jaw. "Just watch the damn movie."

Suddenly, Stella invaded my thoughts. I wondered if she had known a different Denny than the one I was experiencing. His quick temper frightened me, but I convinced myself it was my fault for getting in the back seat in the first place. I adjusted my position on the seat, pressed against the door, and paid close attention to the movie. Now, *Scottie* had a crazy look in *his* eyes as he urged Judy to try on dresses identical to those Madeleine had worn. Nothing was as it had originally seemed in this story. Everything was twisted. The movie strangely mirrored my relationship with Denny in many ways.

* * *

Denny behaved like a gentleman throughout the rest of the movie. He held my hand from afar, but he didn't try to kiss me again. Obviously, my reaction squashed his expectations. I felt bad about that in a way. But this time, I had chosen to listen to the voice Mother Superior had planted in my head. I had to—it was too risky to ignore.

After the movie, a blitz of headlights staggered throughout the theater parking lot. A few cars stayed put. I imagined couples entwined in passionate embraces in the back seat, without realizing the movie had ended. Some might come up for air at the tap on the window from a flashlight-bearing theater manager. They would have a story to tell. One that would cause their friends' mouths to fall agape and their eyes to widen. Mine, on the other hand, would be boring—not even worth mentioning.

We joined the snaking line of cars headed to the exit.

"Did you like the movie?" I asked Denny.

He shrugged. "It was cool."

I had a hunch he really wasn't too keen on it. If I had asked him what it had been about, he probably wouldn't have been able to say. We drove for about ten minutes, then turned onto a street I didn't know, and pulled up to the curb in front of a florist shop.

"Mind waiting in the car for a couple of minutes?" he asked.

"Ok, but don't be long. You heard what my dad said. Eleven o'clock."

He opened the door to exit, then ducked his head back inside. "Lock the doors. Don't open 'em no matter what. This ain't a great neighborhood."

My heart raced again, but not in a good way this time. "What'd you take me here for, then?"

"I just have to pick something up," he said. "It'll only take a minute."

"Pick up what?"

"Don't worry about it."

Annoyed, I pounded all four locks shut with the side of my fist, then slumped in the seat to avoid bringing attention to myself in case someone walked by. Each minute seemed like ten. When two guys corralled in front of the car as if they were admiring it, my heart sped up. One rubbed a hand over the curved headlight. The other kicked the front right tire. The tall guy wearing gray pants and black suspenders cruised around to the other tire and kicked it, too. Then both guys strutted to the front and spat on the windshield. A third guy appeared and spat on the passenger window. I shrank back, trembling. Figurative spiders and snakes crawled over every inch of me. My heart pounded like it was about to pop out of my chest. Horrible visions ran through my mind like a horror film.

The guys began pushing down on the front and back fenders, rocking the beautiful, turquoise car. I practically wet my pants. Not sure if I'd make things worse or better, I pushed and slammed both palms on the steering wheel horn, hoping to either scare them away or draw Denny out to my rescue. The guys backed away at the same moment Denny returned. Now, I feared they'd hurt him.

"Get the hell outta here!" he shouted.

It was three against one. Yet all the guys stopped at Denny's demand and slithered away down the sidewalk. I quickly reached over and unlocked the driver's door. He got inside.

"Why did you take so long?" I broke into heavy sobs. "Why did you even take me here? I could have been killed."

"It's okay," he said. "Those guys are nothing to worry about."

"How am I supposed to know that?" I hollered. "This is not what I expected, Denny. I was scared. I didn't know what'd happened to you. I didn't know what was going to happen to me if you didn't come back out."

He put both arms around me this time. "It's okay. I'm sorry. It's okay." He kissed my cheek.

At that moment, I felt a false sense of safety, but my emotions about Denny continued to plague me. My conscience could not be ignored. Neither could the teachings from my Catholic school. Nor my father's rules.

I released the purse strap from my fingers and sat back in the seat without saying anything else. Denny pulled in front of my house at 11:10 p.m.

CHAPTER TWENTY-FIVE

"Don't walk me to the door," I told Denny. "I don't want my dad to come down hard on you."

He sighed. "You're only ten minutes late."

"You don't know my dad." I turned the rearview mirror down so I could dab the tears I'd been struggling to keep inside. No way could my parents find out I'd been crying. After a few deep breaths, I said, "I'd better go. Thanks for the 'real' date, Denny."

"Wait." He got out and opened the car door for me, then leaned in and kissed my cheek. "See ya at work."

I rushed up the walkway to the front porch steps. When I turned to wave goodbye, the turquoise car had already taken off into the night. I opened the front door and stepped inside. Dad was sitting on the couch watching the eleven o'clock news. He made a big show of lifting his wrist and glancing down at his watch.

"Where's Denny?" Dad puffed on a cigarette and laid it in the ashtray to smolder. "If he really were a *gentleman*, he'd have walked you to the door."

"He wanted to, but I told him not to bother."

Standing meekly in front of my father, I shifted from one foot to the other like a child about to be scolded. My purse strap slid from my shoulder. I wound the thin strap around my wrist. Each turn tighter and tighter as I waited for him to speak again. He only glared and took another deep drag of his cigarette. Each moment seemed the length of a song I disliked.

"Go to your room! As of now, you are punished. We'll discuss this in the morning."

"But Dad, I'm only ten minutes late!"

"Good night, Ivy!"

* * *

Like a bad dream I couldn't wake from, the next morning, I found myself in the same position as the night before. This time, I awaited sentencing for an act so minuscule that I had to pinch myself not to say words I might regret.

"Ivy, you have two choices!" Dad said. The smoke from his cigarette swirled up his nostrils after the word *choices*.

"What? I was only ten minutes late. Is that a crime?" My voice cracked as it rose to a squeak.

"Delores, come out here, please."

Mom walked into the living room holding the Sears bag I had hidden underneath my bed.

"Sit down, Ivy."

My face flushed with a combination of fear and anger. I backed away and sat on the chair with the red cushion, the one no one ever sat in because it was uncomfortable. It was the furthest I could get from my dad without leaving the room. My stomach grumbled. How much more could a person's nerves take in less than twenty-four hours? I just had to harden my resolve and think of it as a test of endurance. Any spy or investigator should expect to endure a grueling interrogation. Since I was tapping into years of techniques embedded in my memory, keeping my composure was as crucial as keeping my mouth shut. My secrets to myself.

Mom marched over to my father and turned toward me. She opened the bag and pulled out her black slacks and sunglasses as well as the items I'd taken from Gramps's trunk. "What are these things doing under your bed?" The sunglasses were clutched in her right hand. She shook them at me. "If you wanted to borrow something, young lady, all you had to do was ask. What concerns me more is the contents of this bag." She shook it as if it too had misbehaved. "It appears you are up to something disturbing. We want an explanation."

As freaked out as I was that they'd found the bag, I was relieved they didn't notice the black book. What made them look under my bed at all? At that moment, I figured the best defense was a good offense.

"Why were you looking under my bed?" I crossed my arms. "I've never done anything to give you a reason to distrust me." My bottom lip quivered, but I blinked and clenched my jaw hard to keep from crying again. "It's nothing to be upset about, Mom. I just wanted to see what it would be like to change my appearance if I were undercover."

"Undercover for what?" Mom shook her head.

"I've been reading about the histories of women in espionage." I sat up straighter. "Do you know who Virginia Hall is?" I raised my right eyebrow. My response sounded childish, but it was all I could come up with. It deflected from the truth without my having to completely lie.

Mom had never finished high school. She was a seamstress when she met my father. I was betting she didn't know the answer.

"Hall?" My mother repeated uncertainly. "Well, I—Ivy, this is not the time to question my memory of high school history."

"Then I'll just tell you," I spoke rapidly. "She was one of the most famous female spies from World War II!" I shifted in the red seat and straightened up. "She disguised herself as an elderly peasant woman to accomplish her mission and then get out of France. She even dyed her hair gray and wore old lady clothes so no one would recognize her."

"That's very interesting, Ivy, but—"

I rushed on, hoping to throw her off completely, and slightly impressed with myself that I had retained all this knowledge. "What about Harriet Tubman? I'm sure you remember her. She was a spy, too! It's not easy being a female agent, let alone a Negro female spy. She worked on the Underground Railroad and saved over three hundred lives by risking her own." I took a deep breath. "Maybe you think I have grandiose ideas, but what if I could make a difference one day, too? Why shouldn't I be allowed?"

"That's very admirable, Ivy," Mom said. "You've always been an inquisitive child."

"Yes, but she's not a child anymore," my father shot back.

"You're right, Dad, I'm not. I'm sorry for taking your things without asking, Mom. I'd planned to put them back. I just got side-tracked."

"Ivy, you're getting too old to be playing dress-up. Or to fantasize about becoming a 'spy,' for God's sake," my father exclaimed. "You're graduating from high school next year. It's just not realistic."

"Detective," I said. "Does that sound more reasonable?"

My father lit another cigarette. "Whatever." The Zippo lighter was shaking in his hand.

"I have no fantasies about becoming a spy. But I do have dreams of finding a career where I can use the knowledge and skills I've acquired," I said with a mature attitude. "There is an entire world of opportunities. And Catholic school is not the most inspiring institution."

My mother straightened up and raised her chin. "Well, if it weren't for Catholic school, I can't imagine how far you would go with these crazy ideas of yours. The nuns and priest keep you grounded, thank God." She let out a sigh of exasperation.

"There are several secretarial schools nearby," my mother said, then tilted her head and bore into my eyes.

"With your grades, maybe you can obtain a scholarship and go to one of those teacher colleges, even," my father said and laid the smoldering cigarette down in the ashtray. Then he held up his hands, palms out, as if he were pleading with me. "Then you'll meet a *decent,* young man instead of a hood like Denny."

"I don't want to be a secretary or a teacher," I said, forcing a monotone voice so as not to yell.

"Honey." My mother sighed. "It's okay to have dreams, but this spy or *detective* business is not going to happen."

"What about an investigator?"

"You are exhausting me, Ivy." She covered her face with both hands.

"You're a beautiful young lady. Take advantage of realistic opportunities that *are* available," Dad said.

"Don't you think our government or police departments rely on women to keep our country safe?" I asked, both hands on my hips. "What about the communists among us you are always talking about?" I shook my pointer finger at him. "Do you really think only men work for the government?"

If my parents only knew what I'd accomplished thus far by *spying,* they would be quite surprised. I knew more about what was going on in our household, our neighborhood, and our town than the two of them together. Maybe none of it seemed important yet. But instinct told me this hard work had a purpose.

"I'm sure it's just a phase," my mother whispered to my father under her breath.

"I refuse to live a mediocre—or worse, a boring life! Maybe that was okay for you, Mom, but not for me."

"Don't speak to your mother like that." My father pointed his finger at me.

I softened up to avoid fueling the fire any further. "Sure, one day maybe I might get married and settle down, but not until I've accomplished my dreams and *I* decide it's time!"

"Enough of this nonsense." My father scooted to the edge of his chair, sitting rigid with anger, jabbing his finger at me. "Forget about this ridiculousness," he said. "You have two choices. Tell your friend Denny there will be no more dates, or tell Mr. Fotopoulos he'll need to find a replacement for you at his store."

Choice number one appealed to me. After last night, I didn't want to date Denny anymore, but I still wanted to find out what he was up to. Quitting Mr. Fudge's would be the worse of my options, not just because I needed to make money, but because I wouldn't be able to monitor his Denny's behavior anymore.

"Fine." I tried to look upset. "I won't see Denny anymore."

Gramps appeared in the living room. "I'm not sure it's such a good idea for you to work with him, either, dear."

"What?" I jumped up from the chair and glared at Gramps as if he were a stranger. He'd never taken my parents' side against me before. I'd always thought he understood me better than anyone.

"But Gramps, I need this job. I'm saving for a car." I huffed. "Laura's father just bought her a *brand new* one for her birthday. I know Dad can't do that, but I'll need a car! How will I get around once I graduate?"

"You'll take the bus like everyone else your age," my mother said, as if that settled it.

"Rest assured, that car isn't for Laura. I bet it's Tom Capri's mid-life crisis gift to himself," Dad said under his breath to my mother. "Saying it was for Laura was his shifty way of acquiring it."

Mom grabbed Dad's hand, pulling him into the kitchen, and turned on the radio, a technique she often used to mute their discussions. I could hear them bickering. Several minutes later, Mom reappeared.

"Ivy, ignore your father's remarks. He thinks he knows everything."

With an eyeroll and a wave of her hand, she marched upstairs.

I stood in the abandoned living room and yelled, "Hasn't anyone heard a word I've said?"

No one responded. I stomped upstairs and slammed my bedroom door shut, locking it.

* * *

I sulked in my room for twenty minutes before my mother knocked on my bedroom door.

"Ivy, let me in."

"Go to church without me!" I hollered. "I have my period and terrible cramps!"

"Open the door this instant."

"Darn," I muttered, and opened the door and sat back down on my bed.

"Young lady, I understand you're upset, but your father and Gramps know what they're talking about when it comes to boys! If they think Denny is bad news, I have to agree with them." Her eyes bore into me. "Maybe you can ask Mr. Fotopoulos to let you work different hours than his. Otherwise, you'll have to quit. It's still early in the season. You can find another job."

"I just started this one. How can you expect me to quit? That's so unprofessional. Mr. Fudge depends on me." I wacked my pillow against the mattress. "This isn't fair at all!"

Mom bit her lip as if she felt sorry but didn't want to show it. "I'll talk to your father some more. Just promise not to see Denny again."

"Okay, okay. Just don't make me quit."

My parents left for Mass. Gramps did not accompany them. He disappeared, somewhere, as usual. I had to get ready for Laura's birthday party, and still had to buy a gift.

The warm breeze sifting through the screen of my bedroom window felt more like July than late May. I put on my favorite sundress, the yellow rayon one covered in a cherry print. Next, I pulled my hair back into a French twist like Madeleine's in *Vertigo* and brushed on a faint layer of mascara. Mostly, family members would be at Laura's party. But I knew she'd invite some friends from her dance class. They always got spiffed up.

After painting my toenails, I grabbed my purse and hurried toward the boardwalk, hoping to find a card and gift for Laura. The streets were alive with people, every shop open and buzzing. Summer had officially begun. Bobby Darin poured from car radios as teenagers cruised with windows down, laughter and chatter spilling from porches where families prepared for backyard barbecues. The music from the boardwalk stands and carousel swelled as I drew closer.

Frank Sinatra's voice drifted from the pool area of the Berkley-Carteret Hotel, serenading holiday guests. I jogged up the ramp to the boards just as a group of girls gathered at Betty's dress shop, swooning over the latest window display. I always preferred Betty's dresses to Laura's, though I'd never admit it. Music shifted with every storefront, speakers trading one song for another as I passed.

The air was thick with temptation—corn dogs, pizza, cotton candy, and the sweet pull of taffy, fudge, and powdered sugar—each scent carried on the ocean breeze and tugging at old summer memories. I couldn't help but smile when handsome young men paused to watch me stroll by. My parents' warning echoed in my mind: settling for a bad boy like Denny when there were so many good ones out there would be nothing short of foolish.

CHAPTER TWENTY-SIX

"Take a chance, spin the wheel!" Workers shouted from their game stands. Passing them by, I stopped at the storefront stands to examine the displays of costume jewelry, searching for a gift for Laura. Suddenly, a marching band thumped down the wooden planks led by a chubby-faced Boy Scout holding the American flag. The drum major parted the crowd like Moses splitting the Red Sea. They overpowered the rock ' n ' roll music streaming from the food stands and transistor radios from beach blankets. As "God Bless America" cranked, each person on the boardwalk stopped in their tracks and placed a hand over their heart until the song finished.

As the last note faded, I started walking again. Teens and families streamed into Palace Amusements. I glanced once more at Tillie's mural, then hurried toward Cookman, hoping to find something for Laura in one of the specialty shops. A furry pair of blue dice dangling from a display in the window caught my eye. I made my way to the salesgirl behind the counter.

"How much for those?" I asked the saleslady, pointing.

"Two dollars and fifty cents."

"Can you wrap them?"

She frowned. "Sorry. We don't do that here."

"Do you have a box, maybe?" She collected the dice and grabbed a white bag from beneath the counter, the kind Mr. Fudge used for taffy.

"If you have a card, I'll tape it to the front, and it'll be just as good."

"Thank you!" I smiled. "I'll be right back."

She nodded. "Sure thing."

I found a suitable card, grabbed a pen off the counter, wrote a note inside, sealed it, and handed it to the salesgirl. As promised, she taped it to the bag.

"Here ya go." I handed her the money. She gave me back fifty cents in dimes and nickels. "Thanks again." I left the store and headed toward Laura's house. On the way, I thought about what my dad had said about Laura's father wanting the car for himself. The car did seem impractical for a new driver, despite how well-off the Capris were. I wasn't sure how much truth there was to the story, though. In any event, I wouldn't say a word to Laura, but I planned to be attentive.

***

Clusters of blue, pink, and yellow balloons bobbed from the mailbox out front. In the driveway, a gleaming baby-blue T-bird caught the sunlight, its paint shimmering like glass. I bent to peek through the driver's window, admiring the crisp white leather seats. Someday, I'd have a car that fine—but it would be one I bought myself. Straightening, I opened the gate and strolled into the backyard, where the guests were already gathered."Happy Birthday!" I hugged Laura and kissed her cheek.

"Oh, I love your hair." She reached out and patted the back of my head. "You look a bit like Kim Novak."

I grinned, even though I knew I didn't look anything like the actress. "Yours looks great, too!" Wrapped in a yellow headband with a bow on top, her thick, chocolate locks draped over her shoulders in fat

180

bologna curls. Her brown halter dress, printed with bumblebees, had a yellow satin waistband.

"Thanks." She grabbed my hand. "Did you see the car?" she asked, beaming with excitement.

"How could I miss it?" I handed over the gift and card. "This is for both of you."

She pulled the card from the bag and read. Then, she opened the bag and lifted the string of dice with one finger. "This is boss," she squealed. "They match the car! Thank you." She hugged me.

"Mmm, love the perfume!" I said after sniffing her neck. "Smells like jasmine . . . maybe rose . . . and a little vanilla."

"It's Chanel No. 5. My aunt gave it to me. It's very chic. Come on." She grabbed my hand, pulled me back to the driveway, and opened the passenger side door. "Go ahead, get in."

We slid inside. I inhaled the new car scent, and Laura hung the dice around the rearview mirror.

"Fantastic," I said.

"I love it." She shoved the key into the ignition and turned the radio on. "Can you believe this is mine? I still can't." She wrapped her arms around the steering wheel, hugging it like a boyfriend, then lay her head on top of it and batted her eyes at me. "We'll go out for a ride later."

I nodded excitedly. "Can't wait."

"It's gonna be the best summer ever!" She winked. "We'd better get back. Guess who's here?"

I dreaded her answer, because I already knew: the cousins from the Black Lagoon, my fresh way of stating their appeal did not entice me.

"My cousins can't wait to see you."

I rolled my eyes as I followed her to the backyard.

"Hello, Ivy. So glad you could make it." Mrs. Capri hugged me and pointed at a long picnic table displaying bowls and platters filled with food. "Go make yourself a plate."

I grabbed a paper plate, took a hamburger from the aluminum pan, lifted the top bun, and spooned a big dollop of ketchup onto it. Next, I added a spoonful of potato salad and an ear of corn drenched in butter. Corn on the cob, another piece of food I hadn't been able to eat since I'd had braces. I carried the plate toward the folding tables beneath a tent. One of the twin cousins pulled out a chair for me. This one was taller and not quite as Grouper-looking. The other twin was already sitting down across from me.

"Thanks." I scooted the chair closer to the table and dug into my food, not wanting to talk.

I had to admit they didn't look half as bad as I'd remembered. They had lost the braces, and their acne cleared up. However, their noses were still too big for their narrow face, and their eyes were too small and close together to my liking. After Denny, it was hard to lower my standards in the looks department, even if it meant getting a better guy. Why did that balance always seem so hard to obtain?

"Great to see you, Ivy!" the one with the blue shirt said.

"Same here. I see you got your braces off."

He lifted an ear of corn. "Sure did. Now I can eat this."

I smiled and bit into my corncob.

Laura reappeared and sat next to me. "You're not going to believe what I just heard."

Always full of information. Maybe her Lois Lane qualities could be valuable to me. Maybe not.

"What made the Capri Review this week?" I joked.

"Stella Lawrence was in the hospital last night." She clapped a hand over her mouth and closed her eyes for a second, as if shocked beyond belief. "She was attacked—this time at her house—by a man!"

My stomach sank. I set my corn down, picturing the man her mother had staggered out of Cafferty's with that night in the rain.

I remember imagining that something horrible might happen, but I'd let the thought leave my mind. Now, I felt sick and saddened. Stella had been through so much. I couldn't fathom having a mother who behaved this way. I could only imagine how Stella must feel.

"Don't tell anyone, but I saw Mrs. Lawrence leaving Cafferty's with a strange man Thursday night," I confided to Laura, before thinking. That was not a smart thing to do. Her loose lips were bound to part quickly. But it was too late to take it back. "What if that's the guy who hurt her? I saw his face. I even saw his car. Maybe I could help the police if they haven't already caught him? Do you know if they have?"

She shrugged. "I don't know all the details. I just heard about the attack, and that it happened at her home. You know, she doesn't live in the best part of town. There've been a lot of break-ins lately, too. I do hope Stella is okay."

"Me, too."

If I wanted to be helpful, I needed to speak with Stella and let her know that I'd seen her mother with a strange man the other night. For the next two hours, I tried to have fun at Laura's party because I didn't want to ruin the mood. But all I could think about was Stella and Gramps's odd behavior. Something didn't sit right. The way he'd acted when Denny arrived, and how he was so down on him now. I had promised to help him in the shed after the party, and that's where I'd finally confront him about the letter as well as Denny.

CHAPTER TWENTY-SEVEN

Laura blew out the candles on her triple-layer chocolate cake with the banana cream filling. To be polite, I took the smallest piece that Mrs. Capri set on the paper plates in the center of the table. I'd lost my taste for sweets since working at Mr. Fudge's.

After we had finished eating, Laura opened her gifts. I don't think I've ever seen anyone receive so many. When she wasn't ripping pretty paper from a multitude of boxes containing decorative pins, silk scarves, or the latest records, she'd tear envelopes filled with Hallmark cards stuffed with cash or checks. I tried not to be jealous, which wasn't easy. It was not so much the gifts as the realization of how much money she must have received that made my blue eyes turn green with envy. All I could think of was how I needed to save money for a car, and Laura had both.

When she finished, she leaned over and whispered in my ear. "You wanna go for a ride?"

I perked up. "Sure!"

She dug the new set of keys from her pocket and dangled them in front of me. The twin cousins looked over and frowned. Thank God the car was a two-seater or there'd be no escaping them.

"Just taking a short ride with Ivy," she said. "I'll be back for you guys in a bit."

Mr. Capri jumped up from his seat. "Where are you girls going?" He shifted from one foot to the next as if to balance the thoughts in his mind as the two of us slid onto the leather seats.

"I'm taking Ivy for a ride, Daddy!" We both shut our doors gently.

"Don't you think it's inappropriate to leave your own party, Laura?" He ended his question with a tight-lipped smile. His tone was somewhat passive-aggressive.

"But Dad, we won't be long," she whined.

He held out his hand, goading her to give him the keys. "We need to drive the car into town, together, a few more times before you rush out on a holiday weekend."

Laura frowned and gazed up at her father like a puppy who'd just been scolded.

"You and I will go out after everyone leaves."

Laura handed him the keys, then turned to me and shrugged. "Oh well, I guess he's right. It wouldn't be right to leave my party.

* * *

After a few more boring conversations with the creepy cousins, I trudged back home on foot, disappointed not to be chauffeured in Laura's new car. The comment my father had made the night before seemed to have some merit. However, even if it were true, I had faith Laura would sweet-talk her dad into giving back those keys sooner rather than later.

Several cars were parked along the front curb of my house—my parents' guests. Smoke from the barbecue drifted through the air from the left side of the house, where the patio connected to the sliding glass doors to the family room. I could hear laughter and chattering. So, I strolled over to the group to show my face and be respectful.

"Ivy—sweetie, come here," my father commanded with a can of beer in his hand. "Everyone, this is my beautiful daughter."

I forced a smile. "Nice to meet you."

It felt as though last night had never happened. My father laughed easily with his guests, and for the moment, I was in the clear. His co-workers and their wives sat scattered around the yard. Some gathered beneath the striped umbrella at the round picnic table; others sank into nylon lawn chairs, snack trays balanced in their laps. Paper plates sagged with the aftermath of the meal—half-eaten hot dogs, torn hamburger buns, streaks of coleslaw and baked beans, and wadded napkins crushed into the corners. The men nursed half-empty beer cans, while the women sipped white wine from flimsy plastic cups, their laughter rising above the hum of conversation.

"She's stunning," a woman with a brassy gold flip wearing a red, white, and blue dress said to my mother. "She looks just like you, Delores."

My mother blushed. "Why, thank you, I only wish I still had her figure."

"Don't we all," the woman said, and the others laughed in unison.

"Are you hungry, Ivy?" my mother asked.

I put my hand on my stomach. "No, thanks. I ate at Laura's birthday party. I'm stuffed."

"Okay, hon."

"Where's Gramps?" I asked and glanced around.

"He must be napping on the porch. Didn't you see him?" she said.

I saw him in the lounge chair. "Go jiggle him. See if the old man's still breathing," my father said.

My mother crossed her arms. "Richard!"

"Sorry, just being facetious." My father turned away and shot an eye roll at his work buddies, who raised Budweiser cans to their lips.

"Ivy, would you mind bringing out the Styrofoam cups, please?"

The scent of coffee percolating alerted me that the party would be wrapping up soon. The tall silver pot sat on a rectangular wooden table up against the house. Several cakes on pedestal glass dishes and plates of chocolate chip and butter cookies with red, white, and blue jimmies surrounded it. I'd learned that once dessert arrives, it's only a matter of time before the first guest leaves and the rest follow. I hurried up the back steps to the kitchen, grabbed the cups off the counter, and set them on the table next to the desserts.

"Need anything else?" I rubbed my hands together nervously as I wanted to get to my bedroom, change my clothes, and re-read the letter once more before I confronted Gramps.

"No, that's fine." She waved her hand as if she wanted me to go on my way.

"Nice meeting you." I waved to the group.

"Same here, Ivy," they responded with a group wave.

I hurried to my room and changed into a pair of dungarees and a St. Teresa's sweatshirt. Sliding my hand to the back of my lingerie drawer, I pulled out the letter. My stomach felt as ill as it did the first time. How could this letter belong to him? Maybe there was another Frances that he knew in the war? Maybe it belonged to that Frances. The idea was highly unlikely, but I wanted to believe it.

CHAPTER TWENTY-EIGHT

Various scenarios ran through my mind of how I would approach Gramps. But nothing seemed right. So, I decided, once all the guests had departed, I'd march into his shed and blurt out my questions and present the envelope to him.

After I heard the last car door slam and goodbyes exchanged, I knew the party was over. I walked out back toward the shed. The sun had set, and the air had cooled. Bluebirds and cardinals chirped and flitted about in our sunflower-shaped birdbath. It seemed as if they were preparing to end their day before entering the summer home Gramps had built for them. The red birdhouse was more like a bird apartment building. Gramps had to cement a tall metal pole into the ground to support the heavy structure.

Sounds of cheering from the baseball game broadcasting from Gramps's transistor radio resonated into the yard from the shed. But when I entered, the shed was empty. I turned off the radio so the battery wouldn't drain. Then, I traipsed around the front of the house and found Gramps on the front porch napping on a lounge chair, as Dad had assumed. The creak from the steps as I approached must have awakened him.

"Ivy." He sat up, stretched his arms in the air, then behind his neck, and yawned. "I worked all day on that red bookshelf. Suddenly, I felt like taking a nap." He yawned again. "How was the party?"

"Good," I said, not wanting to engage in small talk.

"Glad you enjoyed it." He pulled a hanky from his front pocket and wiped the sweat off his forehead. "Would you mind bringing me a glass of lemonade, dear?"

It was strange that he was sweating even though the air had cooled. I laid the notebook on the glass wicker table in front of him, knowing he had no idea of the contents. "Sure," I said, and trudged back toward the house to the refrigerator. I filled two plastic cups with ice, poured us both lemonade, and returned to the front porch.

"Here ya go." I set the glass on the table, picked up the notebook, and sat across from him. I couldn't just jump into a serious conversation only moments after he awoke from a nap, so I sat quietly for a bit.

"Tell me more about the party. Did you get to ride in Laura's new T-bird?"

"Actually, no—Laura's dad thought it was rude to leave the party." I shrugged, not wanting to share my suspicions about the conversation I'd overheard my parents having.

"I have to agree," he said.

"We did sit in it, though. What a car," I said, voicing my envy.

"Some people get things handed to them in life. Others need to work hard for everything. But the ones that do work hard appreciate it more." He pointed at me. "You, my sweet girl, will have a great appreciation for your car when you save for one with your own money. I promise you!"

He was not making it easy to ask him about the letters. I asked myself, *Did I really need to know?* I didn't want to cause conflict, but if I didn't ask, it would torture me to insanity. So, I started the conversation nonchalantly, "Speaking of saving for a car, why did you suggest I quit my job?" I stared him square in the face, trying not to be accusing, but curious to hear his answer. After all, I was annoyed about the way he behaved last night in front of Denny, and I felt I deserved an answer.

"As I said, Ivy, I don't think it's a good idea to work with a boy you are going to break up with. It will only make things awkward between the two of you."

"I can handle it just fine. Denny and I only went on one 'real' date. I don't want to quit my job; I like it there."

Gramps pulled on his mustache and turned away from me.

"I told you, Ivy, I can tell a lot about a young man by the tone of his voice and the way he stands. He's trouble. It's best to avoid him completely."

"Like you avoided Ella?" I asked as innocently as I could, but, shocked, I actually said the words.

Gramps's eyes reconnected with mine. His face lost its color. "What do you mean by that?" He cleared his throat and shook his head as if I'd just tossed sand in his face.

I couldn't believe I said it. Despite my desire for the truth, after seeing his face transition, I feared I had made a terrible decision. However, there was no turning back.

"I found a letter in your box of coins. I accidentally dropped it, and it fell out from behind the balsawood. It doesn't make sense to me because the letter says things that only a girlfriend would write." I pulled the envelope out of the notebook and held it out to him.

Gramps's eyes narrowed. He took the envelope and ran his hand gently over it, staring down at the writing.

"You told me Ella was a young girl," I commented. "This letter leads me to believe she was a woman—a girlfriend—but you were married to Gram. Is this true? Is this also why you don't like Denny—you can tell he's up to no good—because you were up to no good when you were young, too?"

In that instant, I felt sickened by the words I'd hurled at Gramps— the one person I could always rely on, the man whose steady attention and laughter had filled my life with light. My curiosity had twisted into something darker, gripping me with a dreadful urgency.

Whatever his answer, I knew I would forgive him. Yet there was no retreat, no way to unsay what had been building inside me for weeks. The dam had finally broken. Between Denny, Stella, Mother Superior, and now Gramps, it felt as if I were juggling shards of ice—slippery, cutting, impossible to hold for long.

"Ivy, this is not an easy subject to discuss. Things were very complicated during the war." His voice changed from its 'easy-going' tone to the tone of a soldier he once must have been like. "Ella needed help, and I couldn't just abandon her. There are things you wouldn't understand." He wiped his forehead with his sleeve. "It was a long time ago. You don't *need* to understand. You *need* to let sleeping dogs lie."

"Sleeping dogs lie?" I yanked my sweatshirt sleeve, pulling it over my hand, twisting it around my forefinger. "But how can I pretend I never saw this letter?"

* * *

Gramps stood from the chair, unsteady and shaky. He took off toward the shed. I remained quiet and still for a few moments. I figured I'd give him respect and allow him to think in private before responding to everything I'd thrown at him. I released the edge of my sleeve so my hand could breathe again; I was trembling. I sipped the lemonade, sat down, and rested on the chair for about ten minutes. Once I was certain all the guests had gone, I marched toward the shed.

The door was slightly ajar. I could still hear the baseball game blasting out. Still several feet away, I called out, "Gramps, are you in there?" He didn't answer. His hearing seemed to be going lately, so I hollered. "GRAMPS, we need to talk!"

Was he ignoring me? Perhaps the radio's music muted my voice. Suddenly, I didn't like the two-roomed shed as much as I had as a kid. Crickets and spiders made their home in the dark corners. Knowing I might encounter one caused me to shiver. Before I entered, I picked up a long twig that had fallen beneath an oak tree. I used it to plow through potential spider webs. When I pushed the door completely open, bright light from the window on the far side streamed in. Gramps lay on the concrete floor surrounded by bicycles, tools, beach chairs, and a *red* bookshelf.

"GRAMPS! GRAMPS!" I cried, bent down, and grabbed his hand. I placed my other hand behind his head, lifting him. He didn't move, but I could hear him breathing. His hair had flopped to the opposite side of where he normally combed it. I could see more of his scalp than ever before. Clusters of brown age spots covered the bald area of his head instead of hair. The blue part of his eyes peeked out from below his lids. Foamy spit trickled from the side of his mouth toward his patchy white beard.

My stomach twisted into knots, and my teeth began to chatter. *This can't be happening! This can't be happening!* I gently removed my hand from his head and shot out of the shed, back toward the house. Tears streamed down my face. I tore up the steps, yanked the screen door open, and rushed inside the kitchen. I spoke as fast as I could in between tears and sobs.

Mom grabbed the black telephone receiver hanging from the wall and dialed for help. She bolted out the door toward the shed ahead of me. Within minutes, sirens filled the air. A red-and-white ambulance pulled up in front of our house. Two men wearing white rushed out. One carried a stretcher beneath his arm. Neighbors gathered on the sidewalk in front of our house. When I entered the shed, my mother was kneeling on the floor, cradling Gramps's head in her arms. I stood motionless.

"Show them where we are, Ivy!" She waved me out the door.

My feet felt heavy, like trudging through wet sand. I ran as fast as I could to the ambulance. The men followed me to the shed, and I rushed in before they did and bent down next to my mother. She gently released Gramps's head and snatched a syringe that lay on the ground a foot away from his hand. She slipped it into the pocket of her blue dress.

"He must have had a heart attack or a s-s-seizure," she said to the paramedic.

This was the first I'd heard of a seizure issue with Gramps. Maybe he didn't want me to know. Maybe that's why he was injecting medicine privately in the shed. My gut instinct was telling me there were many things I didn't know about Gramps. But it wasn't the time to ask questions. I'd asked enough questions.

Two paramedics gently slid Gramps onto the gurney and strapped him in.

"Stay here with your father," my mother commanded. "I have to go with the ambulance."

"But I want to go, too," I pleaded.

"No!"

As quickly as a yellow light turns red, she climbed into the back of the ambulance and sped away. I returned to the shed, grabbed the letter from the floor, and fell to my knees, clutching my stomach, sobbing. I'd never faced the fear of loss before. I couldn't imagine that Gramps might be gone. And it was *my* fault. All I could do was let out heart-wrenching sobs.

CHAPTER TWENTY-NINE

The following day, I didn't go to school. I sat around the house ruminating and reading about the 1934 SS Morrow Castle shipwreck that burned for days in the ocean in front of Asbury Park's Convention Center, killing over 130 people. Focusing on devastations worse than my own temporarily removed the focus from my situation. Gramps's last words popped back into my head. They repeated like a skipping record. "Ella needed help, and I couldn't just abandon her. There's much you don't know or could understand." And the pain in his eyes was as if I had betrayed him. After all, it wasn't my place to read that letter. I should never have accused him.

Maybe there were things I would never understand. Who was I to judge him without knowing all the facts? But now, I might never know for sure. If he died, I would always know it was my fault. I took out my rosary beads and recited Hail Marys. The phone rang, startling me. I listened to my mother's side of the conversation.

"Yes. Yes. I see. I'll be right there." Mom grabbed her car keys from the table near the front door. "I'm going back to the hospital."

"I want to see Gramps," I cried, tears rolling down my face.

"He's in intensive care, Ivy," she said. "Give him time to rest." She grabbed her purse from the table. "The doctor says he's in grave condition. Any stress could push him over the edge. He's not conscious. You're too emotional. It would upset you both." She pushed the purse up her arm and softened the tone in her voice. "Gramps is hooked up to all kinds of wires and medical equipment. I don't want you to see him like that."

"I'm not a child," I said, and despite my comment, crossed my arms and stomped on the floor like one. "How can it upset him if he's not conscious?"

"He goes in and out of consciousness, the doctor said." My mother took both my hands and clasped them with hers. "Please calm down, Ivy. These next forty-eight hours are critical. All you can do is pray." My mother picked up her rosary beads from the sofa table, unclasped her purse, and dropped them inside. "I'll be back later."

If I had learned anything from all the books I'd read, a good detective must curtail her emotions. Feelings do not belong on sleeves; only, I believed I caused Gramps's heart attack.

The phone rang again, and I grabbed the receiver. Laura was on the other end of the line.

"I heard about your Gramps. I'm so sorry. How is he doing?"

It didn't surprise me that word had already spread to Laura.

"He's not doing too well, but I haven't gone to the hospital. My mother thinks it's too much for me to see him hooked up to those crazy wires," I said as I sniffled and dabbed the tears from my eyes.

"Maybe she's right. I'm sure he'll be okay. We are all praying for him."

"Thank you."

I decided to change the subject. It was the only way I knew how to cope. Compartmentalize. Men at war did it. Doctors did it. Detectives did it. I would do it, too.

I inhaled deeply and said, "By the way, did you see Stella in school today?"

"Y-y-yeah." The tone of her voice dropped. "How can you be

hysterical one second and ask about . . . Stella the next?"

"I'm desperately trying to keep my mind occupied!" I wrapped my arms around my body, comforting myself as I heard this accusation. "You have no idea how difficult this is for me." Like an emotional seesaw, the conflict in my head began to take its toll.

Laura sighed into the phone. "Sorry. Yes, she was at school. She had a bruise on her cheek. Nothing major—not hospital-worthy. The police were at her house, but they must have gotten there before anything bad happened. I shouldn't have blabbed to you without having heard the entire conversation."

Laura was right about that. I feared the likelihood she'd continue making blabbing history. Hopefully, the incident would cause her to take a breath before she rushed off to share personal information again.

"Keep an eye on Stella, would ya?"

"Sure," Laura said. "I'll clue you in if anything happens. Will you be in school tomorrow?"

"Maybe—I don't know for sure."

* * *

Later that night, I heard my parents talking in their bedroom. Their voices escalated.

"He's an old junkie," Dad said. "It's a miracle he hasn't died yet, but he will soon if he keeps shoving that crap in his arm."

What crap were they talking about? The seizure medicine? If he needed it, why was Dad against it?

"It takes away his pain," my mother argued. "He never recovered from that fall from the ladder. The doctors got him hooked on that stuff —it's their fault!"

"Get your head out of the sand, Delores. He's been on it for years."

"That can't be true. He rarely goes to the doctor."

"Doctors don't prescribe junk. He's got a dope dealer!"

"I won't listen to you speak about my father like this."

The bedroom door slammed. My mother's small feet stomped down the steps, and I never heard them return.

Suddenly, my brain started connecting the dots. The bag of powder in Gramps's dresser drawer was the same one in the glove compartment of the car Denny had borrowed. The way Gramps behaved toward Denny—the envelope exchange between Denny and the man at the fudge and taffy store.

The next morning, Mom sat fully dressed at the kitchen table. Dad was gone. He never said goodbye or told me he was going back on the road. I had to get a grip on my emotions; my mother needed me. Maybe Dad was wrong. Maybe I was being paranoid. My mind reeled, trying to connect all the strings that led to this moment. I wanted to believe it was a heart attack or a seizure disorder that sent him to the hospital, but my gut told me there was more. Nevertheless, I made it worse. I had to fix things between us.

"Do you want some breakfast?" My mother asked as she pulled a new strand of gray hair from her scalp and wrapped it around her finger the same way I do. I shook my head.

"At least have some orange juice." She poured a small glass full and placed it in front of me at the table.

"Thanks." I took a few sips, traipsed back upstairs, and got dressed for school. Next, I removed the insinuating letter from my bureau drawer and buried it back beneath the wood on the bottom of the coin box, where Gramps left it—where sleeping dogs lie.

* * *

Laura appeared at my front door, her new set of wheels parked at the curb.

"Want a ride to school?" She grinned.

"So, your dad finally let you take it out?" I said with a smidge of sarcasm.

"He suggested it," she said.

I glanced down, not wanting to meet her eyes. I suddenly felt as if I were causing all kinds of problems based on hearsay. Maybe my suspicious mind had become paranoid.

"Sure." I grabbed my purse and books and followed her out the door.

I slid into the velvet-like seat, and we drove the few blocks to school. Wide-eyed pedestrian students glared at us. Laura's face beamed with pride. There were only two weeks left before school ended. I had been so excited. Now I couldn't focus on anything but Gramps. We parked on the side street outside our homeroom window, next to the enormous cherry blossom tree. Pale pink petals blanketed the lawn like fallen snow. Several classmates rushed over and congratulated Laura on the car. Probably cozying up to her for a spot in the passenger seat this summer. Not many girls in town would be driving a car, especially one like this.

I forced myself to think positively. No news was good news, and Gramps had remained in stable condition. My mother said I'd be able to visit him this evening. I quietly vowed never to mention the letter again. Gramps meant more to me than anything that had happened in the past. I couldn't change that, but I could control how to handle things going forward.

After the pledge to both the United States and the Catholic flag, we sat down at our desks. The air breezed in through the open windows. We could also see Laura's car from the parking lot while we inhaled the scent of the trees and freshly cut grass. The chattering lasted beyond the sound of the bell. Even the nuns had a lighter temperament during these last days of school.

Sister Florinda took attendance and, afterwards, read a list of student names who hadn't returned their books. Then she passed out a volunteer sheet for us to bring home to our parents to sign up to volunteer at the summer fair. Laura grabbed it proudly. Stella sank in her seat, folded the paper in half, and shoved it inside her notebook. I did the same for different reasons. When Gramps got well, I had no doubt Mom would be working in the food tent cooking up sausage and peppers like every year, and I'd collect tickets for the 50/50.

The bell rang, releasing us from homeroom for the chapel. Anxious to kneel and send up prayers for Gramps, I rushed out the door, not bothering to stop and chat with Stella. I'd been praying, incessantly, that everything would go back to normal. My thoughts bounced around like clothes in a dryer.

Stella didn't sit near me in the chapel and hurried out afterwards. As hard as I tried to keep my mind occupied and positive, every step I took seemed to take more effort than usual. After prayer, Mother Superior strolled up to me.

"Good morning, Ivy." She offered what seemed to be a smile, only letting the top of her bottom teeth show.

"Good morning, Mother Superior."

"Why don't you come over to my office so we can chat a bit?"

I wasn't sure what she wanted to chat about. Perhaps Gramps? She must have wanted to ask if my family needed anything. I had to believe that—but then again, she may have discovered the book missing and somehow knew I had it.

"Sure." I followed her. My heart began to quicken. Mother Superior was acting calm and quiet before she dropped the bomb and told me she knew I'd stolen the book. How was I going to get out of this one?

"Please, sit down. You look a bit pale," she said.

A vase of lilies sat on her desk, their cloying scent thickening the air until my stomach turned. Where had they come from? A grateful parent, maybe—someone whose child had escaped the sting of her ruler with nothing more than a warning letter. That ruler, her constant companion before Stella's incident, was nowhere in sight. On the desk lay only a stack of report cards and neat piles of folders.

Above it all, from a heavy mahogany frame, Pope Pius XII—round glasses gleaming, ruby robe blazing—seemed to glare down at me with cold authority.

She shut the office door with a quiet finality, then sat across from me. If the ruler was gone, how did she intend to punish me? Sweat slid down my forehead, and I swiped at it with my sleeve. My thoughts spiraled. Surely she hadn't called me here to deliver yet another punishment—not now, not in the middle of everything else unraveling in my life. With a calm demeanor, she moved the flowers to the side. Then, she clasped her hands and rested them on the desk. "I heard about your grandfather. I'm very sorry. How is he?"

I wasn't sure whether my mother had told her, or whether she had heard the news through the church prayer chain or from Laura. With a sigh of relief, I answered. "He's still in intensive care, but he's not getting worse. I have faith he'll be back to his old self soon." I nodded and grinned slightly, still unsure if she was going to let me have it.

She reached out and placed her hand over mine. "I know this is a difficult time for your family. Your mother must be beside herself with worry. I know your father travels. If you need to talk or share your feelings, I can lend an ear or offer words of wisdom. Stop by the convent any time."

Though she seemed genuinely concerned, the sensation of her hand reminded me of a brief encounter I'd had with a jellyfish; I managed to shake it loose before it stung me. Fearful, the conversation couldn't end that quickly. I sat motionless in my seat, perseverating on thoughts of coming clean. Maybe now would be a good time to come clean and admit I'd taken the book. Tell her the whole story. Obviously, she wasn't a madam. Seeing Mother Superior with the priest who was helping the druggy girl convinced me that there must be a logical purpose for the book. My warped imagination and desire to leave Catholic school had turned me into a lunatic. But Stella seemed to believe the scenario, too. Maybe she hated the nun so much she wanted to believe it. Carrying the load of what I'd done had begun to feel like an anchor to a dead fish.

If I confessed, Mother Superior might be understanding and not come down on me so hard, considering Gramps's situation. Then again, things could go terribly wrong, like they did when I confronted Gramps about the letter. I began to grow tired of sneaking around for answers to questions that no longer mattered in my life. However, I lacked the courage to come clean—at least for the moment.

"Thank you, Mother." I curled my lips into a partial smile. "I appreciate your concern."

* * *

Sister Evelyn passed out yearbooks. The girls zipped around collecting signatures, sharing wide grins, and giggling. I forced myself to keep a stiff upper lip and share in the excitement. After all, when Gramps got well, he'd enjoy reading the silly and heartwarming comments with me; well, maybe not all of them. Stella was nowhere. I had a suspicion she cut out early. At this point, she probably couldn't care less. Besides, I hadn't heard her name called for a yearbook. Most likely, she hadn't paid for one.

The idea of working at Mr. Fudge's had crossed my mind. But until Gramps was on the mend, I had to put that thought on hold. Maybe even forget the whole spy business and plan to be a teacher or secretary, as Dad suggested. After all, I was really in this alone. Stella was part of the problem, not the solution, and I couldn't completely trust Laura. I decided I'd say nothing to Denny. Nothing at all. All my original plans had derailed. Suddenly, life seemed much smaller.

When the last bell rang, I packed up and jumped from my seat. Sister Evelyn, the youngest nun at the school, stood by the door as we all strolled out. Her smooth skin and soft features made her look about the same age as most of us. I tried to imagine her out of her habit, wearing pedal pushers and a ponytail. It baffled me why a female would give up her entire future to serve God. Why couldn't she serve Him without being a nun? As I stepped out of the classroom, I turned back toward Sister Evelyn.

"Is Evelyn the name you chose for yourself as a nun, or was that your given name?"

She strolled over with a friendly smile. "I chose it." She wrung her hands, and her meek demeanor made her small frame appear even tinier. "My name was Mary, just like many of the nuns. I wanted to be different."

"Sure, I can understand that."

"I would have loved an exotic name like Ivy!" Her face reddened.

I grinned. "I don't think a green leafy plant that thrives anywhere and everywhere, even in the darkest of places, is very exotic."

She tilted her head. "I do."

I shrugged, while concealing a tiny smile. "What's Mother Superior's name?" I asked curiously.

"Funny you should ask. The other nuns and I were discussing this subject the other day. We get so accustomed to calling each other 'Sister' or 'Mother,' sometimes we forget we have names." She removed her hands from her habit pockets and used them like a conductor's wand, moving them with each syllable as if stringing together a melody. "Her name is Mother Sister Theresa Mariella—not sure which is her given name." She scratched the side of her cheek with her thin finger. "Pretty, isn't it?"

"Yes. Very." Even though I'd seen Mother Superior out of her habit, I couldn't picture her young as Sister Evelyn.

"I've always detected a slight accent in Mother's voice," I said. "Do you know what it is?"

"German, I believe. She mentioned it once briefly." Sister Evelyn guided me out the door and closed it behind us. "You are very astute, Ivy. No one else has ever noticed."

Though she had just complimented me, I felt as if I'd suddenly been smacked. Though Mother Superior was not a madam, something about the book and the way she abruptly changed from the hard-hearted nun to a softer and kinder version of herself intrigued me. As the strings began to weave together, I feared I might have inserted myself into a situation more complex than I could fathom. At that moment, I decided I'd pursue my path in espionage just a little longer.

CHAPTER THIRTY

After school, I opened the front door to an empty house. Gramps's transistor radio wasn't playing from the kitchen as usual. No smelly cigar smoke fogged the air, stinking up the house. His ugly green recliner sat forlorn next to the standing ashtray.

The fear I might never see him jingle change in his pockets when the ice cream man rang or find him sitting on the front porch burping his cigar into the ashtray, or hear him cursing from the shed when he hammered a thumb or spilled paint, caused me to tear up.

I couldn't bear to sit in the empty house waiting to hear word from Mom. I pictured her sitting next to Gramps, holding his hand and talking to him, whether he could hear or not. I opened the refrigerator and took out the leftover chicken and macaroni salad. Only able to stomach a few bites, I tossed the rest in the trash.

The phone rang. I grabbed it quickly, hoping it was good news from Mom.

"Gramps is doing well, Ivy. He's going to be okay."

Tears of joy filled my eyes. Having come so close to losing Gramps made me realize how lucky I was to have a second chance. Though I wanted to know the answers to those letters I found, I'd never bring them up to him again. Never. I rushed to the phone to call Laura.

She quickly picked up the phone.

"Do you want to go out for a little cruise on the circuit?" she asked.

I got giddy at the thought that Laura and I could finally join the action, driving up and down Ocean Avenue and Kingsley Street. Though I knew our parents would have a fit if they found out.

"Twice in one day," I said. "How did you manage that?"

"My parents are too busy with the boys tonight," she told me. "Can you be ready in an hour?"

"Sure! See you soon."

"Great." I placed the phone back in its cradle and wrote a note for my mother, our new way of communicating.

Dear Mom,

I couldn't just sit around, so I went for a ride with Laura.

Love,

Ivy

I placed the note on the kitchen table, bolted upstairs, yanked my hair into a fresh ponytail, and dabbled pink balm onto my lips. When Laura's car rolled up, I slid into the passenger seat, where the warm, leathery scent wrapped around me like a secret too big for the house to hold. We took off toward Ocean Avenue to join the onslaught of teenagers cruising the streets and blasting their car radios. We rolled down the windows and let our hair whip in the wind like wildflowers.

"Do you mind if I turn on the radio?" I asked.

"Nothing you can do about Gramps right now," she said. "Might as well enjoy the night."

Surprised by Laura's free-spirited attitude, I grinned. "Sure."

We sang to the song pouring from the radio and waved our arms out the windows as if we were the center float in the holiday parade. Guys driving by honked their car horns at us. Girls in less appealing cars looked away and back again, with envy.

Gramps would be okay, I told myself, and enjoyed the moment. Just when I didn't think anything else could knock me from my temporary cloud, Denny pulled up next to us in the turquoise Buick with Stella in the passenger seat.

Even though I'd made up my mind to forget about dating him, a sick feeling welled up in my stomach seeing them together.

I ducked into the seat. "Look who's next to us!"

Laura turned quickly to the right. "Oh my Gosh!" Her jaw dropped. "Where did Denny get that car?"

"Denny's full of surprises."

The light turned green, and he sped off.

"Was that Stella?" Laura asked.

"Yes!" I shrieked.

"What do you care?" She peered down her nose, avoiding eye contact with me.

"I don't care!" I uttered. "Follow them!"

Laura turned toward me with wide eyes. "You just said you don't care. Why do you want me to follow them?"

"I can't say."

I had long wondered how Laura always knew about everyone's business. But I never pressed her on it. I figured that her mother, a boardwalk store owner and the church's social chair, was the one who had access to all the community news. Not to mention, the prayer chain always had a broken link that led to gossip. This time, I just said it right out.

"How do you always know what's going on before everyone else?"

She looked down at her lap, then sheepishly glanced back up. "My dad has a police radio."

"And you've never mentioned this before because . . .?"

She shrugged. "Because he told me not to."

Yet she *was* telling me. I shook my head. At this point, I was glad she told me. It might come in handy.

Laura turned the corner and followed Denny's car, with one car in between. I wasn't worried he'd notice us tailing him. He had no idea Laura had a car. I didn't think he even knew who Laura was.

"What's going on, Ivy?" She stepped on the gas and ran through a yellow light on Main Street, continuing to tail Denny. "I thought you were over that hood."

"I am, but I did go out with him a few times. I didn't tell you because I knew what you'd say."

"I can't believe you kept this from me." She beeped her horn at the driver ahead of us.

I pulled her hand off the horn. "Stop, you'll draw attention to us."

"Sorry."

"He's turning down Cookman." I pointed to the left.

No longer "cruising the circuit," we entered the next town, Ocean Grove. "If I'm going to do this, you need to tell me what else you've been keeping from me."

"Like what?"

"Like what were you doing in Mother Superior's office the other day?" Her voice turned high-pitched. "You looked at me as if I were a stranger and ran out," she said. "And what about Stella? I see you talking to her all the time. How did the two of you suddenly become so buddy-buddy?"

"He's turning down Central. Don't lose him," I said.

The speed limit sign changed to twenty-five miles an hour. The car in front of us turned. Now, we were directly behind Denny.

"Go slower, or he's gonna see us."

"We won't lose him in Ocean Grove. It's too small, and he's obviously headed to a destination." Laura slowed down even more.

Denny pulled into a parking spot on Central, near Wesley Lake.

"Pull over," I directed Laura.

She parked on Atlantic, a one-way street facing away from Central. Laura and I turned around in our seats to spy on Denny and Stella. I wished I had Gramps's binoculars. Within a minute, a car pulled up next to Denny's car. A man around Dad's age stepped out. It was the same man who'd come into the fudge and taffy store the night Denny put money into the bag with the fudge.

Next, Denny and Stella got out of the car. The three of them walked to the bridge over Wesley Lake. I couldn't see well, but I could see they were making an exchange. The man cocked his head to the left and pointed. The conversation did not seem cordial. Denny backed away, and Stella moved behind him. My gut told me Denny was using and selling drugs. Was Stella involved, too? I began to twirl my purse strap around my finger, clutching it at the base. My hand turned numb.

Laura looked at her watch. "I've got to get back, Ivy."

"I'm sorry," I said. We both turned around in our seats and faced each other. "I didn't mean to do this to you."

She turned the ignition back on and began driving home. "You've got to tell me everything. It's like you've been leading a secret life these past couple of weeks."

"If I tell you, you have to promise not to tell *one* soul!" I shook my finger in her face. "I mean it, Laura. This is serious stuff; I need to know you are not going to blab to anyone!"

She made the sign of the cross on her chest. "I promise. Now spill!"

"It's complicated." I breathed in a deep sigh. "It all started with the book." I went on to explain the whole story.

Laura repeated the phrase, "Oh my gosh," so many times I had the urge to shake her.

"I can't believe you've done all these things while keeping me out of everything." She glared at me while we were waiting at a stop sign. "I thought I was your best friend."

"You are," I answered, "but you have to admit, you do have a hard time keeping a secret."

Laura looked down, clutched her fingers, and rolled her thumbs together. "Well, now that you won't be playing detective with Stella anymore, you can bring me along." She glanced back up and grinned widely. "Think about it! I have a car. We can get around and find out so much more."

She had a point. It wasn't easy walking everywhere. Band-aids covered the blisters that had formed on the backs of my heels and were beginning to crumble. Now that Denny had a car, I'd need one, too, if I wanted to continue following him.

"Okay," I said. "We'll talk more tomorrow."

The one thing I did keep from Laura was the letter I'd found in Gramps's coin collection. That, I would never share.

Laura grinned and glanced over at me. In the snap of an instant, she ran up a curb and hit a mailbox. "Oh my God!" she screamed and backed the car down the curb, and dashed onto Main Street.

"What are you doing? You can't just leave the scene of an accident!"

"I took the car without asking." Tears streamed down her face.

"You what?" I placed my hand over my mouth in utter shock.

"It's just—my dad keeps making excuses about why I can't drive it. Since everyone was out and wouldn't be home until late, I thought I'd just—take it out—for a while. And then you got us all wrapped up following Denny and Stella."

"So, it's my fault you hit the mailbox. And my fault you drove away?"

All this time, I had believed Laura was the perfect angel who got everything she wanted. Now, I considered what my dad had said must have been true. Was he also right about Gramps?

"You can't tell anyone about this."

Now the tables were turned. Laura wanted me to keep a secret.

"I won't."

Now, Laura drove slower than an old woman looking for her dog.

"We'll be back before my parents get home. I'll act like I know nothing when my father discovers the car."

"How can you pull that off? Your father keeps the car in the driveway." My eyes practically fell out of their sockets at her comment.

"My dad backed it in yesterday. The car was facing the street—someone could have driven over the curb and hit it."

"Like you did?"

"No, he can never know!"

"That's crazy. Not to mention, I left a note for my mother saying you were coming to pick me up."

"Please, say I met you at the boardwalk instead." Her eyes pleaded. "You have to stick with me on this. We both have secrets now, Ivy."

Laura was right, but why did she feel like she had to say it?

CHAPTER THIRTY-ONE

Though summer was near, New Jersey weather made no promises, and the boardwalk didn't guarantee a bustling crowd until after Independence Day. When I got to Mr. Fudge's, the door was wide open, and two policemen stood at the counter. My heart stopped. Did they come to see me about Gramps? Had my mother been too distraught to drive? Or were they here because of Denny? A pit formed in my stomach, yet again.

"Ivy," Mr. Fudge waved me in.

My heart quickened. But neither Mr. Fudge's voice nor body language indicated that the police were there about Gramps. A thick-necked policeman with light brown hair and a bushy mustache produced a notepad. He scribbled in it as Mr. Fudge answered questions. A colored officer with a long, thin face approached me.

"Have a seat, Miss Munroe." His front tooth was chipped at the corner. Had he broken it on the job in a struggle with a bad guy, or had it been a remnant from a fall off his bike during a childhood mishap?

"We're looking for information on Denny Carson."

Gramps and Laura had been right. Even I had been right. Only I kept refusing to accept my gut instinct.

"What would you like to know?" I asked.

With his left hand, the officer grabbed a pen from his front pocket. "What was your relationship to Denny?"

I breathed in deeply, scared that anything I said could cause trouble. "We were friends and worked together." I clasped my hands the same way Mother Superior had while she sat at her desk that morning.

"Did you ever see Denny with this man?" He laid a picture on the table.

My eyes widened. "Yes, sir."

"Where and when?"

"One time, the man came into the store and purchased fudge from Denny." I squeezed my hands together tightly to stop them from shaking. "I also saw Denny talking to him in Ocean Grove. I couldn't hear anything they said, though."

"You didn't see them make an exchange of any kind?" He stared deep into my eyes as if he didn't believe me.

"I was a block away inside a car. It looked like they exchanged a large envelope. I couldn't see for sure."

He turned the page of his notebook. "Miss Munroe, do you know a Laura Capri?"

Oh my gosh! What had Laura told the police?

"Yes. She is my friend." I let my purse drop from my shoulder onto my lap. Then I caught the strap and twisted it around my finger.

"Miss Capri told us you both saw Denny make an exchange with the man on the bridge. She also told me Denny was with a girl." He peered down his long nose, glaring at me. "Is this correct?"

"It was hard to see what they were doing," I said. "I told you we were almost a block away."

"Do you know where Denny Carson is, Miss Munroe?"

"I have no idea." I swallowed, but the lump in my throat didn't dissolve.

The officer continued to write in his notepad.

"Do you know Stella Lawrence?"

"Yes. She is a classmate," I said, keeping my voice steady.

"Was she with Denny on the bridge?"

"Yes, she was. I've seen them together several times," I said, to make matters worse.

"Miss Munroe, did you steal a book that belonged to the Mother Superior at St. Teresa's School?"

Suddenly, the floor seemed to disconnect from my feet. I felt as if I were spinning. How did he know this? Only Stella and Laura knew about the book. It had to be Laura. My face grew hot with anger.

After a long pause, I answered, "Yes. It was just a schoolgirl prank." I tried to minimize what I had done.

The officer cocked his head to the left and said, "Well, Miss Munroe, your schoolgirl prank has caused some disruption with the school, the church, and even the police." He scratched his nose and looked cuttingly into my eyes. "Where is that book?"

"It's at home."

At that moment, I realized Mother Superior must know everything as well. Laura may have ruined my life and any future I would have if I couldn't get myself out of this.

"We called your parents. They should be here any minute.

"My parents!" I exclaimed.

"You need to obtain that book and take it to the station," the long-faced police officer stated.

"My parents can't deal with any more stress. My Gramps is in the hospital," I cried. "Please let me go home, and I'll explain everything to them. I'll bring the book to you tomorrow."

"I'm sorry, Miss Munroe. It's not that simple. They are already on their way," he flipped the page in his notebook. "Do you know where Stella Lawrence is?" He held the pen steady, waiting for me to speak.

"She's probably with Denny," I shot out. "She's always with him; I'm sure she has something to do with any of the trouble he is in."

He pulled another piece of paper from inside his notebook, laid it on the table, and pointed to the names. "Do you know who Jo and Viv are?"

You are Mata Hari. You are Harriet Tubman. I said these words to myself to remind me that I had to be as strong as these women had been. Never had I thought my actions could turn into such a mess. What had I done?

I sat up straight. "I have no idea." I lied, frightened to death.

"Okay," he said, and shrugged. "If Stella should contact you at any point, please call us, immediately." He handed me his card.

I bit down on my lower lip when my mother walked in. She seemed small and fragile as she stood before the long-faced policeman.

"Officer, we are willing to cooperate," she said.

The officers turned toward one another and nodded.

Officer number one said, "We need the book your daughter removed from St. Teresa's School. We spoke to the head nun. She told us there is information in it that may be helpful with our case."

"My husband will be back late tonight," Mom said. "I'd like him to be with me at the station. Would it be possible to bring the book in the morning?" Her voice was soft like a church mouse.

"Fine."

The officer cocked his head toward me. "Miss Munroe, if Denny or Stella contacts you, call us immediately."

I released the purse strap from my finger and let the blood run through it, once again.

"Yes, sir," I said with conviction.

The thick-necked policeman who had been talking to Mr. Fudge the whole time marched over to the table. "You done here?" he asked.

"Yup." The long-faced cop followed us out the door.

Like Scottie's dream in *Vertigo*, pieces of moments flashed through my mind with no cohesive stream or clear sense. I wasn't sure why I lied to the police officer, but I needed time to make sense of everything before I risked sharing any information that might cause trouble for any or all of us.

In the background, I heard Mr. Fudge say, "I didn't know what was going on with Denny. I thought he was a good boy."

Before I followed my mother out the door, I turned to Mr. Fotopolous. "What do they think Denny did?"

"They say he sells drugs at my store!" He said, grabbed a napkin from the holder on the counter, and wiped his face. "From my store! This is bad, very bad."

Everything my father had said was true. Everything Gramps had said was a lie. Everything I knew in my gut about Denny I had ignored. And Laura betrayed me. I had no idea how all this was going to pan out.

* * *

The ride home was quick and quiet. The minute we walked through the door, my mother dropped her purse on the kitchen table. She glared at me, caressing the cross around her neck. "Where is this book, Ivy, and why in the world would you steal it?"

I swallowed hard. "It all started innocently—I just–I didn't want to spend another year at St. Teresa's. You've known I wanted to go to public school, but you refused even a conversation about it. I figured, if I took the book and removed anything bad about me that had been recorded, Mother Superior would seem like a liar when she tried to convince you otherwise."

My mother ran her fingers through the bottom of her shoulder-length hair. "This is unbelievable! You are unbelievable!" Her church-mouse voice was replaced with a shrieking maniac's. "What has

215

happened to you, Ivy? I raised you better than this." She paced the kitchen, flailing her arms. "Seems your goal to set up a nun as a liar has backfired!" She slapped her hand down on the counter. Her lips were tightly closed, white in color, and her eyes crazed.

"I'm sorry." I began to sob.

"You are incorrigible! Lying—stealing from the church—stealing from me! Forcing your best friend to follow a derelict boy and girl in her brand-new car who were dealing drugs! I don't even know you anymore. You say this was all because you wanted to leave Catholic school! My God, I believed that would have been the only place that might have saved you. Obviously, it hasn't. There will be repercussions for your behavior."

My entire body began to shake as the tears continued to roll down my face. "What do you mean?"

I wanted to tell her that Laura had taken the car out because she "wanted" to go out. Not because I'd forced her. I wanted to tell her she hit the mailbox and that I told her to lie. But I didn't say anything. She wouldn't have believed me. At that point, my mother looked at me with a disappointment I'd only seen her use on my father.

Eyes closed, she clutched her cross again as if she thought she'd get a message from God. "Get me the book!"

I scurried upstairs, bent down by my bed, pulled the book from its hiding place, and carried it downstairs. It was the albatross around my neck. The Book of Ill Repute. Only, whatever it contained had nothing to do with me or anyone I knew—except maybe Denny.

CHAPTER THIRTY-TWO

"Your father will be here soon," my mother said. "We spoke long into the night about this situation. We feel your imagination has gotten out of control—you have lost your way. It's our job, as parents, to help you find your way back." She wrung her hands and rocked back and forth.

"What are you saying?"

"You are right, Catholic school is not the place for you—not now, at least," she said. "Your grandfather agrees." She rubbed her right temple with her fingers. "He doesn't have much time left on this earth, but you do! We need to save you."

"You spoke to Gramps about me?" I perked up. "How are you planning to save me?" I asked with a shaky voice.

"We're taking you to a place that'll teach you to appreciate the good life you have." She glanced away, but not before I could see her eyes well up.

"Where?"

She opened the closet door and pulled out the gray suitcase I used on our yearly trips to visit cousins in Florida. "I've packed everything you'll need. It's for the best, Ivy." She handed it to me.

"I don't need saving!" I yelled. "Gramps knows the truth—Please talk to him! He understands me!"

"Gramps doesn't remember much of anything," she said. "In all honesty, we are grateful he had the heart attack. I know it might sound terrible, but he needed to get his life in order, too."

"This is insane!" I shouted. "I heard you talk about him. I found the dope in his drawer."

My mother's eyes widened, and she hugged herself, then turned away.

"Only I didn't know that's what it was at first. I knew Denny was his dealer. Only I didn't know that at first, either. If anything, Gramps wanted to *save me* from Denny."

My mother's face reddened. She held up a plastic bag containing a white powdery substance. The bag I had taken from the car Denny had driven us in the night of the movies. "It appears he was too late!"

"It's not mine!" I shouted. "Please! There's more to this than you know! I'm not crazy. Let me explain."

"Ivy, I don't want to know any more." She wrapped her hand around her forehead. "Not one more word. I can't trust anything you say."

My mother transformed into a hardened woman. I didn't know her. She pointed toward the staircase. "Get your bathroom essentials. Quickly—take my old cosmetic case from the vanity."

I marched upstairs and sat on the edge of my bed. What if I refused to go—locked the door and stayed put? Would my father break it down and haul me to the car, screaming? And would it even matter? As much as I wanted to, I did as Mom instructed.

Once inside the bathroom, my gaze flickered from one thing to another, unable to settle. Everything felt strangely unreal as I swept items into the bag. After I finished, I looked over and noticed Gramps's bedroom door open. At that moment, I slipped into his room. Quickly opening the cigar box, I grabbed the letter and shoved it into the case. If my suspicions were right, there was only one person who could help me. Once I showed her the letter, she'd explain everything and maybe forgive me.

"Ivy, let's go!" Mother hollered up the stairs.

* * *

Tiny raindrops began to fall onto the windshield. I felt as if each drop symbolized a countdown to my fate. Then my mother began to speak.

My father sat stoically behind the steering wheel.

"You should know that Mother Superior was working with Father McVee, a priest who has been trying to help troubled girls get off the street. He has been using his own money to prepare this place—a halfway house to shelter them—working to find them jobs—so they won't return to pros . . ti . . tution," she stuttered. "And you interfered." She let out a hard sigh.

"But the names in the book were all men. That's what confused me." I grabbed the string from an umbrella that lay next to me and wrapped it around my finger. "And the odd notations–you would have thought the same."

"The names of those men in the book are men in a nursing home across from Sunset Lake," she said. "They're old and feeble. The notes were for training the girls to assist them with basic needs, and some simple requests to make their last days more comfortable—innocent requests."

"You have to understand how it looked from my perspective," I said.

"It was never your business to begin with. The men have no family members—no loved ones to pay attention to them. The nursing home's staff is small. Father McVee believed that if the girls had a purpose–a job—a place to live, he could get them out of prostitution and off drugs, while providing a decent service that paid them."

I wanted to throw up. My mother was right. I had assumed the most obscene scenario, all because of my inherent aptitude to spy and desire to leave Catholic school. But I couldn't shake one detail. I remembered eavesdropping on a conversation between the nun and the priest. Mother Superior had said to the priest, you *help me, and I'll help you.* But how was he helping her? What my mother shared made sense, and I was ashamed. Only, I couldn't forget the letter.

"You have no idea how sorry I am," I said and released the string that was cutting off circulation to my finger. "If the names in the book are innocent men, why do the police care about the book?"

"There were other names in there, too."

Then, I remembered the name on the car registration matched the other name in the book, along with notes I didn't understand.

"You have to believe me, I'm so sorry. I'll go to confession. I'll explain everything to Mother Superior."

"We are past apologies, Ivy." My mother turned on the radio. A newsman overrode the conversation. Other than that, the car remained quiet for the rest of the two-hour drive up the Parkway. The radio spewed depressing information about unemployment. President Eisenhower's voice hummed into the car, discussing political affairs. Every fifteen minutes, George Burns and Gracie Allen promoted Betty Crocker's marble cake mix. Everything I'd done to bring me to this faraway place played on a loop in my mind, tormenting me.

Finally, we turned off an exit, and the scenery changed. Nestled behind split-board fences and large oak trees, sprawling ranch houses dotted landscaped neighborhoods. The flat yellow line splitting the road in two *disappeared,* and the road snaked up a hill around several bends. We reached a stop sign, and my father let out a nervous cough.

Eyes glued to a map, my mother waved her arm. "Turn left here."

My father followed her directive.

"Make another left."

He slowed down and turned the steering wheel again. The rain eased up, and I opened the window for air. The scent of eucalyptus and lavender emanated from the green fields. These palliative fragrances lost their power to quiet my nerves. A group of ducklings glided across a small pond, their tail feathers fluttering in the wind. All tranquil sights, sounds, and scents surrounded me. However, I felt no peace. Suddenly, the homes disappeared, and rows of tall oak trees lined the empty streets.

The sweet fragrance drifting through the window turned sour with the stench of manure. Horses, cows, and even llamas roamed the vast countryside, meandering behind the fence as we approached the property. Several brick buildings came into view. Each was labeled A, B, C, D, and E, with E being the furthest from the road. Gravel replaced the smooth asphalt entry. The car rocked over the uneven ground. We entered through an ornate iron gate that read "Meadowlark Haven." Where had my parents brought me? I wrapped my arms around my knees like a petrified child.

* * *

My father cut the engine and sat for a moment. He squeezed my mother's hand. She squeezed back and then turned toward me.

"Ivy, this place will teach you how to put others first. I'm afraid we have spoiled you as an only child." She took in a deep breath. "And, I'm sad to say, the nuns did not do a good job nurturing the benevolent spirit within you—I suppose I didn't either."

"No, that's not true, I care about people. I want to be helpful." I'm not a horrible person.

My mother turned away from me and took in another deep breath. This time, she opened the car door, got out, and came around to the back seat. She bent down and took my hands in hers. "This was not an easy decision, Ivy. But there's no turning back now. I'm confident you'll come back a better person."

My father remained quiet—so unlike him.

"I don't even know where I am. What about my job at Mr. Fudge's? What about school? There are still two weeks left. I'll fail. Why would you want me to fail?" I cradled my face with both hands.

"You'll finish school here," she said. "You're practically finished anyway—just review—perhaps one of the nuns will check in on you. I'll contact Mr. Fotopoulos. I'll explain that you needed to leave the job for personal reasons. That's all he needs to know. He'll understand." She nodded matter-of-factly.

"When will you be back?" I whimpered.

My father stepped out of the car and grabbed my bags. "We'll be back after we receive a good review from Mr. Dodge, the headmaster," he said. "This summer program has benefited many girls like you. You'll have experiences here you could never have back home," he stated and then repeated. "It's for the best." This time, almost as a question. He hugged me and kissed my cheek.

My arms stayed glued to my side. He let go of his embrace and stepped back. The sound of footsteps approached us. A man in a navy pin-striped suit strolled over and shook my father's hand. He introduced himself as Headmaster James Dodge and extended his hand to me. "This must be Ivy."

I reached out. My hand, a dead fish. He gripped it tighter and harder than anyone ever had before and turned it slightly to the right, then let go. My hand pulsed from the jolt.

He pointed to the suitcase. "I'll take that and show Ivy to her room."

"Thank you, Mr. Dodge," my mother said.

"We love you, Ivy." Mother hugged me. "It's for the best. You'll see."

My parents stood by the car and watched as I left with the strange man. I shivered as I focused on the large black eyebrow covering his entire forehead. The man smiled wryly, showing a set of gray teeth.

"Follow me, dear," he said.

My nails dug into my palm as I clenched my fist. I was that lost child in a department store again—a girl caught in a nightmare, pleading to wake up. If I could start over, I'd never take that book. I'd never date Denny or snoop on Gramps. The unknown ahead left my thoughts tangled, like a delicate knotted necklace at the bottom of a purse. But then it struck me—this was the life I had chosen. Women of espionage who came before me had endured far worse, and now, it was my turn to follow their path.

CHAPTER THIRTY-THREE

My suitcase sat in front of the door, staring at me. Empty of all the dreams I'd hoped for this summer. I rocked on the bed and wept. Gramps always said, "It's okay to dip your toe in the lake of despair—just don't leave it there." When I reopened my eyes, I glanced out the window. The last glimmer of sun sank behind the oak trees, like a wilting flower. My eyes readjusted to the change of light, and I heard a rap on the door.

"Miss Munroe," the voice demanded. "It is time for supper."

I jumped from the bed. A thin, mousy young woman, not much older than I was, stood there outside the door. Her hair, ash-brown with a widow's peak, framed her face into a heart shape. She wore cat-rimmed glasses. Her hair was held back in a bun. She wore a white blouse buttoned to the top and a plaid skirt that almost reached her ankles. She looked like a child pretending to be a schoolmarm. I didn't know how to react.

"Hello, Ivy, I'm Miss Genevieve," she said. "I will be in charge of your itinerary while you are here." Her hands remained clasped at her waist. The glasses covering her almond-colored eyes made it difficult to read her. "First, I'll take you down to the mess hall for dinner. Meals will be served three times a day in Building C." She pointed toward my suitcase. "You might want to grab a sweater; it is chilly outside."

My stomach growled, but I didn't feel like eating. With no idea when I'd get another chance, I didn't argue. The cold farm didn't strike me as a place filled with midnight snacks. Perhaps my mother packed cookies or pretzels in my suitcase. I quickly rummaged through my possessions while she stood at the door. A week's worth of underwear. Two bras, long johns, socks, another pair of dungarees, and old short-sleeved shirts. Also, two button-down sweaters. A plaid dress that I abhorred and a pair of Mary Janes neatly packed at the bottom. No snacks.

"Breakfast is at eight. Lunch at twelve. Dinner at five. If you miss dinner, you won't eat again until morning."

No need for me to respond. She was loud and clear.

"Time management skills are important at Meadowlark Haven. If you can't follow the basic rules for mealtime, how can you expect to prosper in life?" She asked rhetorically with no expression, only a blink behind her glasses.

I pulled the sweater from my suitcase. "Yes, Ma'am," I said, standing at attention to let her know I was a rule follower.

"Read this cover to cover when you return." She handed me a pamphlet with white letters on a green background that read, "Meadowlark Haven." A photo of the sprawling farm with a building behind the title.

"Yes, Ma'am," I said and followed her out the door.

* * *

Rows and rows of long rectangular metal tables and chairs lined the room. Bright incandescent lights hung from the ceiling. The windows stood high. No chance of opening them, like the ones in St. Teresa's. All the tables were roped off and labeled with the same letters as the buildings. First, the Letter A was written on white cardboard the size of a piece of paper. It stood nearest the kitchen. Letter B behind it, and Letter D, all the way in the back. The girls sitting at those tables looked washed-out and tired. Some had gashes on their faces and puffy, black, and blue eyes. Shivers ran up my arms as my gaze flicked from one to the next.

Ms. Genevieve pointed to a stack of orange trays. "You'll sit in Section A and wait for your table to be called." She pointed toward the short man dressed in a gray janitor-type uniform. "If you are late, you must wait until the last table is called." With a mocking smile, she tilted her head and said, "Don't be late."

I shuddered. My growling stomach twisted with fear. I traipsed toward the second table in Section A. Several empty seats were available. A boyish-looking girl with a burnt-orange mop for hair and round, wiry glasses pointed toward a chair.

"Welcome to lovely Meadowlark Haven; I'm Peg." She flicked her hand up without moving her elbow from the table.

"Ivy," I simply answered. The girls at the table giggled under their breath and raised their chins in acknowledgment. And they went about whisper-talking to one another.

"Where ya from?" Peg asked.

"Asbury Park." I grinned slightly, hoping she knew of the popular beach town.

She picked food from her tooth and flicked it beneath the table. "Is that New Jersey, New York, or Connecticut?"

Disappointed, I answered. "It's New Jersey—by the ocean."

"I've never been to the ocean. What's it like?"

"Nice—wish I were there now," I sank in my seat. "How 'bout you?"

"The Bronx."

I nodded. "I've been to the zoo—never a farm, though. What do the animals have to do with us?"

She smirked. "You don't know?"

I shook my head. "I haven't read the pamphlet yet."

Peg let out a sardonic chuckle under her breath. "We're the farm hands—though it doesn't exactly say that in the pamphlet."

I raised my eyebrows, and a lump settled in my chest. "But I don't have a clue how to work on a farm."

Peg patted my shoulder. "Don't worry, you'll learn."

"A," the man up front shouted.

The girls made a beeline to get their food. I followed with my orange tray. A colored woman wearing a hairnet dropped a piece of chicken on my plate. *I don't like drumsticks. White meat is all I eat.* But I didn't see an alternative in the metal bin. Next. The woman dropped a spoonful of mashed potatoes on my plate and a pile of green beans.

"Thank you." I hated green beans, as well.

At the end of the line–dessert. One sugar cookie per paper plate. I grabbed one and followed the girls back to our table. With a fork and no knife, I picked at the chicken and shoved a spoonful of mashed potatoes into my mouth. I gagged—powdered potatoes with no butter or salt. Not about to complain, I watched the girls around me eat as if it might be their last meal.

"B," the man called. He sneezed, then blew his nose in a handkerchief and stuffed it into his pocket.

The "B girls" scowled at our table as they marched toward the food.

Next, he called "D." These girls were much thinner than the rest. Making no eye contact with anyone, they trudged past us, slouching. If Mother Superior were here, she'd be tapping her ruler on the table, hollering, "Up straight, girls."

The portions on their plates were minuscule compared to everyone else's. None had a cookie. Some, not even a piece of chicken.

I whispered in Peg's ear. "That's not fair."

"What's not fair?"

"Why isn't there enough food left for Section D?" My eyes widened with concern. They looked undernourished and roughed up. "What's going on?"

"That's the Degenerate Table," she said nonchalantly. "They're here for different reasons. "It's best to keep quiet about them. You certainly don't want to be transferred."

I pulled the napkin tight around my finger. Considering I had already been transferred from St. Teresa's against my will, I did not want to repeat history. Curiosity had become my downfall thus far in life. Yet, I needed to understand why necessities like food were withheld from these girls. They looked so battered.

After we ate, a bell rang, and the girls pushed their chairs in and formed lines in front of their sections. All but D.

"Why isn't Section D standing?"

"You sure ask a lot of questions," Peg huffed. "The degenerates have to clean the tables and mop the floors," she whispered. "It's their inducement."

"What's that mean?"

"Just worry about yourself," she said. "Not everyone starts in Section A—consider yourself lucky."

Since Peg was the only person speaking to me, I thought it smart not to push.

"Where do we go now?"

"The first night, 'A-girls' go back to their room to take a shower and get a good night's sleep," she said. "So, you have time to read the pamphlet and reflect." She tilted her head to the side as if she were going to smile, but didn't.

Something about the way she said *reflect* made my stomach jump again. The word choice sounded like something a superior would say, not a classmate.

"Enjoy it." She glanced at me the way I imagined the mother of a baby bird about to nudge her offspring from the nest.

Miss Genevieve reappeared and directed me to follow her. I glanced back at Peg.

She winked.

* * *

The day had drained me emotionally, physically, and mentally. After a shower, I fell into bed with the pamphlet and read it cover to cover. The school's mission statement focused on humility, appreciation, and caring for the farm animals. Exercise, education, and routine seemed to be the other main components.

Still bothered by the sickly condition of the girls in Section D, I'd take Peg's advice and keep my thoughts under wraps. My plan—obey and go home. Despite my curiosity, it wasn't my job to investigate the girls in the other sections. After believing I had come to terms with that, I fell into a deep sleep.

* * *

The next morning, a knock on my door woke me abruptly. Miss Genevieve let herself in immediatcly after. This time, dressed in overalls and work boots. She held articles of clothing tucked under one arm and an empty bucket in the crook of her other.

"Good morning, Ivy," she said without a smile.

I stared at her blankly.

"You'll need to put these on." She held out the folded clothing. "A second pair will be waiting for you at the group cabin. Each girl is allotted two."

"What's a group cabin?" I asked.

"Did you think you were so special that you were the only girl to have her own room?" She smirked.

Without an answer to her rhetorical question, I accepted the clothes and placed them on the bed. Then I unfolded the flannel shirt and a pair of clean, but stained overalls, and held them up in front of me. They were just like the ones Miss Genevieve had on. Only, these fell to the ground much beyond my five-foot frame.

"Looks like you'll have to roll up the bottoms." She pointed at her own cuffed pants. Another grin appeared on her face. "Go put 'em on." She motioned with her chin. Miss Genevieve continued to speak through the closed bathroom door. "Introduction day is over. Today, you begin working with the others on the farm."

Introduction day? Miss Genevieve hadn't offered a proper introduction to this God-forsaken place. Other than the flimsy pamphlet and the information Peg shared, I didn't know quite what to expect at Meadowlark Haven.

"The lead girl in your group will guide you."

I opened the bathroom door and stood before Miss Genevieve, waiting for approval. She inspected me, furrowing her brow.

"Go braid your hair." She pulled a rubber band from her pocket and dangled it in front of me.

Why in the world did my parents think sending me to a farm would be a good thing? I wrapped the band around my finger several times. How bad could it be? I was an "A-girl." After I washed my face, I braided my hair and shook the blood back into my blue finger.

"Will we be having breakfast first?" I asked, fearing the answer would not be one I'd hoped for.

"No, Ivy. Breakfast is served after your morning chores. It's a good incentive." She pointed at my suitcase. "Make sure all your things are packed. You will not be returning here."

One piece of unexpected news after another. How much did my parents really know about this place? My confidence began to shrink. I had never even been to sleep-away camp. Laura had gone one summer and told me that sharing a room and bath with another girl was a nightmare. I tried to think positively and hoped I'd get to know the others better. With any luck, I'd be rooming with Peg.

I followed her out the door. She walked at a fast pace, much quicker than I would have so early in the morning.

"I'll be back after chores."

"You're not staying?" I pointed at her, insinuating the overalls suggested that.

"Oh, these?" She chuckled. "I just wear them to set the mood." She clapped her hands. "Chop, chop. Lots of work needs to be done before breakfast."

The sun had just risen, but I had no idea what time it was. I covered a yawn with my tired hand and followed Miss Genevieve across the dewy grass to the farm. The loud ringing of a bell startled me. It rang six times.

CHAPTER THIRTY-FOUR

The heavy stench of manure emanating from the barn caused my stomach to lurch. Miss Genevieve didn't seem to notice or care and handed me a shovel.

"Peg," she called. "Show Ivy the ropes."

"Yes, ma'am."

Peg was dressed just like me—and, like every other girl in that dank barn. Most had a single braid trailing down their backs, though Peg's short hair set her apart. The stench was unbearable, thick and sour. Each breath twisted my stomach tighter. I gagged again and again, whispering silent prayers not to vomit.

The shovel felt clumsy and impossibly heavy in my hands, far more than the fishing pole. I wasn't used to roughing it. It was my first true taste of hard labor, and, already, it threatened to break me.

Suddenly, helping around the house and cooking with my mother didn't seem so awful. Perhaps if I confessed this to my parents, they'd come back for me. Only, I didn't know how to reach them. I didn't see any telephones—not even a payphone. There must be one in the main building, I thought. Once I grilled Peg, despite her suggestion not to ask so many questions, I could find out more. I hoped.

Peg waved me over. "Good morning, Ivy." She seemed perky—too perky.

"Good morning," I said dryly.

She tilted her head and grinned. "Is this your first time cleaning a horse stall?"

"This is my first time on a farm." I shrugged, almost embarrassed.

People all over the world perform these chores daily. I wasn't proud of the fact that the thought of doing this work repulsed me.

"That's okay. I'll help you. First, you need to take out the water and feed bowls." She bent down, grabbed one bucket, and pointed for me to take the other. "Next, you'll have to sift through manure with the pitchfork and put it into the wheelbarrow. Make sure you shake it so not to take out too much wood shaving. And don't forget the wet spots—and put fresh shavings in the stall."

Just when I thought she was finished explaining, she continued with more directions.

"Then, put piles from the top of the bedding into the muck bucket." Peg pointed at the pail I was carrying. "When it's full, dump it in that wheelbarrow. Oh, and you need to replace the wood shavings in the stall for bedding, but don't forget to sweep up the old hay first. If there's any hay left, rake it into the corner."

"Did you work at the Bronx Zoo?

She laughed. "Nope."

I pulled my shirt up over my nose and took a deep breath.

"Don't worry. You'll get used to it." She disappeared, leaving me alone in the stall.

My eyes darted in every direction. The girls from Building A zipped around. They shoveled, dumped, and swept at the speed of light. I suddenly remembered that if I didn't pick up my pace, I would miss breakfast.

* * *

A loud bell rang in the distance. Girls began to vacate, and I was left alone in the barn except for a large black girl in a stall behind me. She was singing "Amazing Grace." How anyone could sing while picking up horse crap was beyond my comprehension. Hunger and hard labor forced me to my knees. I upchucked into the pile of fresh hay I had just shoveled into the stall. Tears fell onto my crusty face as I picked up another batch of hay and covered my indiscretion.

After finally completing my morning chores, I heard another bell ring. All the girls trampled back into the barn. I gazed around, and Miss Genevieve appeared before me.

"I see you didn't make it to breakfast." She tilted her head. "The first day always takes a bit of getting used to." She glanced around, taking stock of my workspace, then began to walk away.

I followed like a scared puppy.

"You can take a bathroom break now." She pointed to an area away from the barn. "If you pick up the pace, you might make lunch."

I wanted to scream. I wanted to slap that widow's peak right off her forehead. No, I imagined pushing her face down into the pile of manure. But I knew if my actions matched my thoughts, my stay at Meadowlark Haven might get worse. At the same time, I was slightly ashamed of my thoughts. The pamphlet I'd read suggested I would learn to be humble. Maybe this was a test.

Miss Genevieve led me to the bathroom. A room filled with several stalls, each containing wooden boxes about two feet high with holes—holes to hover over. Each box was above the same creek where others before me had left their business. After I finished, I turned on the faucet in the rusty sink to wash my hands. A metal mirror hung above it, offering a blurred vision of my face. Only one day in, and I barely recognized myself. I was ten years old the last time I'd seen my face so filthy. I'd been helping Gramps dig ditches in the yard to build a fence. Suddenly, I missed him so.

"Let's go, Ivy," Miss Genevieve snapped. "You need to speed up and get to the next chore if you want to make lunch."

I quickly dried my hands, then followed her toward the chicken coups, pig pens, and goats. Peg reappeared. She handed me another bucket, this one filled with feed. The thought of the animals eating lunch before me added to my annoyance.

Peg handed me yet another bucket and pointed to a hose. "After you fill the pens, fill the tubs." Though we all wore overalls, Peg seemed the most natural in them.

I went up and down the rows of animals, dropping food and water. After a couple more hours of doing this, another bell rang. The girls began to disappear. Once again, I was left with the black girl who obviously worked as slowly as I did. She was singing a hymn. Her voice was raw and emotional, but melodic and hopeful.

"You have a lovely voice," I said. Though it was true, I offered the compliment in the hopes she'd talk to me. I desperately yearned for camaraderie.

She did a quick curtsy. "Thank you.

"What's your name?"

"Billie—my mama named me after Lady Day—you know, the jazz singer."

"If you don't mind me asking, how can you sing?"

She peered around as to make sure no one was listening. With a deep tone, she whispered almost under her breath. "It's better than crying—plus it makes me happy."

I detected a southern accent and wondered how she ended up in New York. She gazed up toward the ceiling and closed her eyes for a second.

"Nobody seems to mind, anyway," she said. "And it's nobody's business what I do." Billie folded her arms across her chest. "That's what Lady Day says." She stood up straight, raised her chin in the air, and grinned, displaying the whitest teeth I'd ever seen.

I smiled for the first time since my parents abandoned me at the farm.

She put down her bucket and swatted the back of her hand at me. "Better get movin' if you wanna eat."

I dropped the last bit of feed into the chicken coup, wiped my hands on my overalls, and followed her out.

* * *

After we washed up for lunch, I sat at the table with the same girls from dinner the evening before. This time, the seat next to Peg was taken by a tall girl with thin lips and no expression. Billie sat next to her, and I plopped down next to Billie. Since I'd missed breakfast, I tossed back lunch like the pigs I'd just fed in the pens. No one spoke to me. Not even Billie. No one spoke at all. All I could do was ruminate on how to convince my parents to return and take me home.

After we finished, Miss Genevieve appeared at our table. She goaded me with her finger just as everyone stood to get in line to leave. I let the others pass me and tentatively teetered up to her.

"Afternoons at Meadowlark Haven s are dedicated to education." She handed me a notebook and a pencil and marched toward the door. A forceful wind smacked me hard when the door opened, nearly knocking the notebook from my hand. I pulled it tightly against my body, fearing that if it flew away, something bad might happen. Concerned about my schoolwork from St. Teresa's, I got up the nerve to question Miss Genevieve.

I cleared my throat before speaking. "My mother said a nun from St. Teresa's might visit. Has one been here?"

Miss Genevieve walked briskly. Tired and still hungry, I breathed heavy, trying to keep up. The cuffs at the bottoms of the overalls kept unfolding, causing me to trip several times. I wanted to remove the disguising, filthy clothes, and sit in a hot bath, but the possibility did not exist.

"No one has been here," she said. "You'll follow the same curricula as the other girls. If you've already done the work, consider it a review. If you haven't, consider it a challenge. Either way, it's a positive endeavor." She turned toward me, tilted her head, and glared at me as if to tempt me to question her more. The small, austere woman caused me to shiver in a way even Mother Superior never had.

"After class, you'll follow the girls to Group," she stated.

I couldn't fathom going to class dirty and smelly. But I couldn't imagine cleaning animal stalls before the day began, either. And the way she said *Group* made my stomach lurch. Though I didn't question her.

"After class, you'll go to the showers, change, and go to the mess hall for dinner." She picked at her teeth with a piece of hay. "Peg will be your guide. Your suitcase is next to the bed you've been assigned. Once you've removed only the *necessary* items, I will be back for the suitcase." She paused. "We have limited space, so choose your items wisely."

As we trekked toward the classroom, the girls from Group D passed us going in the opposite direction. All were pushing the wheelbarrows that the girls from Group A had filled earlier with manure. Each girl hunched over with sour frowns and eyes of exhaustion while following Mr. Dodge, who was dressed in dungarees, with a light tan bomber jacket and a cowboy hat. He looked more like a sheriff than a headmaster. The girls resembled convicts—the kind I'd seen chained together, on the side of the highway, gathering trash.

I tried not to stare, but I did a double-take when I recognized a face. My heart stopped. With a dull gaze, Stella followed the group, last in line. Her hair, a wiry mess, shot out from the braid running down her back. Her body, now frail, showed no signs of the former appeal I'd seen only a week before. I wanted to yell her name, but I knew it wouldn't be wise. Did she see me, too? I had to talk to her, but I'd wait until dinner and try to slip her a note.

CHAPTER THIRTY-FIVE

Building E sat north of Building D, a small cottage akin to a 19th-century one-room schoolhouse. The scuffed and faded wooden floor creaked as each girl entered. Two small windows covered with overgrown ivy and cobwebs offered no charm to the space. Only large enough for one section of girls at a time. Despite being a temporary resident at Meadowlark Haven, I wished Stella were sitting next to me, as she always had in class.

Three rows of five beat-up wooden desks and chairs sat in the middle of the room, leaving a wide gap on the perimeter. An odd setup, I thought. A man in his mid-twenties stood before a podium and a blackboard—the teacher. Tall and lanky, a pale blond crew cut covered his head, and acne scars plastered his hairless cheeks like slabs of pizza. His beady gray eyes bore into each girl as they strolled in.

"Get seated, girls." He pointed toward me. "Looks like we have a new addition to the class. "What's your name?" he asked with bland enthusiasm.

"Ivy."

"You can call me 'Mr. Ross.'" His eyes scanned over me as if I were a slice of lemon chiffon pie.

He didn't introduce me to the class. Instead, he walked up to the lectern, pulled out what looked like a small skull from the shelf inside, and placed it on top. Next, he strutted up to the blackboard and sketched a picture of a monkey. "This, young ladies, is where it all started."

He called on Peg, who sat in the first row toward the podium. "Pass this around."

Peg strolled up to the front and picked up the skull.

"Careful now," he said. "It's very delicate."

She laid it down gently on her desk and rubbed one hand across it. She swirled her long pointer finger in each orifice as if she thought she might find a prize. An odd, perverted smile seemed to appear on Mr. Ross's face.

Peg picked the skull back up, held it next to her head, and made googly eyes. Then she let her tongue fall to the side of her mouth like an overheated dog. Everyone chuckled. She handed it to the girl behind her.

One by one, we examined the skull. Some with raised eyebrows. Others rolled their eyes and shook their head. During our observation, Mr. Ross circled the students, caressing his chin as he moved along the perimeter of the desks. His ominous and menacing glare hovered over us. When the skull returned to Peg, she carried it back to him.

Mr. Ross pulled out another skull from inside the lectern. "You," he pointed to Billie.

With her shoulders slumped, she slowly stood up without making eye contact with Mr. Ross and walked to the front of the classroom. She carried the skull back to her desk and tentatively touched it the same way Peg had.

"What can you tell me about the differences between these skulls?" Mr. Ross asked.

Billy shrugged.

Peg raised her hand.

"Yes, Peg."

"One's bigger—just a little."

"Do you think it's a bigger monkey?"

"Maybe–I don't know."

Mr. Ross turned back to the board and drew a stick figure of what appeared to be a child. Next to that, he drew an even bigger one. And next to that, he drafted another, adding the letter "U" twice, and drew small circles beneath it, simulating breasts.

I swallowed hard. His drawing made me uncomfortable. The teacher and his class unsettled me in a way I'd never felt in Catholic school—not even during science lessons. Then Mr. Ross, with his disturbing grin, licked his lips after finishing the addition to his stick figure. A chill ran through me.

"The difference," he said, "One is a monkey skull, and the other is a human. Do you know which sex it is?"

How could we possibly know that answer from examining a skull? Despite my thoughts, I had no plan of verbalizing them. And where in the world had he gotten it from? Chills ran down my arms.

"This is a female skull." Then he pulled out an even larger one. It seemed as though the inside of the lectern was a bottomless graveyard pit.

"This is a male. Do you know why his skull is larger?"

No one answered. Each girl's face appeared expressionless, which spoke volumes.

"Cat got your tongue?" He held his arms out, palms up. "The male species is bigger because it's stronger and smarter. If you look closely, you will see the cavity for the brain is larger."

Peg waved her hand again. "Are you saying that even a smaller man has a larger brain than a woman?"

"Yes, Peg. Even the male monkey has a larger brain than the female. Because that's where it all started. The evolution process." He held out the "s" sounding like a piece of meat dropping into a frying pan.

Whether true or not, Mr. Ross's bizarre lecture was disturbing. If my parents knew the school was teaching evolution, they'd surely come pick me up. Though I'd known of such teachings, it had never been a topic that my family or St. Teresa's discussed.

Mr. Ross went on to talk about human and animal reproduction and taped to the board pictures of animals mating. The eerie grin plastered on his face led me to believe he was fascinated by our facial reactions as he spoke. The more explanation he offered, the more uncomfortable the class appeared. Though none of the girls engaged with him. He went on talking about queer topics for the entire class. My stomach burned with hunger as much as it did with disgust. When the bell finally rang, I rushed toward the door. Mr. Ross grabbed my arm.

"Ivy, how did you enjoy your first day of class?" His beady eyes glimmered at me, amused.

"Fine, sir," I said.

He released my arm. "Good to know."

I clutched the notebook to my chest to hide my body from his long, inappropriate gaze.

"See you tomorrow." He smiled with his mouth, but not his eyes.

After stepping out the door, I rushed up to Billie. "Is he always this creepy?"

"I don't pay him no mind," she said. "I've had cousins more bothersome."

Her comment seemed odd. Even more so since she didn't answer my question.

"Best to keep your head down and let him do his thing," she said in a sing-song southern drawl.

I quivered at her comment and changed the subject. "Where are we going next?" I asked.

"It's shower time, praise the Lord." She placed her hand on her voluptuous chest.

"Thank God," I whispered.

I burned with the urge to scrub away the disgust clinging to me—deeper than skin, in ways I couldn't yet name or understand.

CHAPTER THIRTY-SIX

uilding A contained two adjoining rooms. We shuffled inside. I paid attention to the chatter, hoping I'd learn something about the girls and how they ended up at Meadowlark Haven. Two sets of bunk beds and two dressers, each with four drawers, filled the room. As promised, Miss Genevieve left my suitcase, along with my cosmetic bag, next to the beds near the window.

"Your bunk is on the top," Peg said. She pointed to a dresser. "The bottom drawer is empty."

I grabbed my suitcase, sat on the floor, and opened it. Piece by piece, I transferred my belongings into the drawer.

"You can keep your cosmetic bag underneath the bed," Peg pointed out. "The only thing you'll need from there is your personal effects."

It was apparent I would not need all the clothing I'd brought. So, I transferred my most important belongings to the dresser drawer and left the rest in the suitcase for Miss Genevieve to take. However, I didn't know where she'd be taking it, so I removed Gramps's letter. Fearful it would be displaced, I slid open the zipper at the bottom of the cosmetic bag and hid the letter inside the lining.

The chatter continued while the girls began disrobing in front of one another. Not accustomed to this, I turned my back. I dropped my clothing to the floor and quickly draped the clean bathrobe over my filthy body.

"Where are the showers?" I asked Peg.

She grinned as she stood naked in front of me. It was hard not to observe her small breasts and the orange bush between her legs. Though all my life, I'd gone to a school with only girls, I'd never seen any nude before. Once, I'd found a *Playboy* magazine hidden in the garage. I flipped through the pages, examining beautiful women with flawless bodies. The girls at Meadowlark Haven did not resemble those in the magazine, nor did I. And I felt oddly embarrassed. However, no one else showed unease.

Peg led me to a communal bath area, where the girls stood under pouring spouts, soaping up their grimy bodies. "This is it."

I gasped, knowing I'd be washing my private parts in the open space with others.

"You'll get used to it," she said, and strode over to an unoccupied shower head.

Brown-tinted water idled beneath each girl as it cleansed away the day's work. Billie stood under the streaming water; her woolly hair covered with a white plastic cap. Her curvaceous body captivated me with its large, tawny nipples blending into her dark chocolate skin—another sight I'd never witnessed. No one seemed to be staring but me. I quickly readjusted my gaze, disrobed, then scrubbed away the shame that enveloped me from the inside out.

Afterward, we brushed and braided our hair and dressed in our own clothes. The ones our parents packed—modest outfits—plain gray or tan wool and cotton skirts with buttoned-down shirts to match. Most girls wore penny loafers; some wore white tennis shoes.

"I'm starving," Billie hollered into the air.

Another girl yelled back. "Seems you have enough fat to keep you going for another meal and then some."

Several girls laughed, but Billie shot back, "You've got to have something to eat, and a little love in your life to find joy . . ." She grinned. "Guess you girls ain't got neither if you need to feed your soul by jabbing at mine."

The girl rolled her eyes but said nothing more. No doubt everyone in the bunch was hungry and didn't want to waste energy bickering. Once the bell rang, Peg led the pack to the mess hall like a scout leader. From what chatter I overheard and the behavior I witnessed, Peg had risen in the ranks at Meadowlark Haven. In which building had she begun her stay? I imagined the higher you rose, the closer you were to going home. Not sure if this was a spoken rule or one achieved by observance. However, I intended to follow the rules while creating a clandestine plan to reach Stella and contact my parents.

* * *

Dinner wasn't much different from the one we had the night before. This time, meatloaf instead of chicken. Unlike Mom's, the inside was dry. The lack of gravy made it worse. A cup of chocolate pudding served as dessert. Those grabbing their lot *ooohed* and *aaaahed* as they placed it on the tray. I sat down between Billie and Peg, hoping to learn more about what to expect next from at least one of them. Since the night before, Miss Genevieve had sent me to my room after dinner, I had no idea what the evening's routine would entail. Most likely, the one-day transition was to allow me the opportunity to contemplate, cry, assess, build fear, and accept that, until further notice, Meadowlark Haven would be my residence.

I tapped Peg on the shoulder. "So, what's next on the itinerary?"

"Group."

"What's group?"

"It's where you share the reason you're here and how you can become a *better you*," she said and shoveled the rest of her pudding into her mouth.

* * *

We gathered in a large shed outside the barn, behind the chicken coup. The girls referred to the spot as The Outhouse. The leader, a young nun named Sister Connie, did not wear a habit. She sat in the center of the room, which was squared off with old, brown sofas. All the girls from Group A grabbed a seat. I stuck close to Peg and sank into the worn-out cushion next to her. My nose twitched from the musty smell of the damp, cold room. Only one electric heater warmed it slightly.

"Good evening, girls," Sister Connie said. "We will pick up where we left off last week. Before we begin, please stand up and introduce yourself to any newcomers."

After introductions, the meeting got underway. Several girls shared the wrongdoing they believed sent them to Meadowlark Haven. After each one had outed their transgression(s), Sister Connie asked if they thought they deserved to be here.

"No, my mother is crazy," one girl whined. "She's the one who should be sent away. All she does is bark orders all day and expect my sisters and me to do her job."

Sister Connie rubbed her chin, giving thought before responding. "Perhaps your mother is overwhelmed and needs help?" she suggested. "Can you think of ways you could help her lighten her load before she asks?"

The girl shrugged and rolled her eyes.

"For our next session, I expect you to bring a list of three solutions."

One by one, the girls shared their issues. Most seemed to have misbehaved with boys, skipped school, or gotten caught drinking alcohol.

"Your turn, Ivy." She clasped her hands in her lap and tilted her head.

I struggled to sit upright on the springless couch. "I stole a book that belonged to the head nun in my school, and I spread a rumor about her," I spoke quietly, but loudly enough for all to hear.

Gasps filled the room.

"What compelled you to do this?" Sister Connie asked.

When I answered her question, I sounded exactly like the spoiled brat my parents had accused me of becoming.

"Do you think you deserve to be here?"

All along, I had not believed I deserved to be there, but after listening to myself and observing the others' faces, my thoughts were in question.

"I guess—I think. What I did was wrong, but I didn't intend to cause harm to anyone. But the punishment is not worthy of the crime," I stated.

"Until you can come to terms with the fact that your parents know better than you, and have decided it *was* in your best interest, you have some work to do."

After we completed confessions and psychological exercises, we concluded the session with a song. Billie's beautiful voice kept the bunch of us on key. After we finished, Peg led us back to our dorm. Sister Connie's pretty eyes and kind demeanor reminded me of Sister Florinda. However, despite the nonthreatening group meeting, the other teachers and staff at Meadowlark Haven seemed off. On the way back to our dorm, a light flickered from another small building like The Outhouse in the distance. A man's voice was shouting, and then female voices shouted back. Then, in unison, all the female voices seemed to be chanting something.

I froze in my tracks, trying to hear what they were saying. Peg grabbed my arm, pulling me toward our dorm.

"What is that?" I asked.

She pulled harder. "Come on. Just be glad you started here."

"What do you mean?" I stopped and stared into her eyes, waiting for an answer.

Peg's comment confirmed my suspicion of a hierarchy at Meadowlark Haven. From the discomfort on her face, I gathered she had worked her way through and up. I, on the other hand, was fortunate to be placed in Group A from the start. But Stella was not. What had she done that was worse than my wrongdoing?

CHAPTER THIRTY-SEVEN

Each day bled into the next. I learned to work smarter and faster. Stella and the other girls from Group D trudged past our table during meals to collect the meager scraps left behind. The girls looked more and more ragged. Stella seemed sluggish, almost mechanical.

I tried to catch her gaze, but she never looked my way, appearing lost, drifting in a trance as she followed the line. Desperate to reach her, I tore a napkin from the stack and scrawled a message with the pencil I kept hidden in my notebook. I knew she'd be cleaning our table after breakfast with the others from Group D. To protect us both, I wrote in code—using names only she would understand.

Jo,

Meet me behind Building B at 8:00.

Viv

I shoved the napkin beneath my plate, hoping, again, to make eye contact on her way back from the food line. Heart racing with intense focus, I willed Stella to look at me. She did. With a quick motion, I tapped the side of my plate, hoping she'd understand my intent. She blinked.

Afterwards, I followed the group to class.

"What is on the agenda today?" I asked Peg, sounding like a broken record.

"Physical education class." Peg walked at a fast pace. I wasn't sure whether she wanted to get away from me or feared being late.

"What kind of activities do we do there?" Dressed in work boots and overalls, I couldn't imagine what they would be.

She shrugged. "It's different every time," she said. "Last week, we had to catch a pig."

I scratched my cheek. "How is catching a pig physical education?"

"You have to race."

"Against the pig?"

"No—each other. Whoever catches the pig in the least amount of time wins."

I couldn't have been further away from home if I'd taken a rocketship to the moon. Gym was not my favorite class. Beads of sweat began to form on my forehead.

Mr. Ross led us out to a field on the other side of the farm. "Today's lesson will be on obedience and empathy."

The furrowed eyebrows and twisted mouths of my classmates demonstrated they were as curious as I was.

"You will be given a task. If you do not complete the task, your partner will be reprimanded."

My heart rate increased to the speed of a running pig before I even moved a finger. Not knowing who would be assigned as my partner frightened me. Peg and Billie were the only girls I'd spoken to. I did not want to ruin a relationship that had barely begun if I failed the exercise.

"You will begin with isometrics." Mr. Ross pointed at the brown dirt with patchy grass. He didn't offer us a mat.

"When I blow the whistle, you'll begin doing pushups. The goal is to complete twenty. You will have one minute, and your partner will count. At sixty seconds, I'll blow again, and you will stop."

I'd never done push-ups before and feared what would happen if

I did not reach twenty. Surely, he couldn't expect us all to meet the outrageous goal. However, if we didn't, what kind of reprimand would our partner receive?

Mr. Ross paired up the girls. Billie and Peg were together, and I was with a girl named Ann who looked like a female linebacker. This could go two ways. Ann would do great, and I'd fail miserably. She'd receive a scolding on my behalf, or I'd do great, and she wouldn't, and I'd reap the wrath of Ann. Either way, I was not confident that the exercise would turn out well for either of us.

"You first," Ann said.

"On the ground," Mr. Ross commanded and blew the whistle.

By the time I reached five push-ups, I collapsed in the dirt.

"Get up!" Ann shouted. "You can do it."

Groaning, I forced myself to do another five push-ups, then dropped again.

Ann stomped her foot. "Come on!"

After a deep breath and one last attempt, Mr. Ross blew his whistle before I completed the exercise. Red-faced with anger, Ann scowled at me in a way that made the hair on my neck stand. Before I was completely upright, she clocked me on the side of the face. I fell back to the ground.

An odd grin of satisfaction formed across Mr. Ross's face before he blew the whistle again.

"On the ground," he hollered to Ann.

Miss Genevieve appeared from the seat she'd been keeping warm while observing. "Let's go." She guided Ann away.

Neither Mr. Ross nor Miss Genevieve asked whether I was okay. Holding my cheek in my hand, I stood in shock. Instead, he directed the class to sit on the ground and face him.

"Because of Ann's lack of discipline," he said as he wagged his finger at me, "she neglected to experience empathy." Mr. Ross held his arms out, as if he wanted to hug us. "Both are essential for becoming a 'better you.'"

The phrase, "a better you," would become a mantra I'd hear repeatedly as the weeks went by.

"Billie—walk Ivy to the nurse's building," he instructed.

Too shaken to speak, I staggered to my feet and followed her. The girls watched us as we trudged toward the medical building. On our way there, Billie walked behind a bush and vomited.

I put my arm on her shoulder. "Are you okay?"

"Guess all that running around in the heat got to me," she said.

Together, we trudged along the path toward the nursing building.

The nurse placed a bag of peas in my hand and said, "Hold these for fifteen minutes." She pointed at a chair, motioning me to sit.

Billie held up her hand to signal she was leaving, but didn't say a word about her ailment. At dinner that evening, Ann did not sit with us. Waiting in line for food with Group B, I assumed she'd been demoted, and "that" was our lesson for the day.

My cheek ached as I tried to chew the rubbery leftover chicken. This time, served over rice. We gathered after dinner and played games intended to build strength and character, as per Sister Connie. I followed the others and kept my mouth shut. Billie crooned a hymn while Sister Connie accompanied her with a guitar. Like zombies, we sang along while Billie seemed to be in a world of bliss.

Finally, the gathering ended, and I was free to meet with Stella. I prayed she'd show.

✳✳✳

After walking back to the dorms with the others, I ducked outside without anyone noticing. Without supervision, the girls were blowing off steam. A full moon lit the sky, and the dew on the grass glimmered in the light. The scent of pine and lilies almost tricked me into believing all was well. My heart jumped at the sounds of Stella's footsteps creaking along the brush.

The moonlight shone on her creamy white face, accentuating the dark circles beneath her eyes. She looked like a patient who'd escaped a lunatic asylum. The once pink pout I'd envied so much had vanished into a frown displaying a despair much worse than mine.

"Stella, oh my God!" I hugged her. My action was out of character; however, the act came naturally. "How did you end up here?"

She kicked a pinecone. "Don't play stupid, Ivy."

When I told the police about seeing Stella and Denny, I had no way of knowing she'd end up here, too.

"I'm sorry, I never meant this to happen. Things got so out of control."

She rubbed her hands together to keep warm. "This place is a Hell-hole."

"It is, and I know it's worse for you!" I reached for her hand.

She backed away. "You don't know anything." A fire sparked from her eyes that frightened me.

"The police came to my house. I was watching Molly. They carted us both off to the police station because no one was home. Now who's gonna take care of her?" Stella stammered.

Tears began to well up in my eyes. I didn't say anything—just listened.

"Someone told them I was helping Denny," she said, squinting her eyes at me. He loves me, and I'd do anything to help him. We were gonna skip out of town in just a few days. Now, how's he gonna find me?"

"Stella, he's a bad guy. He doesn't love anyone. He would have ruined your life."

"And this life is better?" She folded her arms, her eyes spitting daggers at me. "Even here, you got it better than me. Perfect little Ivy Jean Munroe. It must be so awful for you having to take care of the animals and sitting in class with the other 'A' girls."

"You're right, it is better for me, but it's still awful—never been punched before." I pointed to the bruise on my face.

"Get used to it," She grinned sheepishly, exposing a chipped front tooth. "At least they'd send you to a dentist."

My heart sank as I looked at her once beautiful smile.

I blurted, "You can work your way out of 'D.' You just have to follow the rules. There are girls in 'A' who started there—I just don't know how long it takes."

Her eyes narrowed. "Not for girls like me."

"What do you mean?"

"Not for girls who don't have parents—or any that actually give a shit." She shook her head, and her hair fell, covering her face.

"They can't keep you here forever," I said.

"Oh yeah? My mother handed me over to the cops. They brought me here. No one is checking in on me—like you—Ivy." Her tone made me uncomfortable.

Had I not met Stella's mother, I might not have believed her. It made me think how many girls from homes like hers were in the same situation. Though angry and hurt that my parents had sent me to Meadowlark Haven, I believed they had no idea how terrible it really was. They would come back for me. However, *when* was the question? Offering hope to Stella was all I could do. Then suddenly, a crazy thought entered my mind.

"What if Mother Superior can help us?"

Stella gazed up at me as if I had just picked a bug off the ground and eaten it.

"I know it sounds crazy, but we were off base about her." I tugged at the bottom of my sweater, stretching it over my finger. "Yes, she was tough on you. I know she's the last person you'd think could help, but we were wrong about her—about everything. She was actually helping those girls on the streets—trying to get them off drugs—the drugs Denny was pushing on them."

Stella perked up. "Then it's her fault I'm here."

"What do you mean?" My eyelid began to twitch.

Stella started pounding the toe of her shoe in the dirt. "So, what if I was helping Denny?"

Though I'd seen Stella and Denny together, it never occurred to me she'd been helping him.

It felt as if I had been clocked in the face a second time. "What?"

"It's true," she said. "But I didn't know he was pushing drugs onto those girls."

"But you said one of them jumped you."

"I lied." She shrugged.

I dug my fingernails into my palms. "You were helping him push drugs?" I asked again, still shocked.

"Not exactly." She began kicking the dirt her shoe had made loose.

"But how—why?"

"You wouldn't understand."

Stella was right. I didn't. I had been jealous of her and Denny, but I never would have thought she was helping him. As shocked as I was, I felt sorry for her. The realization flashed through my mind that it easily could have been me whom Denny conned. My parents had tried to protect me. No one stepped up for Stella.

Then I thought Mother Superior must have known about Stella, Denny, and her mother's behavior. Maybe she was trying to help Stella, too. Maybe she'd help again.

I grazed her arm. "I don't believe she wanted you here. She couldn't know how bad this place is. If she had, she wouldn't have told my parents about it."

"No one cares about me, Ivy. I'm getting out of this place on my terms. If you know what's good for you, you'll keep your mouth shut this time."

"What are you gonna do?"

"Why the hell would I tell you?"

The night bell rang. "Please, Stella, don't do anything stupid."

"Leave me the hell alone."

Lost for words, I turned away and headed back to my dorm.

CHAPTER THIRTY-EIGHT

Several weeks passed, and Stella ignored me. I'd learned through the grapevine that girls came and went at Meadowlark Haven without much fanfare. Some had stayed for as long as a year. Some never went home at all. They became staff members who had started in Group D and worked their way up, but had nowhere else to go—girls like Stella. Mr. Dodge, the Headmaster, provided them with food, shelter, and a small stipend. Sister Connie seemed to be the only "trained" professional on staff aside from Mr. Ross, who had the run of the place with no supervision, and seemed to run his class by warped instinct rather than ability. Whenever I asked questions about him, I was met with downward stares and a quick change of subject.

Missing out on summer at home was painful. The thought of Laura cruising the circuit with someone else in *my* seat brought me to tears more days than I care to admit. I wrote to my parents, but their replies were always brief—never a phone call, despite my pleas. Sometimes I wondered whether they had even received my letters. And telling them the truth about the horrors of Meadowlark Haven felt far too dangerous.

Peg and I palled around, but sometimes she looked at me longer than I thought she should, which made me uncomfortable. The light in Billie's eyes started to fade. Her songs weren't as uplifting as they used to be. One evening, on my way to group, I spotted Sister Connie speaking with another woman. She was tall with silver hair, and my heart stopped. I hadn't recognized her at first. When I looked closer, I realized it was Mother Superior without her habit. My heart sped up. It all began to make sense. My instincts were right. She had to have been the one who told my parents about Meadowlark Haven. *Should I approach her? Should I beg for forgiveness? Should I yell for help like someone who had been capsized on a desert island and take the risk?* This might be my only chance to connect with the nun. So, I quickly did an about-face.

Without much time to spare and the risk of being discovered, I rushed back to my dorm. Not allowed in the room during the days, I feared I'd be caught. Counselors often made their rounds to check for "strays." If they found any, punishment could be expected.

I tiptoed inside and pulled Gramps's letter from my suitcase. and shoved it into my pocket. As I pushed back the suitcase, a mouse ran across the wall behind the bed. My instinct to scream was halted when I heard a whimper from the showers. With baby steps, I crept into the bathing area. Out of the corner of my eye, I saw something much worse. Billie lay on the shower floor, naked, with blood seeping from her wrists.

A scream much louder than any warranted by the sight of a mouse escaped from my throat. "Billie," I cried and knelt beside her. "Oh my God?" I screamed over and over.

She tried to talk, and blood began to pour quickly from each of her wrists. I grabbed several towels and wrapped them around her self-inflicted wounds, then covered her body.

All I could say was, "Why?" as I choked on my tears.

Bille responded with a garbled whisper, "Meadowlark Haven ain't no place to raise a baby." She closed her eyes for the last time.

* * *

My screams carried across the farm, reaching all the way to The Outhouse. In moments, staff and students from Group A swarmed around me, escalating the chaos. Headmaster Dodge and Sister Connie ushered everyone out of the dorm just as the ambulance arrived to take Billie away. I couldn't stop sobbing. Mother Superior appeared, slipped an arm around me, and guided me to an office.

The room—unlike any I'd ever seen at Meadowlark Haven—held two cushioned chairs angled slightly toward each other with a round wooden table between them. An elaborately decorated leather-bound Bible rested on top. A desk at the far end sat beneath a large window overlooking the property's entrance.

She pointed to one of the chairs and took the seat across from me.

"This is a tragedy, Ivy. You must be traumatized. I can't imagine why the girl would take her life." She shook her head slowly. "Were you friends?"

My hand trembled uncontrollably. I sniffled several times, fighting for words. "Her name is—was—Billie," I said. "And she told me why she did this before she passed. Billie was pregnant." I looked up and swallowed hard.

Mother Superior lifted a hand to her mouth and gasped.

"This place is not what you and my parents think it is," I said, meeting her gaze. "Billie became pregnant while she was here. And we both know there are no boys at Meadowlark Haven."

Mother Superior stood, pulled a wad of tissues from a box on the desk, handed them to me, and sat again. "Sister Connie told me about some terrible things happening here." She bowed her head and clasped her hands. "Evil finds its way in, even when intentions are good. Though this is not a Catholic institution, Sister Connie and I volunteered to guide the girls. Only recently did she share the darker details of what some of them had confided. I promise you—we will make sure things are corrected and that those responsible are held accountable."

I wrapped my arms tightly around myself. "But that won't bring Billie back."

"No," she said softly. "But it won't ever happen again—not at Meadowlark Haven."

I swallowed hard, gathering the courage to say more.

"Despite the horrors, I have learned some lessons, the ones my parents and you knew I needed to learn." I dabbed the tears with the tissue and continued. "My interference with your mission is inexcusable. My mother told me about your work. I sincerely apologize for that. My selfishness and inquisitive mind collided."

"God forgives you, Ivy." She nodded. "So do I."

"Thank you," I said. "But there is still one thing I don't understand."

"What is it?"

Having read the letter a hundred times since discovering Gramps's connection to Denny—and after learning Mother Superior's first name—I needed to know if my suspicions were right.

I pulled the letter from my pocket and held it out to her. "I never meant to read this. I found it by accident, and ever since, it's caused one problem after another. I'm not trying to create more trouble." I swallowed hard. "I just want to understand what it means—for me. And as Gramps said... once I do, I'll let sleeping dogs lie."

CHAPTER THIRTY-NINE

Mother Superior gingerly unfolded the letter, and her eyes began to fill with tears, just as Gramps's had. Her face transitioned from light peach to pale. After she finished reading, I waited for her to respond. Each second seemed an hour. Finally, she blinked, and a tear fell onto her cheek. My eyes welled up again, and a second flurry slid down my face.

She placed her hand over mine again. "I've always known you were special, Ivy. Why wouldn't you be with a man like Francis for a grandfather?"

Barely breathing, I sat at attention waiting to hear more.

"This is why I've been so hard on you. If I'm to trust you, you need to give me the same respect."

I nodded with all sincerity. "Yes, of course."

She pressed the letter against her cheek. "It's hard to know where to begin." She closed her eyes and shook her head, almost in slow motion. "First, I'll start with that boy, Denny Carson." She wiped the tears from her face. "I've known what he was up to for some time. When I discovered he was supplying your grandfather with drugs, and you had a seemingly romantic interest in him, I had to step in."

"Truly, I'm so sorry for the trouble I've caused."

"It seems you do have a penchant for spying, Ivy." She inhaled and exhaled slowly, her hand rising and falling against her chest.

"Please tell me more about Gramps." I pointed to the letter. "Was I right? Did you send him this letter?"

The Mother Superior I'd known seemed to vanish, replaced by a simple woman burdened by a painful memory. When she finally spoke, her voice was soft, the words struggling to get past her lips.

"I was only sixteen, your age," she said. "Francis—your grandfather—was a young soldier. Each day, I sat on the front steps, waiting–waiting for the war to stop. Waiting for a long-lost family member to find us. Help us. Take us away. Perhaps I waited for God to send someone to save us. To save me."

I sat quietly in awe, yearning to hear more of the story, trying to contain my own emotions.

"After ten each morning, Francis walked by, dressed in his uniform and hat. He always greeted me with a smile. He carried himself with a gentle confidence, strolling down the wounded streets, cracked sidewalks, and piles of rubble. I wondered whether he had imagined them the way they once were. Clean, bustling with mothers strolling their babies, and children skipping home from school. Aside from his good looks, it was his smile that impressed me; it exuded hope. I'd dreamt he would stop, and one day, he did." She broke the trance and looked at me, embarrassed.

"Please go on," I said softly.

"'Hallo. Mein Name ist Francis,'" he said, using German words to the best of his ability. In gentlemanly fashion, he removed his hat. The golden eagle on the rim sparkled in the sun. His hair, perfectly parted on the right, was longer than the other soldiers I'd seen. Her ashy face turned pink. "I was so young."

I blinked and nodded, trying to let her know I was no longer a threat.

"I hesitated at first, then, I finally said, 'My name is Mariella.'" Surprised he cared to know the name of this tall, awkward teenage girl with saggy clothes." She waved her hand dismissively. "He stroked his mustache several times with his finger as if it were a comb and held out his hand. 'Nice to meet you,' he said. At first, I was frightened, but my fear ended as if God whispered in my ear, *It's okay.*"

I pictured a youthful Gramps and smiled at the image in my mind. Always cheerful and kind, how could I have thought any different?

"Our first meeting was short and formal, but each day after, we spoke more. A friendship formed amidst the rubble and pain that surrounded us. Each time he strolled by, I'd hear him whistling. He told me he looked forward to our chats. He said he whistled because of me. And he nicknamed me *Ella.*"

"He was so much older than you," I said, surprised. "Didn't you find it odd?"

"I didn't know how old he was, nor did I care." She grinned slightly. "Times were different then. And, the skin on his face was soft, not hard like the other soldiers that passed by. I assumed he must not have been in combat. And he treated me like a young lady, not a child."

The conversation was hard to hear, but after all I'd been through, I understood life has no clear path to our destiny. Nor does it fit neatly into a perfect box in our memory, as we imagine it should.

"To this day, I can remember the scent of his cologne, vanilla, and citrus. It wafted through the air each time he approached my stoop," she said.

The nun smiled, lost in her memory. I glanced down, not wanting to cause her embarrassment as she shared the intimate memories of my grandfather *with me.*

"The day I first walked with him, he bought a cigar and coffee for himself. White chocolate wrapped in red cellophane for me," she said.

Mother Superior continued sharing. "'I knew I could make you smile,' he said.' I hadn't remembered the last time I'd smiled before or after him." She pulled the tissue from her pocket again and dabbed her eyes.

The Gramps she spoke of was no different from the man I'd always known. However, the nun I'd known all these years had no resemblance to *Ella*.

"He never forgot you."

"Thank you for sharing that, Ivy." She reached out and squeezed my hand.

"Please tell me the rest," I urged.

She took a long sip of water, then started again.

"Several days passed, and I didn't see him. I tried not to be sad. I tried to believe the rain kept him away. Each day without the whistling was like a day without the sun. Eventually, I promised myself I would wipe him from my memory. The cold moved into my home and my heart. When Francis finally returned, the snow and all that had happened had buried my hopes of seeing him again. The day he reappeared, my teeth had been chattering so loudly I could barely hear him call my name."

"You were all alone in that house?" I whispered. "Gramps told me of the terrible circumstances he found you in."

"Yes, Ivy. I was alone, scared, and starving. I had layered on sweater after sweater until I emptied all my dresser drawers. I had done the same with my socks. Every pair. My coat wouldn't fit over my clothing. I spread it out on the floor to make a warm place for Apsel, my little dog, when we weren't huddled together."

I began rocking in my seat as I wrapped the tissue around my finger. Finally, I was going to hear the part of the story Gramps had never finished.

"Before I had even met Francis, my father had lost the use of his legs and couldn't leave our home to seek a doctor. One day, my brother left to find help. He never returned. That last horrific day, when I found my father dead of his own hand, I prayed to God to forgive him. Then, I vowed to repay God for my father's sin. I also prayed he would not leave me to die alone."

I covered my mouth in shock. "I'm so sorry," I said.

"For three days, my father lay across from me before Francis appeared," she said. "My stomach was a hollow ache. Fear enveloped me beyond any nightmare. The painful memory etched a black chill and filled my soul with unending sorrow. I began to understand why my father had done what he'd done. Temptation lured me to pick the gun from the floor and use it on myself, as well."

"But you made a vow to God to forgive your father."

"Yes, Ivy, that's true. And that's why I'm here today. If Francis had not returned, perhaps I wouldn't be." She rubbed her hands together as if she could still feel the chill, though the stagnant air from the hot summer day hung heavy in the room.

I'd wished someone had been able to save Billie from the same fate.

Mother Superior seemed to disappear into a trance. Although she still faced me, the memory of her past seemed to be unfolding in real time.

"Day after day, I stared at the snow-covered sidewalk. The footprints of people passing by appeared and disappeared beneath the snow, until the day I heard that familiar whistling. At first, I thought it was my imagination playing tricks on me. The beautiful tune emanated from his lips."

I sat at the end of the seat, mesmerized as Mother Superior shared the story. The nun seemed to transform into a person I'd never met before.

"When Francis returned, I was sitting inside the crook of a window-less casing covered with soot while Apsel lay on the floor beneath me. I can't remember how long I'd been sitting there. My cheeks burned from the cold wind, which had tugged the ragged white curtains outward."

"Yes, he told me this exact story. I can see it all again."

"He stopped in front of my house," she said. "He glanced toward the stoop, and then I saw him look up. 'Ella, are you okay?' he shouted. I couldn't speak. He rushed to the front door and stepped inside. His frantic eyes assessed the situation. My father lay frozen stiff in a puddle of dried blood."

I gasped.

"In the gentlest voice, he beckoned, 'Come here, Ella. Let me help you.'"

My heart quickened as the vivid story gripped my emotions. "How did he help you?" I asked. "And how did he bring you to America? The letter doesn't make sense to me. Although only twenty-three, Gramps was married before he went to war. My grandmother was still alive. My mother had been just a toddler."

"Dear Ivy, when I talk to you and the other girls about the sin of the flesh, it's because I know it firsthand. That's why I had to serve God for the rest of my life. To make up for what I'd done."

Her hands began to tremble; I grabbed onto them. Strange at first, but I no longer felt as if I were touching the hands of a pain-inflicting, mean-spirited nun.

"Before I found Gramps unconscious in the shed, I had confronted him with the letter. It's my fault he had the heart attack. He tried to tell me to forget I saw that letter. He said I wouldn't understand."

Mother Superior glanced around the room as if she expected someone to interrupt us. We had been talking for at least an hour. Her voice picked up speed, and she continued the story.

"The air was frigid in the orphanage. Children of all ages surrounded me. All lost in despair and fear. Why had he brought me there? Each night, the others' cries pierced my ears. They echoed throughout the desolate halls. I cried too, into my pillow while I held Apsel for dear life. He seemed to understand the importance of his quietness. I feared they would take him from me."

The room grew gray as the sun began to sink behind the office curtains.

Transfixed, Mother Superior continued. "The days were uncertain. We'd sit in class, forcing our minds to be attentive, only to be led into the basement the moment the sirens rang out. It must have gone on for a month or more. I lost track of time until the day Francis returned. I heard his voice from the common room."

"'I am Colonel Francis VonBartels, and I'm here to take Mariella,' he said. The matron asked where he was taking me. He answered in my native language. 'Ich werde sie heiraten und dann wird sie mit mir nach Amerika kommen.' I jumped off the rigid chair I'd been sitting in. The matron stepped into the room and said, 'Bekommen Bitte, kommen Sie Mariella.' I followed her and saw him. He was dressed in a crisp blue uniform with medals on his chest. A hat covered his blond hair, including the right part. He appeared older than I had remembered."

The nun paused and looked down at her hands.

"What did he say? What does that mean?" I asked, my heart pounding.

"He told the matron he had come to take me to America," she whispered, and continued the story with more urgency. "My hands shook. My mouth went dry. I had nowhere else to go. No one to care for me. I believed God sent him. All I had was an imagination I'd stolen from books that imprinted images of places and wonders I'd never known nor believed I would experience. A rush of excitement rained on me like liquid sunshine. I had to leave with him, or I would die. I asked if we could bring Apsel, but he told me we couldn't. He explained that he now belonged to the children at the orphanage."

Tears reemerged from her eyes.

"Francis moved close by my side. 'It's okay.' His thumb brushed away my tears as I wept and sniffled and said, 'Goodby mein bester Freund,' (goodbye, my best friend) and handed Apsel to a quiet girl who reached out for him and bid goodbye to the country I would never see again."

"So how did Gramps bring you here to America?" I adjusted myself in the seat. Hives began to form beneath my chin. I scratched, waiting to hear more.

Mother Superior sat up straight, breathed in deep, and said, "He married me. That was the only way he could take me away from the orphanage. Away from Germany." Her head slumped over her clasped hands again.

My jaw dropped. "B-b-but—he was already married."

She lifted her head and placed her hand on her heart. "I didn't know that at the time. He only did it to save me, which I didn't understand at the time, either. When we arrived in America, he told me we were no longer married, and I mustn't ever tell a soul. He left me with a good family, and he returned to your grandmother."

My heart stopped. Not so much because of the shock of what she was telling me, but because it hurt for the young Mother Superior.

She shifted positions in her seat. "One day, he appeared at the home of the family he had sent me to live with. He came inside, but he didn't ask to speak to me. The man who had been caring for me like a father forbade me to join them in the parlor. So, I wrote a letter begging Francis to rescue me, and slipped it into the pocket of his overcoat hanging in the hall closet. At the time, I was young and had no understanding of why he could never bring me into his life. And I never again heard from him."

"So how did you know he lived in Asbury Park? How did you end up in the convent?"

"I didn't know he was there. It wasn't until several years ago. I'd heard him talking to Father McVee. Something about him drew me to follow him into the sanctuary. I stood outside the confessional and listened; God forgive me." The nun crossed herself. "Then, I knew. Though when I witnessed his meeting with Denny and the exchange of hands, I also knew what he'd gotten himself into. Perhaps after all these years, he couldn't silence the guilt in his mind. Perhaps the addiction began after he'd been hospitalized after falling from the ladder. I didn't know, but I decided to help Father McVee with the girls, if he would help me save Francis."

"How did you plan to do that?"

"We were working with the police to get Denny. He may be young, but he's been working with a man named Joseph Finetti, who is the one supplying him with the drugs. We hoped to help the police get this man."

"Does Gramps know that you are here?" I asked.

"No, Ivy. Too much time has passed. Respect his words . . . Let sleeping dogs lie."

I wrapped my arms around my body again, needing comfort. "I will."

She reached around her neck and pulled a chain hidden behind her blouse. "He made this for me."

A coin from Gramps's collection hung from her neck.

She gently clasped it in her hand and smiled. "All these years, I've worn it. This was the only tangible piece of Francis I had left."

I'd thought it was lost somewhere in my room, but it was with Mother Superior the whole time.

"Now, God is leading me to continue to help these girls. I've completed my work at the school. It's time to pass the torch. Father McVee has received funding from a group of well-to-do families to continue his mission. He has asked me to join him in his efforts in New York City. After school is out, next June, I plan to leave. I beg you, never share what I've told you about your grandfather. No good can come from it. The most important thing is that he is no longer a slave to Denny and his drugs. In a sense, Ivy, you did help him. His body is cleansed from that poison, and your mother has confided to me that the memory of it has disappeared."

"Do you mean he doesn't remember anything?" Panic gripped my heart.

"No, he still remembers his family, but his memory is fading." She blotted her eyes with a tissue. "It's okay, Ivy. It's a part of life that many must face. Now, it's time for healing and love." She reached out and squeezed my hand.

Tears burned my eyes. "I'm sorry. I was selfish. My parents were right. Everyone was right. Even Stella. Despite all I'd gone through, I can see it was God's way of redirecting my path."

Mother Superior nodded thoughtfully. "Perhaps, Ivy. We never truly know God's plans for us while we are in our trials. But we must always seize the chance to do what's right for all. Not just ourselves."

The sky had grown dark, and I saw a girl's shadow crawl out from the window of the office next door. I squinted. It was Stella.

CHAPTER FORTY

Police cars were still scattered across the property. Sister Connie was trying to gather the girls into some semblance of order. I caught sight of Peg out of the corner of my eye and ducked behind a bush, hoping to avoid her while keeping Stella in view. When the girls finally formed a line and began heading toward Building C, I slipped out from my hiding spot and took off after Stella.

Far from the building, walking toward the fence near the street, I called out. "Stella! Wait!"

"What do you want from me, Ivy?" she yelled without stopping.

"I was right, Mother Superior will help us. She knows what's been going on here. It's gonna be okay."

"What's going to be okay?"

"Us—all of us."

Stella laughed, mocking me. "And you really believe her?"

"It's true."

"Sure, Ivy. Keep telling yourself that. You're more stupid than I thought."

"I know you don't want to believe me, but you'll see. The police know everything, now."

"And how does that change my life?" Stella looked back at me, annoyed.

"Meadowlark Haven will be held responsible for all the terrible things they've done."

Stella snickered. "Again—how does that affect me?"

I couldn't answer. So, I asked, "Where are you going?"

"Why in the world would I tell you?"

"I swear, Stella. I want to help you."

"Well, Ivy, you can't."

The last police car drove out through the front gate with Mr. Ross in the back seat. The commotion died down. The dinner bell rang, and the girls and staff disappeared into the building.

"You'd better get back, Ivy. No one will come looking for me, but if you're missing, they'll send out the brigade. You'll ruin everything. Again."

"It's getting dark, and there is nothing around here for miles. If you leave, you'll get lost, or picked up by some nut case."

"Let me figure that out. Now get the hell out of here. If you really want to help, you won't say a word to anyone."

* * *

After lights out, I climbed through the window and headed to Stella's dorm. I'd hoped she'd gotten cold feet and changed her mind about leaving. When I got there, I peeked through the window. Her bed was unmade. Though I couldn't imagine she'd still be there, I trudged back to the spot I'd last seen her. Maybe she was still there waiting— waiting for someone to pick her up. She must have used the phone in the office where I'd seen her crawl out. Perhaps I could still talk some sense into her—I'd at least try once more.

The sounds of the farm animals kept me company as I crept along the fence toward the street. It was darker and far quieter than it had been earlier, the faint starlight, my only guide. Sticks cracked under my shoes, and my feet dipped into the small mounds where groundhogs had burrowed their tunnels. Heat lightning flickered across the sky, and the earthy scent of the farm trailed me all the way to the gate.

A car drove past, its bright light shining toward me. I crouched down by the bushes, slapping mosquitoes and fidgeting with tall patches of crab grass. Difficult to find the spot again, I feared I might get lost. Without a watch, I had no way of knowing what time it was. Not that it mattered. I began whispering loudly. "Stella, are you out here? I promise you, Mother Superior will help you. Stella, are you here?"

No responses. Just crickets and the sound of an occasional car passing by. While kicking pine cones along the fence, I noticed a small, pink book face down in the grass. I bent to pick it up. It was a diary. Stella's diary.

CHAPTER FORTY-ONE

Though I'd been home for days, waking in my own bed gave me a new appreciation for life. After leaving my "pretty seaside bubble," as Denny once called it, I could never see it the same way again.

I followed Mother Superior's advice to do what was right and told her about my conversation with Stella, believing she would help. I was too late. Stella was missing—and I had no idea where she'd gone.

My parents had no idea of the horrors that had been taking place at the farm and were grateful nothing worse had happened to me, as it had to Billie. But now, they understood my need to explore life beyond the boundaries they had set for me.

"Being parents does not make us all-knowing," my mother admitted. "Maybe you will experience that one day, or maybe you won't. Whatever happens, it's okay."

Dressed in my usual summer outfit—a sleeveless cotton top and culottes—I rushed downstairs and joined my mother in the kitchen without complaint. Gramps watched his morning show from his big green chair while Dad read the paper on the couch. I came up behind him as he turned the page, and my jaw dropped at the headline.

SEXUAL ABUSE AND TRAGEDY AT MEADOWLARK

HAVEN'S UPSTATE NEW YORK GIRLS RETREAT

Retreat?!

Dad must have heard my footsteps and laid the paper down on the coffee table. I attempted to pick it up. But his quick hand thumped on the paper. "I'm not sure you want to read this."

"Dad?" I tilted my head and stared him blankly in the eyes.

He moved his hand away. I picked up the paper and sat down in the red chair across from him.

The article mentioned Mr. Ross and the school administrators' names, but did not mention Billie. A smaller article beneath stated:

ASBURY PARK RESIDENT, MADDIE LAWRENCE, KILLED IN AUTOMOBILE CRASH IN NEW VESTAL, NEW YORK

I continued to read. The article stated she hadn't been driving the car registered to Joseph Finetti of Newark, New Jersey, who claims he lent it to a friend. It appeared the driver of the vehicle had left the scene of the accident and was missing. Chills ran down my arms. Why was Stella's sister driving Finetti's car? Where was Stella? Where was Denny?

After I finished reading, I told my parents about seeing Stella at Meadowlark Haven—everything except finding her diary. They already knew about Stella's mother and the discrimination she'd faced after her husband's death, which led the widow to drink. The rest they'd learned from Laura.

In the final weeks of summer, police came and went, questioning me about Denny, Stella, Mr. Ross, Billie, and Meadowlark Haven. Sister Florinda visited often, offering guidance and comfort. Though the time at the farm—and what followed—was tragic, I believed God had a plan for me. My purpose felt clear. Every book I'd read had taught me what no school ever could: I was at the helm of my own destiny.

The police called one afternoon and asked to speak to me. My parents accompanied me, and once again, I was face-to-face with the same long-faced policeman who had interrogated me months before.

"You are a lucky girl, Miss Munroe," he said.

"Yes, I know."

"Denny used his charms to get all these girls hooked on him—then on drugs. Once they were addicted, he'd tell them they had to pay for the stuff. When they couldn't pay, he'd send them to Finetti, who got them to prostitute themselves for the money. Denny would get a cut of that in addition to the drugs he sold."

Thinking that I could have been one of them made my stomach hurt, but it helped me understand how it could happen to other girls, especially those without a loving family.

"Denny was washing money at Mr. Fudge & Saltwater Taffy for Finetti," he said.

I was right after all.

The officer showed me a picture of two men. "Do you know these people?"

"One is Denny," I said, "and the other is the man I saw him give envelopes to on several occasions."

"That is Finetti," he said. "We just wanted to confirm this."

"Did you arrest them?" I asked.

"Unfortunately, this case is still under investigation. However, the two minors are missing," he said.

Though he didn't mention their names, I knew he was referring to Stella and Denny. Neither of them had been seen since that night.

"If you hear anything from either of them, please contact us immediately."

My heart dropped. Though he didn't say it, I knew Stella was with Denny—somewhere.

"Do you know anything else?"

"I'm sorry, we can't go into any further detail," he said. "Thank you for your help, Miss Munroe. This is all we needed. Good luck to you."

My dad explained that the newspaper couldn't mention Denny and Stella's names because they were minors. Would anyone ever know who Billie was? And why was she sent to Meadowlark Haven? Who robbed the world of her beautiful voice? And what about the other girls in Groups B and D? This became a mystery I found difficult to shake. Nevertheless, I chose not to pursue the thought.

One day, after the investigations and the funeral, Stella's mother appeared at our door holding Mollie, a diaper bag in her arms, and another woman standing next to her. With a milk mustache and sweaty curls stuck to her cheek, Molly's light brown eyes twinkled when she saw me. She reached out. I swept her up in my arms while my mother spoke with Stella's mom. Mrs. Lawrence choked back tears. Her hands shook while she chain-smoked at our kitchen table, while the other woman spoke.

"Ivy, can you take Molly upstairs for a bit?" my mother said.

"Sure." I scooped up Molly and her bag. She smiled easily as we trudged upstairs to my room, where I showed her a few of my childhood toys. The old red rubber ball quickly became her favorite. We sat on the floor rolling it back and forth, Molly giggling each time it bounced back into her hands.

Before long, a rancid smell wafted up from the sweet toddler. I hesitated, not wanting to interrupt my mother, then rummaged through Molly's bag for a fresh diaper. To find it, I had to pull out several of her belongings. Nestled among them was the picture of Stella dressed in Gramps's Navy clothes. Why had Stella's mother put it in the bag?

When my mother's voice called from downstairs, I quickly shoved everything back into the bag—everything except the photo. With Molly in tow, I headed back down to see what was happening. Near the front door sat a grocery bag filled to the brim with more of Molly's clothes and toys.

My mother stood with both hands pressed to her chest, grinning as though I hadn't seen her happy in years. "Looks like Molly will be staying with us," she said. "The woman with Mrs. Lawrence was from social services, and they both agreed Molly needs a stable home while things get sorted out. Rather than send her to strangers, they asked if I'd take her."

A bright light shone in Mother's eyes, steady despite the uncertainty ahead. It hadn't crossed my mind that Mrs. Lawrence's visit would end this way, but I knew—deep down—that Mom was thrilled. Thrilled to share the burden. Thrilled to have Molly.

Later, that same day, Laura appeared at my door, too.

"Hi Ivy," I'm so glad you're home. The ordeal must have traumatized you."

"What do you care," I said as I dug my fingernails into my palms, trying to avoid shaking her or worse, smacking her in the face, not that I would. I reminded myself that I had made my own mistakes and decided to hear what Laura had to say.

"I didn't mean to hurt you," she said with tears in her eyes. "Please forgive me."

After standing there for a while, I thought about all that had happened. Staying angry with Laura wouldn't do me any good. So, I accepted her apology.

After Laura left, I placed the photo of Stella inside the diary. Until that moment, I had tried to respect Stella's privacy. But something in my gut told me maybe she wanted me to find it. So I began to read.

CHAPTER FORTY-TWO

Stella

I wish I could run away. My mother wouldn't notice, nor would my sister. But poor Molly would suffer. What kind of life would she have? It certainly wouldn't be any better than mine. Maybe one of the neighbors will complain again, and they'll take Molly away from this hellhole for good this time.

They'll see how my sister leaves her sitting in a dirty diaper for hours on end. And how Molly lives on cereal and canned fruit. I love my sister, but she's turned out to be just like my mother. But if she's taken away, I may never see her again. Maybe I'll run away and start a new life and come back for Molly.

Denny's done with school, same as me. The nuns only care about punishing me, not making my life better. It's no different for Denny. He has money coming in now. Much more than he earned at the fudge shop where he worked with Ivy. At first, he told me he was a delivery boy for a grocer, but I soon learned that he was delivering drugs. And then he said if I helped him bag the white powder, he'd share his earnings. There's nothing I wouldn't do for Denny. Now, he's talking about leaving town and going to the city where he could make bigger deliveries. Mother Superior will have to save her stick of justice for the next troubled girl who hates her life as much as I do.

Now that Denny has that nice car and money, we could take off. I don't care about waiting until school is out. It's not like I plan to finish, anyway. We're perfect together. He just doesn't know it yet. And Ivy—well, she's nothing but a spoiled brat. She makes me sick. Maybe she's gotten one or even two whacks from Mother Superior—if any. She has nothing to complain about, though she always does. Her big grievance about wanting to go to public school is a joke. It was fun playing detective with her. Letting her believe that Mother Superior was a madam. How naive could the girl be? For a minute, I thought we could become friends. Then she turned like the weather and grew cold toward me. It must have been that friend of hers—Laura. She's even more spoiled than Ivy.

I know Denny didn't mean to hit me the other day. My fist flew out first. It was my fault. My bad temper—inherited from my dead dad—the dad I hear stories about. Denny confuses me. One minute, he's cozying up to me, and the next, pushing me away.

My nosy neighbor saw it happen and called the police. She's always interfering with our lives. Last summer, she called family services on us for letting Molly sit alone in her playpen in the yard. For God's sake, the house was a hundred degrees, and I only ran inside to use the bathroom. What does this woman think she's going to accomplish by calling the cops every time our family does anything imperfect?

* * *

It had never occurred to me that Stella would pour her thoughts onto paper like this. That she was so desperate for love and attention, she would chase it anywhere—even when she knew it was an illusion. And it had never occurred to me that she understood more about me than I did myself.

One day, I would find her and tell her that her prayers had been answered. Until then, I tucked the diary and photo behind a loose board in my closet, hidden away for safekeeping.

CHAPTER FORTY-THREE

When senior year began, Sister Florinda had taken Mother Superior's position as the head nun. The wooden ruler no longer had a place in the classroom. Sister Florinda also brought her creative ability to the school. She encouraged us to sing and act, allowing us the opportunity to put on plays for the community. We donated the proceeds we received to the halfway house supported by Mother Superior and Father McVee in New York City.

I had forgiven Laura; her intentions had never been malicious. She simply wasn't built to keep a secret. Before long, she was spending less time at her mother's boardwalk shop and more time at the school, helping with the plays Sister Florinda produced. Laura had discovered a knack not only for acting, but—more impressively—for marketing. My own contributions were gathering hard-to-find props and helping write the scripts. Writing had become an even deeper passion, right alongside my steady longing to be a detective.

Days slipped into weeks, then months, and still no word from Stella. The remarkable women of espionage who'd come before me were remembered because someone had shared their truths. I held tightly to Stella's diary, certain that one day, I would share hers with Molly.

At last, graduation day arrived. I slipped into a light blue dress beneath my mustard-colored gown and rode with my parents to St. Teresa's. They sent me off with a stiff but loving hug, which was their way. Then I joined my classmates and waited nervously behind the curtain in the all-purpose room.

Mother Superior presided over the ceremony, calling each student forward in alphabetical order and announcing their plans—teachers, brides-to-be, nurses, and secretaries. The girls wore neatly set curls and mid-length ponytails, tied with ribbons to match their graduation gowns. One or two more progressive girls wore it with a short fringe like Audrey Hepburn's. I chose the soft shoulder-length wave. My heart ached that Stella wasn't beside me, as she had been for so many years. She would have gone with the bouffant, the new trend making its way from New York City.

One by one, Mother Superior draped a scarf around each graduate's neck, St. Teresa's name embroidered in black along with the year 1959. When my turn came, she placed the scarf gently on my shoulders, then paused. She stepped back, hesitated, and smiled—a rare, unguarded smile, wide enough to show both rows of teeth.

Taking a deep breath, she leaned toward the microphone. "I'm so proud of all the graduates today," she said, her smile unwavering. "But it gives me special joy to announce St. Teresa's very first scholarship recipient—Miss Ivy Jean Munroe."

The room seemed to hold its breath as she handed me a crisp envelope, then drew from her pocket a shimmering rosary. She lifted it reverently to her lips, kissed the cross, and pressed it into my hands.

"These are for you, Ivy," Mother Superior said. "As a woman, you will have to work twice as long and twice as hard. But I have complete faith in your future success as you pursue a college education at Marymount College to become an investigative journalist."

I looked out at the audience as they cheered. My father nodded with approval. Though undoubtedly, he helped me fill out the scholarship application, hoping I'd find a husband, not a career. Nevertheless, I continued working summers at the fudge and taffy shop to help with tuition.

My mother teared up, grateful I'd remain in a Catholic institution. Gramps's blue eyes twinkled as he combed his mustache with his bottom lip. He nodded as if a faraway memory popped into his mind for a moment's visit. I accepted the beads, kissed them, and wrapped them around my fingers, not to quell my nerves this time but to embrace the gift I'd been given. A chance to do something extraordinary—to make a difference.

While living in New York City, I wouldn't need a car after all—one less thing to focus on. Father McVee and Mother Superior promised my parents that they would keep an eye on me while I helped at the women's halfway house between my studies. I also planned to pay attention to newspapers' coverage of underserved women as I prepared to learn and use the skills I had acquired throughout my privileged life. If Nellie Bly could do it, so could I.

Just as I began to exit the stage, Mother Superior pulled me aside. She bent down and pulled out a thin square box the size of an eight-by-eleven picture frame from a shelf inside the podium. She handed it to me and nodded. I removed the top, and inside was a leather-bound black book. With a gleam in her eye, she lifted it from the box. She positioned her thumb and yellow-nailed pointer finger to fan through the empty pages like they were a hundred invitations for opportunities. After placing the book back in the box, she laid her hand on mine and said, "You are going to need this."

CHAPTER FORTY-FOUR

1973

After our beach walk, Molly and I returned with two full buckets of sea glass. She sat down in the Adirondack chair on the front porch and placed her bucket between her legs. I put mine on the ground next to the chair. The silence between us was heavy.

"I'll be right back," I said.

She offered no response.

I got up from the chair and rushed upstairs to obtain the remaining piece of the story—the clipping.

When I returned, I removed the clipping from the pages of the black book Mother Superior had given me on my graduation day and handed it to Molly.

Her eyes widened. "Why didn't you ever tell me all this before?" She asked, then refocused on the bucket of sea glass.

"How could I? When your grandmother dropped you off, you were just a toddler. Over time, you flourished. Your only memories were of the new family you had become a part of—us. How could we disrupt your life by allowing you to wonder about an aunt who may or may not have been alive?"

"Did you know my mother?"

"I'd known of her, but I didn't *know* her. I'm certain she loved you. She brought you home from that hospital after her boyfriend ran out on her. It's no secret that the nuns worked hard to convince her to give you up. Think about it, she was your age, Molly, with a baby, no husband, and she didn't have the best home life."

"So, you said." Molly glanced up and wiped tears from her face with the back of her hand.

"The odds were against her, but she tried," I said. "Your mom had a job, and Stella watched you when she could—which was often. Your grandmother never recovered after her husband, your grandfather, took his life. She didn't leave you because she didn't care about you— she couldn't care for you."

"She brought you to us knowing you'd have a better life. Mom had always made it known in the church that she loved children. She often helped young families and commented that she wished she had more children of her own. Your grandmother did visit you for the first few months, but it was all too much for her to lose an entire family. Not long after, she went into a nursing home and passed away from lung cancer."

"What about Stella? Didn't anyone look for her? Did anyone even care?" Molly gazed up, tears streaming down her face.

"Yes, Molly, I did. I never stopped looking for her." I opened the black book Mother Superior had given me all those years ago. The pages were filled with notes—notes from years of following leads that sent me nowhere. "During that time, when I wasn't studying or working at the halfway house, I searched for Stella. I'd hoped she'd turn up there one day. My gut always told me that if she were alive, she'd be in New York City."

First, I handed Molly the picture of Stella dressed as a sailor. "This is what she looked like when we tried to disguise ourselves while following Mother Superior."

Molly cracked a smile and rubbed her thumb over Stella's face. "I do see a resemblance."

Next, I handed her the newspaper clipping. "Here. No more secrets. Read for yourself."

Molly gingerly took the clipping from my hand, unfolded it, and read:

UPPER WEST SIDE CULT EXPOSED

A group of men and women living in a ten-bedroom apartment have been living in a commune setting known for experimenting with psychotherapy, psychedelics, and sharing sexual partners, has been shut down for alleged kidnapping.

Several younger women in the commune had been directed to care for the children of married couples. The group leader separated parents from their children, allowing them only minimal time together. They intended to raise a generation of followers who no longer bonded with their parents, but instead with the commune. The oldest surrogate was discovered to be Stella Lawrence, who was named missing in 1958 after an escape from Meadowlark Haven, a girls' behavioral retreat that was later exposed for its abusive practices.

After a police interview, Miss Lawrence stated that thirteen years ago, her boyfriend brought her to the commune to hide out from an arrest warrant. After several months, she refused to leave with him, and she has remained with the commune since. "The little ones need me," Miss Lawrence stated. "This was my family and my home," she told police.

Several of the women are being treated for drug detoxification at the local hospital. For more information, please call. 212-555-0100.

Molly clutched the paper to her chest and looked up angrily. "How long have you known about this?"

"I just found out, Mo."

"But you kept her existence from me for my whole life! How could you? This is my aunt. She was a part of my life once, and now you tell me she's been out in the world all this time. My only real family member—with no one to help her."

I placed my hand on her shoulder. "By the time you were in school, you had no memory of anyone, and Mom and Dad thought Stella must have been dead. They believed it was best to leave the past in the past."

Mo pushed my hand off her shoulder. "Just like what Gramps said to you when you found out about Mother Superior?" She asked rhetorically with anger and turned away from me while remaining seated. She had paid great attention to every detail I had just shared. Except for the crickets and light music bouncing off the ocean from the boardwalk, silence filled the next few moments. When I tried to conjure up words to defend myself and my parents—our parents—nothing came to mind.

"My entire life has been a lie," she said in a deep monotone voice.

"That's not true, Molly. We told you about the accident, and we told you about your grandmother being too ill to care for you." I grabbed the string from the bottom of my sweatshirt and wound it around my finger.

"That wasn't until I was nine years old. If that friend of yours hadn't mentioned it when we were shopping for a dress for my communion, you would never have told me at all."

I remembered the day I'd run into Laura all those years later. Her parents had sold the store and moved away. I never expected her to show up out of the blue with her new husband, taking a walk down memory lane.

"You're right. Mom and Dad adopted you and always saw you as theirs completely. They have loved you as much as they loved me; maybe more." I cracked a tiny smile. "They couldn't see how knowing the truth could add value to your life. Remember, they thought Stella was dead. The police gave them every reason to believe this."

"I still had a right to know. How would you feel if it were you?"

I suddenly thought of Gramps and Mother Superior and how I felt when I discovered their history. But I kept the secret for the good of our family. Though now Molly knew. Gramps and Mother Superior had been dead for years, and I still believe that her statement, 'no good could come of it,' was true. My parents felt the same about telling Mo about Stella, but I had always disagreed. However, I had respected their wishes—until now.

After several seconds, Mo looked up. "You're just as bad as them. What you did wasn't right. All of you. Not right at all."

"Molly! I wanted to tell you—I would have told you—it just was never the right time. You have to see that. Now, we can help Stella.

We can help her—together."

Molly stood up from the chair, and the bucket of sea glass toppled to the ground.

"Wait, there's one more thing," I said and handed her the diary.

She took it from my hand and rushed into the house.

* * *

The sun dropped low in the sky, leaving behind a sherbet-colored glow. Mom and Dad stepped onto the porch, their night robes covering them.

"Where's Molly?" Mom asked. "I thought I heard yelling."

"No, everything is fine." I lied. "I think she went to take a shower," I said, hoping I was right. "We were out on the beach, and we're both pretty grimy."

"Tell her good night for us," Mom said. "See you both in the morning."

"Night," I said.

For some reason, I didn't think Molly would confront them, yet, and I believed she'd come back. So, I waited.

* * *

Molly appeared with wet hair and fresh clothes and sat down in the same chair as before. She picked up the bucket, grabbed the scattered sea glass from the ground, and dropped the pieces inside. Calm and quiet, her hand sifted through the broken relics of smooth and colorful glass that had lived a life much longer than either of us. With her thumb and forefinger, she grabbed a triangular grayish-red piece. It was curved at each point, almost making it appear heart-shaped.

"Where do you think it's been?" she asked, as she caressed it between her hands as she was comforting it after a long voyage through time. The more she warmed it with her touch, the redder it became. "Look, she opened her palm. You don't often see glass this color—if ever," she said, continuing to examine it. "Maybe it was a perfume bottle that sat on the vanity of the Queen of England." She laid it in the palm of her other hand and held it out to me.

I gingerly took it and rubbed its smooth surface. "Or maybe it was a wine glass that belonged to Victor Hugo." I joked, hoping to keep the moment light.

Mo chuckled for a second, then her face became somber. "Do they know about the article?" she asked, referring to our parents.

"No, I wanted you to know first. They didn't keep the secret to hurt you, Molly. Please don't be angry with them."

Molly rocked back and forth. Her eyes closed. "We can tell them about Stella in the morning."

"And we'll go see her together and let her know she's not alone," I said, pressing the red sea glass back into Molly's hand. "Here—it's yours. You know, it's possible to make new memories with someone else's past. Look at the sea glass table over there." I gestured toward the half-finished mosaic leaning forlornly against the side of the house. "Each shard of sea glass washed ashore from some faraway place, whispering its own untold story. We may not know their journey, but we could give them new meaning now. It's not too late, Molly. We can still make something beautiful with what we have."

Molly walked to the table and carefully placed the red piece in the center. I followed, setting down one more fragment on either side, as if sealing the promise between us.

The End

CHAPTER FORTY-FOUR

Whispers of Sea Glass
Study Guide

1. Understanding the Setting

Where does the story take place? How does the setting affect the mood of the book and the way characters think and act?

2. Connecting with the time period

Did you connect with the book's historical time period? How did the time period affect behavior then vs. now? What are instances where the past reflects the present?

3. Explain how the author alludes to the figurative and literal uses of "Sea Glass."

What does the book suggest about whispers? Share an example of how the author uses whispers in a figurative sense.

4 . Main Character's Growth

How does the main character change from the beginning to the end of the book? What are some examples? How do her experiences or realizations lead to this change?

5 . Relationships

Choose a critical relationship in the novel. How does it help reveal the characters' personalities, beliefs, or struggles?

6. Character Development

Choose one central character and trace their internal journey. How do their thoughts, moral struggles, or relationships evolve over the course of the novel?

7 . Faith, Belief, and Questions: Provide examples where the characters question their beliefs or values. Why is this questioning critical to the story?

8. Moral Responsibility

What moral questions does the novel raise about responsibility—to oneself, to others, and to one's beliefs? Are any clear answers offered?

9 . Community vs. Feeling Alone

Even though characters live among others, some feel isolated. Why do you think this happens? Use an example from the book.

10. The Role of Memory: How do memories influence the characters' actions or thoughts? Why do past events matter so much in the present?

11. Silence and Secrets

What are some examples of when characters avoid speaking honestly? What effect does this have on their relationships or the outcome of the story?

12. Author's Style

The writing is thoughtful and reflective, but also fast-paced. How does this style affect how you experienced the story? Did it make the book more or less engaging for you?

13. Language and Style

How does Decker's candid but straightforward lyrical prose shape the reading experience? Provide an example of a passage where language deepens meaning rather than advancing plot.

14. Supporting Characters:

The supporting characters played an important part in shaping the main character's journey. Provide one example of how directly or indirectly their connection did so.

15 . Title Meaning

What do you think the title Whispers of Sea Glass means? How does it connect to the message of the novel?

About the Author

Wendy Lynn Decker was born and raised in New Jersey. She lives a bike ride away from the Asbury Park, New Jersey, boardwalk. She's the author of the young adult novel, SWEET TEA, and the FaithWriters Award-winning middle grade book, THE BEDAZZLING BOWL. When Wendy isn't writing, you can find her singing at local beach establishments or entertaining friends with her husband on their hillbilly yacht.

You can connect with me on:

- https://www.wendylynndeckerauthor.com
- https://www.facebook.com/wendylynndeckerauthor
- https://instagram.com/wendylynndeckerauthor
- https://tiktok.com/wendylynndeckerauthor

Also by Wendy Lynn Decker

Wendy's writing style centers on realistic, emotionally honest fiction with vivid imagery and a warm, down-to-earth voice that often reads like intimate, conversational storytelling. If you enjoy *Whispers of Sea Glass* or any of her books, please find it in your heart to leave a review on Amazon.com or Goodreads.

SWEET TEA

The anniversary of Olivia's daddy's death happens to land on the same day the world remembers John Lennon. While TV stations replay Beatles songs, in 1984, Landon, Georgia, Olivia's mama gets swept back into her own memories—and her behavior grows harder for Olivia to explain away.

A chance comment on a talk show flips a switch in Olivia's mind: Mama might not just be quirky—she might actually be sick. Suddenly, sixteen-year-old Olivia is thrown into an adult world, searching for answers and strength she didn't know she had. With no family to lean on, she finds help in the most unexpected places: a peculiar but kind stranger, and a friend Mama makes inside the psychiatric ward.

Balancing her mother's struggles with the shaky excitement of first love, Olivia learns that courage and intuition—plus a little faith—are sometimes enough to light the way.

THE BEDAZZLING BOWL

Aly M. Bellisher, a ten-year-old teller of tall tales, discovers her best friend is no longer attending public school. Aly fears she will now be the only Christian kid in her class. When she begins to act out, her mother hangs a special bible verse on the refrigerator door for her to memorize, or she won't be allowed to sing at the church cantata. Matthew 5:14, "Be a light for God . . ." With many obstacles in the way, Aly fails in her attempt to memorize the verse. Only when faced with a situation at school of befriending the new girl does Aly truly learn its meaning.